Their Protective Dom

Club Decadent Series Book One

K.C. Ford

PSA, while this book features elements of kink and BDSM, it is NOT a how-to manual. This is a work of erotic fiction, and everything written here should be treated as such. Always do your research and ALWAYS practice in a SAFE, SANE, and CONSENSUAL manner.

eBook ISBN: 978-1-7780290-3-5

Paperback ISBN: 978-1-0691328-1-9

Cover Design: Katherine Ferguson

Edits: Katherine Ferguson

Formatted with Atticus

About

This is Book One in the Club Decadent Series. Each book in the series focuses on a specific relationship and can be read as a standalone. However, the series is best enjoyed in order.

Xander Ward took on a private assignment away from his security company. That was over three years ago. The day Penelope Fergusson walked into her father's office to be informed she now had a bodyguard is the day Xander swore to protect her with his life. From what? He isn't sure, leaving him on guard 24/7. With each day, his obsession grows. He tried to keep his distance, but then Penny took him to New York with plans of seduction, and Xander couldn't resist her any longer.

Penny had a plan. A plan to seduce her bodyguard before it's too late. Is it a perfect plan? Not even close, but she didn't have a choice. She's running out of time. Penny's father has arranged a marriage for her to a man she's never met, and she wants to experience a world of pleasure all in one night. What better man to do it with than the stoic bodyguard she's been half in love with since the day they met? Xander is also a member of the exclusive and luxurious Club Decadent, the hottest adult club in New York... and Penny wants enough memories to last a lifetime. When another man offers to join them... Penny wants the most out of this one night and goes for it, throwing caution to the wind, doubling her pleasure and her memories.

Alexandre 'Lex' Ricci took the unexpected announcement from his father that he now had a fiancée in stride. If in stride meant selling the majority stake in the company he built from the ground up to his CFO, and walking away to marry a stranger, then, sure. He needed a night to let loose, and he knew his CFO, Andrew, belonged to an exclusive club Lex wanted access to. It's not like he has much to look forward to by being strong-armed into marrying a stranger. When he's persuaded to introduce himself to the most striking couple he's ever seen, Lex finds them both impossible to resist.

When fate and a bit of intrigue guide three lost souls together, the collision is explosive. The fallout is just as hot. And one night at Club Decadent will never be enough.

Author's Note

This story is a high-heat, MMF, insta-love romance with a protective, dominant bodyguard MMC, a mafia princess FMC (though, with almost nothing to do with the mafia its self), and a bratty, Italian switch who rocks a pair of slutty little glasses. If that's all you need to know, skip ahead. If you need more details, please refer to the list of contents and tropes on the next page. Happy Reading!

This book is written in Third Person and multi-POV. There is an age gap (MMC is 35, FMC is 25, MMC is 30). Italian is used with English translation. Tattooed MMC. Yearning and pining. Adult language and situations. Explicit sexual scenes between consenting adults, including elements of BDSM and Kink (including: Shibari, multiple orgasms, cum sharing, period sex, DP, pegging, and more). Scenes involving – MF/MMF/MM. Consent. Good girl praise mixed with a bit of degradation. There is some violence, and a secondary character's on-page death. There are off-page deaths from cancer. Pop culture references and a guaranteed HEA.

The Playlist

Music plays a big part in this author's and these characters lives. If you enjoy some great club bangers, love songs, songs to 'get it on' to, and dash of Canadian hits. This is the playlist for you. Enjoy!

Club Decadent Series Playlist by K.C. Ford

Contents

Chapter One

Penny

The bane of Penny's existence is also her obsession, and from the moment her father introduced Xander Ward to her, she couldn't escape him. Stuck to her side as if he's glued himself there.

It's what a bodyguard does best.

Six-foot-six, muscular, and intimidating with strawberry blond hair, he kept braided beneath the collar of his shirt. His black signature suit was pristine and tailored to fit his massive frame. Xander Ward is in a league of his own.

Penny wished the heat in his gaze equaled desire, and not the constant search for a threat to cause her bodily harm.

Her seduction plan is outrageous.

Yet, desperate times call for desperate measures. Last week, Penny's father informed her he'd chosen a husband for her. She still seethed at his audacity. She's supposed to take over their family empire. Her father believes she requires a husband at her side to do so.

Now Penny counted each grain of sand slipping through her internal hourglass, knowing with each passing moment, her chance to have what she wanted lessened.

Alexandre Ricci is his name. Sounded pretentious. Penny's father wanted the union to strengthen their position, telling her it must be this way when she tried to argue. No pressure and no choice for Penny. She's his heir after all.

She almost wished he didn't love her mother the way he did. He might've remarried, giving him the chance for more children and the son he always wanted.

Penny believed her father blamed her for that choice, too. In two weeks, he'll announce her pending nuptials on her birthday. *Her fucking birthday.*

The wedding date's already set. Penny will be married in less than two months, and the stark reality made something inside her snap. She refused to enter this archaic arrangement without doing something for herself.

Wild, raw and real.

Penny had her share of boyfriends throughout high school and college, but none stirred her desire. The all-consuming kind she read about whenever she escaped into the books she loved. During her second-to-last year of university, her father insisted she have full-time security, and Xander became her shadow.

His presence alone shut down all chances of someone asking her out. Not that it mattered. The first time he oozed those *touch her and die* vibes, Penny declared herself swept off her feet. And now she's on the cusp of turning twenty-five without ever....

It's not like she saved it for marriage... though maybe she saved it for Xander in the hopes he'd... he'd what? Control her and seduce her the way he did... Penny gave herself a mental shake. Thankful for the thick sweater she wore to hide her hard nipples. She's almost out of time.

Hence the plan.

Her. Xander. New York. And about seventy-two hours to convince him to give her enough memories to last a lifetime.

No big deal.

Super big deal.

Amidst the preparations she wanted no part of, Penny convinced her father to let her take this trip. She must've caught him at the right moment, busy and distracted - the usual, and he agreed.

Now she rushed to pack her bags in case he changed his mind.

Phase one of her plan is to get Xander to come with her to New York. Since the man followed her everywhere, she figured phase one would go off without a hitch.

The clincher? Phase two. A night of utter debauchery and seduction she hoped would check many firsts off her list.

In her haste to pack, Penny bypassed her assistant, Freya, on a mission to grab another outfit. She marched to her bed, where her overflowing suitcase lay.

She didn't need fifteen outfits for three days, and she planned to buy what she needed for her grand seduction. It's not like she can pack those kinds of things with her present company.

"You know it's one of my jobs to pack your cases," came Fraya's soft reprimand from behind her.

Penny ignored Freya and grabbed her black Gucci slacks. The ones that emphasized her legs and the curve of her ass, and she swore Xander's eyes drifted to her backside from his spot beside the door, like he approved of which pants she picked.

Freya gave a disdainful sniff. "Penelope, since you've got things under control, I'll leave you to it."

The moment Freya closed the door, it took Xander less than half a dozen steps to stand in front of her.

Penny's pulse quickened.

"Ms. Fergusson...."

Penny ignored him and shoved a cotton t-shirt into the case.

"Penelope, at least listen to reason."

Xander knew how much she hated it when he tried to remain impersonal with her. She gave him a long-perfected side-eye and kept stuffing her already overstuffed case.

"Princess," Xander growled, causing her thighs to clench.

While Penny's not actual royalty, Xander started calling her Princess not long after he took over her security detail. It did wicked things to her girly bits. And when he growled it? The sound went straight to her core. Did she have a voice kink?

Not. The. Time.

"You're my bodyguard. I'm traveling to New York. Therefore, you're coming with me."

"The threats against you are real, and I wish you'd take them into consideration. It's too dangerous."

Penny sighed, facing him with her hands on her hips. A sad attempt at her own intimidation.

"Months have gone by since anyone threatened me." Somehow, Penny kept her guilt hidden, having just told Xander a lie.

Xander took another step, standing toe-to-toe with her. His frustration at her casual dismissal etched his face. "Whoever wants to harm you is biding their time, waiting for the right moment. The danger to your life isn't over."

No matter how convincing Xander's argument may be, she's not budging. "Taylor arranged everything. A suite at the St. Regis, a car, and the jet's ready to go." Penny gulped when Xander's jaw clenched.

"Guess you've got it all figured out," he said through gritted teeth.

Xander hated not being in control. She even worried he might get pissed at his second in command, Taylor, for helping her. Taylor laughed it off and assured Penny he'd handle anything Xander threw at him, be it a fist or verbal lashing.

Penny pushed it a bit more. "Besides, my father gave his permission."

"Your father chooses the oddest things to indulge you in."

Oh, hell no. Xander wanted to piss her off? "I am an adult capable of making my own decisions."

Xander stood close enough that her breasts brushed against him with each breath she took, and a gasp slipped past her lips. *When did they get this close*?

For the first time, Penny caught the desire darkening Xander's gaze. Yet it did nothing to lessen the iciness of her words.

"My father has dictated decisions that are supposed to be mine to make. Ones that will shape the rest of my life." The unspoken elephant in the room plunked itself in the tiny space remaining between them.

Xander at least looked chastened, though it didn't stop him from arguing his point further.

Stubborn man.

"There's more to this than a last-minute shopping trip on the eve of your engagement."

Penny sucked in a breath. His bitterness equaled hers, yet Xander knew more about this Alexandre than she did, and his refusal to tell her about him... hurt.

During times like this, she missed her mother the most. This arrangement would never have happened. Penny didn't believe her father to be cruel, yet what he's forcing her to do speaks of his cruelty. She didn't want to dwell on her father right now.

"Please don't fight me on this." Determined to lighten the mood, she said, "Besides, I told my father it's the perfect opportunity to get to know the man who keeps me safe every day. For educational purposes, of course."

Penny's ridiculous statement had the desired effect when she heard his reluctant chuckle.

"If that's what you told him, I'm surprised your father didn't lock you in this room and fire my ass." Xander sighed. "Look, whatever you said worked. Despite all my protests, he wants you to go. This doesn't change the fact--"

Penny raised her hand and stopped the speech she'd memorized a long time ago. She stepped around Xander and returned to her packing. If he wanted to dance around the subject, fine. Penny could tango.

She crossed her arms and faced him again. “It doesn’t change how you have information about the man I’m expected to marry and won’t tell me a damn thing about him.”

Chapter Two

Xander

Xander knew he'd lost the battle, and damn it, he didn't want to fight it anymore. He cleared his throat and conceded. "I'll pack my bags." Then he turned and walked out of Penny's room. The moment the door closed, he leaned against it and rubbed a hand over his face, tugging his beard.

Fucked. He is so fucked.

He raised his phone to his ear, barking when the call connected. "I'm going to pack. I assume you'll have everything covered here."

"Oh? Going somewhere?"

"Nice to know how easy it is to manipulate you, Tay." Xander's eyes darted along the hallway, ensuring no one lurked, then he growled, "Fucking traitor." Which made Taylor's laughter louder.

"Enjoy your time in New York, brother. Don't let Penelope take advantage of you."

"You're one to talk."

More laughter filled his ears.

Xander didn't get the chance to tell him to fuck off when Taylor said, "I'll take over rounds and be outside Penny's door in two minutes." Then Taylor disconnected.

Taylor never questioned the strict protocol Xander demanded for protecting Penelope Fergusson. This is her home, and she ought to be safe here, yet with his Princess...nothing is ever enough.

Hell, the reason he even called her Princess to begin with is because she lives in an honest-to-god, fucking castle. Xander reached his room in record time. The secret passages he memorized during his first week on the job cut his route in half.

When he closed and leaned against his door, the memory of when he first met Penny came to the forefront of his mind.

Xander stood off to the side when Penelope walked into her father's study. First impression? She's a goddess among mortals. Dressed in jeans and a t-shirt, with her rich auburn hair in a sleek ponytail, falling to the center of her back.

He wanted to wrap the silky strand around his fist.

Xander took an uncontrolled step toward her. If Taylor hadn't gripped his forearm, he would've closed the distance and done it. Did he want to get fired on the first day?

Penelope's father shuffled the papers on his desk, making her wait for the explanation of why he'd summoned her. Xander knew very little about his business. It's something they both planned to rectify.

An old acquaintance recommended him for this job, and Xander found he couldn't refuse. Not after he saw Penelope's photo. He left the day-to-day operations of his security company back in New York in the capable hands of Everly Hayes, another member of his team. Taylor volunteered to come with him, and the two of them now stood in an honest-to-god castle complete with its own village a few hours from Glasgow.

"We've dealt with the breach in your security," Penelope's father said, breaking the oppressive silence settling over the room.

"Thank you, Father. When you first made me aware, I took the liberty and applied to other schools."

Her voice. Oh, fuck, her voice resonated like the sweetest of melodies, something Xander wanted to hear for the rest of his life.

Penelope's father grunted. "Where did you decide?" Her eyes widened in response, surprised by his question.

Did her father not show interest in her life?

"Erm, I'm sticking close to home and decided on Edinburgh. My course selection took a bit of time, which is why I'm late."

Her father didn't like the reminder of her delay. "While your initiative is impressive, your safety remains at risk, and I've decided; if you want to complete your education, you will not leave these grounds without twenty-four-hour security."

Penelope's creamy complexion heated while she worked to keep her emotions under control. His Princess is strong.

Wait, his Princess? The impossibility of Penelope ever being his didn't lessen how right it felt to call her his.

"Wait, father-" Penelope tried.

Her father's face turned molten. "This is not up for negotiation. Despite your mother's best efforts, you are my heir, and we cannot risk you flitting about while you fill your head with useless information."

"Father, please. My education is to your benefit."

Xander wanted to pump his fist in the air and cheer her on when she held her ground against her father. No matter how futile her attempt might be, he admired Penelope's tenacity.

"Securing a marriage is more suitable," her father muttered, and Xander clenched his fists. A surge of possessive jealousy coursed through his bloodstream at her father's callous words.

She's *his* Princess.

The energy rolling off him brought her attention to him, and when Penelope's amber gaze met his, logic told him he needed to decline this job.

While other parts, like his heart, soul, and cock, let him know how difficult walking away would be.

Penelope marched up to him, and Xander took in her height. Tall women were his weakness. Her luscious curves checked all his boxes, and he knew she'd handle whatever he gave her. Like all nine fucking inches. *Shit.* He needed to lock ideas like those away.

There's at least a decade of age and a lifetime of experience separating them, yet Xander wanted to corrupt this woman.

What he didn't expect was the slender index finger poking him square in the chest or the harsh words accompanying it. "You are going to stick out like a sore thumb."

His expression shifted to a scowl. Yeah, at six-six, he's a big fucking guy, but he knew how to blend into the background.

She turned back to her father. "Father, please be reasonable."

"I am. I contemplated pulling you right out of school. Consider this a generous compromise."

Penny squared her shoulders, shrugged off her father's words, and turned back to face Xander with her hand extended. His hand engulfed hers, and he relished her soft skin against his calloused palm. "It's nice to meet you. I'm Penelope Fergusson, though please call me Penny. Welcome to Castle Fergus."

A smirk teased his lips. "Alexander Ward." Xander tipped his head closer. Despite her height, he still maintained several inches on her, and he caught a whiff of her flowery scent. "Call me Xander."

He nodded toward the man beside him. "This is my associate, Taylor Benson." Xander didn't let go of her hand, not allowing his friend to touch her.

Mine.

Funny thing, Penny let him. "Pleased to meet you, Mr. Benson," she said, giving Taylor a nod.

Without a care in the world, Taylor gave her a bright smile. "You too, and it's Taylor."

"Mr. Ward," Penny's father, James, said, standing behind his desk, now done with their meeting. "Geoffrey will show you and your associate to your quarters and introduce you to the rest of the staff. If you'll excuse me, I have another meeting."

Xander let go of Penny's hand, and with a gesture toward the door, James Fergusson dismissed them from his presence.

Penny didn't budge. "Father, I'd like to attend the meeting. Like you pointed out, I'm your heir. Aren't I expected to be there?"

"You'll attend council meetings when I deem it acceptable for you to do so."

Penny seemed to shut down when she replied, "Yes, Father."

They left in a procession, with Geoffrey leading the way, followed by Taylor, Penny, and Xander. Walking behind, Penny gave him a front-row seat to her justifiable rant.

"Damn him and his archaic ways. It takes more than a penis to get shit done."

Penny's head whipped around when Xander chuckled, and her molten amber gaze pinned him in place. Then she turned back and kept talking to herself.

"My last two years of university, I'm stuck with a shadow who eclipses the sun. One look at him, and no person will dare come near me."

"Damn right, they won't," Xander grumbled.

Then Xander almost tripped when Penny exclaimed, "I'm never going to get laid at this rate." She veered away from their procession, heading in the opposite direction to where Geoffrey led them.

He wanted to follow Penny. Press her against the wall and caged her in with his body. He wanted to be the first to do things to her. For her. Wicked things, dirty things... things which beckoned his inner Daddy Dom. It'd be best for everyone if he walked away.

He never did.

For three years, Xander fought this pull between them. He can't anymore. If Penny asked for what they both desired, his resistance would crumble.

Chapter Three

Xander

They boarded the jet a few hours later.

Penny kept her distance, sleeping in the bedroom at the back of the plane while Xander sat in one of the club seats in the main cabin, staring out the small window into the blackness of the night.

When they landed, a driver waited beside a black SUV on the tarmac and drove them to the hotel.

Xander grabbed their keycard and escorted Penny into the exclusive elevator behind the St. Regis butler, carrying their bags. He thanked the man when he set their bags inside the door. Xander declined the unpacking service and sent the man on his way.

He checked the suite over while Penny waited by the door. At least she listened to him regarding her safety. Satisfied no recording devices or anyone were in their suite, Xander locked the door and grabbed her bag, setting it inside the larger of the two bedrooms.

"Try to get some more sleep. Lots to do tomorrow."

Is Penny smirking?

"Yes, lots to do. Goodnight."

Damn it, she is.

Xander didn't have the energy to figure out what Penny's up to. Not getting any sleep on the plane is catching up with him. The comfortable mattress lured him, and he crawled between the soft sheets. He succumbed to the need for sleep, knowing Penny slumbered on the other side of the wall.

Xander woke with the sun and ordered a carafe of coffee, letting Penny sleep a little longer. With their time here limited, he knew she'd want to make the most of it.

He gave her door a firm tap and pushed it open. Nine in the morning, and his Princess remained a lump beneath the bedding in the dim room.

His Princess.

No, not his. Penny's marrying Alexandre Ricci in a matter of months.

Despite the knowledge, Xander's gaze raked over her. Penny's hair spread out behind her on the pillow. Her right arm lay above her head, and her fingers tangled in some strands. The soft snore made him smile.

Xander traced his finger from her temple to her cheek, sweeping her hair away from her eyes. Penny looked innocent and unaffected while she slept.

"Princess...it's time to wake up." He kept his voice low, not wanting to startle her.

Penny let out a soft moan, her face scrunching in protest, not ready to wake. "Five more minutes," she groaned, pulling a pillow over her head.

Xander chuckled. "I guess you don't want this cup of coffee after all."

Penny's caffeine obsession had her flinging the pillow away and sitting up against the headboard. "I'm up, I'm up."

Shit. So is his dick.

She'd slept in a pale peach top, which did nothing to hide the rosy color of her pebbled nipples when the blanket fell to her lap.

Xander cleared his throat and handed her the mug. He didn't realize until she sat up that the reaction to her thin top was level with her face. He turned away.

Not quick enough.

"Thanks for the...erm...coffee." She giggled, taking a healthy sip. Then Penny let out a moan, which exacerbated the situation. "Oh man, it's the good stuff."

For his sanity, Xander kept his back to her. "I'd uh... like to take you to breakfast at one of my favorite places. Once you finish... uh... enjoying your coffee, we'll head out."

Xander pointed to the pile of clothes he'd tossed on the bench on his way out. "Wear these and make sure you use the runners you brought. We'll be doing a lot of walking today."

With his hand on the door, Penny stopped his exit when she called his name. Xander took a deep breath and turned to face her. Disappointed yet relieved, she pulled the covers over her tempting breasts. "Yeah?"

"You got me an outfit to wear, despite all the stuff I packed?"

There's no sense in denying it. "Yes, and I know you hate when Freya does it, but-"

"No, no, it's fine. I like it when you take care of me." She leaned forward, and the blankets dropped again, giving him another eyeful of her hardened peaks.

Xander swallowed. "It's just clothes."

"I know. It's also...more. Thank you for everything, Xander."

Xander gave her a sharp nod. "I'll give you some time to get ready." Then he closed the door between him and his temptation.

Xander checked the time, then knocked on Penny's door. "Come in."

He found her in the bathroom with her arms in the air and her hair tangled around her fingers as she tried to braid her hair. Xander stepped behind her and met her frustrated gaze in the mirror. "Here, let me."

Penny's arms dropped to her sides, and braiding her hair became a lesson in restraint when she let out a quiet moan when he pulled a brush through her hair, freeing it from knots.

"Thank you. I can never get a braid right."

"You look good in the clothes I chose for you." Penny looked like the sexiest Yankees fan. Faded jeans with tears at the knees and rolled-up cuffs paired with a Yankees jersey with the matching ball cap waiting on the counter.

She blushed, and it became a little harder to keep the way she affected him a secret. "I know nothing about baseball, though I have heard of the Yanks."

"Yankees," Xander said with a laugh, finishing her braid. "If we had time, I'd take you to a game. Elastic?"

"Right. Right, Yankees," Penny agreed, handing him the band from around her wrist.

Xander tugged on the end, and he couldn't resist wrapping it in his fist. His other hand dropped to her shoulder, and they stared at one another's reflection. "There, all done."

Penny spun to face him. The grip he kept on her hair tipped her head back, and it brought their mouths close enough that Xander could taste her minty breath. He cleared his throat and let go of Penny's hair.

He reached for the ball cap and put it on her head, tapping the brim. "Come on. I have the perfect breakfast spot in mind."

At that moment, Penny's stomach rumbled. They both laughed, and it broke the ever-present tension humming between them. "Thank goodness, because obviously I'm starving."

Penny slipped her small black purse across her body, and Xander grabbed his wallet and room key, ensuring the door locked behind them. If Penny wants to get to know him, the place he's taking her to will provide some answers.

When they stepped outside the hotel, Penny took a deep breath as the noise and energy of the city surrounded them. "I love New York. Every time I come here, I find it harder to leave."

Penny glanced at him from beneath the brim of her hat. "If I ever got the opportunity, I'd move here."

Xander smiled and admitted, "It's one of my favorite places." He missed New York something fierce. He grew up here. His friends and family are here. It's his home base, his sanctuary between missions while in the military. Hell, the office for his security company is here. The one thing keeping him from this city is the fiery redhead beside him.

So, yeah, he'd fucking like it if she lived here too, but her future's set, and Xander must accept that.

They walked several blocks to his uncle's diner, becoming one with the flow of pedestrians. Xander enjoyed seeing the smile on Penny's face. It's the most relaxed she's been in a long time.

Xander's earliest memories are of his uncle and the diner he owned and lived above. His uncle Dimitri raised him after his parents died in a fire when he was two, and despite his tragic beginnings. He grew up happy, working at the diner until he joined the military a few years after 9/11. In the elite special forces team he belonged to, Xander found the extended family he needed.

The bell jangled above the door to Ric's Diner when Xander held it open for Penny to enter ahead of him. "Mm, it smells delicious in here," she said, clapping her hands. "Excellent choice for breakfast."

Xander smiled, grabbed a couple of menus off the counter, and took Penny to a four-seater in the corner.

The place hummed with conversation and the comfortable, chaotic hustle of a busy restaurant. Xander was about to tell Penny his connection to the place when a firm hand on his shoulder caught him off guard.

"Shouldn't be able to sneak up on ya, boy. You're slippin."

"You're the only one." Xander stood from their table and embraced the man.

"I'd better be."

Xander chuckled and tightened their hug. "It's good to see you, Uncle."

"You didn't tell me you were coming."

"It's last-minute and-"

"Bah. I don't want to hear sorry excuses. Even I know how to text Alexi." No matter how old Xander got, his uncle still chastised him like he's ten.

Dimitri's tone changed the moment he spied Penny behind him. "Now, who do we have here?" he asked, stepping around Xander to offer Penny his hand.

"This is Penelope." His uncle's head turned back around to pin him with a stare, aware of whom Xander worked for.

"Penny, this is my uncle Dimitri. He owns this diner. This is where I grew up."

"Ah, Alexi, this is your home, no matter how old you get."

Xander hugged his uncle again. "Thank you."

Penny stood and held out her hand. "It's a pleasure to meet you, Dimitri."

"The pleasure is mine," he replied with a kiss on her knuckles, making her blush.

Xander chuckled. "Enough, uncle. Don't scare her off with your flirting." He gestured for him to join them. "Have you stopped long enough to eat breakfast?"

"I'll stop when I'm dead, but I'll spare some time to share a meal." Dimitri waved one of his servers over. "Any allergies?" he asked Penny.

"No."

"Allow me to order for you, then."

"Alright, thank you," Penny agreed, setting her menu down.

Dimitri studied Penny as if he possessed the ability to read her food preferences by the number of freckles on her face, and Xander tried to hide his smirk with little success.

"The lady will have the Salmon Benny with the garlic roasted potatoes, and a fresh fruit cup. Do you want your usual, Alexi?"

"Yes, uncle."

"He'll have the Western Omelette, and I'll have yoghurt with fresh fruit and granola. Bring a round of fresh-squeezed orange juice and espressos."

When the server left, Dimitri turned his attention back to Penny. "Alexi has never brought a woman here to meet me. Ever."

"She's my job, Uncle." Damn it, he didn't want to put that look of hurt on Penny's face. And he knew the lie for what it was because she's so much more. "Penny wanted to come to New York for a little getaway."

Dimitri gave him a look, and Xander knew he was about to get called out. "Oh, she's far more than that, I'd wager."

Fucking mind reader.

"*She'd* appreciate not being spoken about like *she's* not here," Penny snapped back.

"I'm sorry, Penelope. That was inappropriate and uncalled for."

"Thank you, Xander." Penny captured Dimitri's attention. "Now tell me, did Xander show up this way? I can't picture him as a small child."

Dimitri laughed and regaled her with stories of Xander's youth, adding a few embellishments to keep the tales tall and Penny entertained.

Xander set his napkin on his plate, done with his meal and stories of his awkward childhood years. "You ready to go?"

"Yes." She turned to Dimitri. "My compliments to the chef. You chose exactly what I wanted, Dimitri. Delicious, thank you."

"I'm going to use the restroom. Penny? We're going to be doing a lot of walking."

"No, I'm good."

Xander threw a stack of folded bills onto the table.

"Alexi, your money is no good here." Dimitri protested. "It looks like enough to buy everyone in here their meals and then some."

"It is." Leaving no room for argument.

Dimitri waved their server over, sending her to the till with instructions to divide it among the staff.

"I'll be back in two minutes."

"I'll keep her safe," his uncle said, answering his unspoken request.

"Never any doubt, Uncle." He glanced at Penny. "I'll be right back." Xander left their table, maneuvering through the others scattered along the way to the hallway at the back.

Chapter Four

Penny

Penny adored hearing about her elusive bodyguard. When Xander headed to the washroom, she believed Dimitri planned to regale her with more stories when he pulled his chair closer and placed his hand on top of hers.

"When he says two minutes, he means two minutes," Dimitri said, pulling her attention back to his sharp gaze.

"You know, fate is a crafty siren. When Alexi signed on to guard you, I knew she had a hand in it."

"What do you mean?"

Dimitri gave her an assessing look, then a sharp nod, seeming to agree with whatever conclusion he'd come to. "You are Alexi's, which means I will lay my life down for you."

Penny's heart ached. She wanted it to be true; belonging to Xander is her ultimate desire. She didn't know how to accomplish such a thing when she was supposed to marry someone else. "I don't know what to say…Xander and I are not…my father hired him to keep me safe."

Dimitri met her gaze with finality. "You are Alexi's. He'll figure it out…even if he is being stubborn about it," he said, tracking Xander on his way back to the table where he stopped to talk to some of the staff he knew well. "You've got your cellphone on you?"

"Yes."

"Well, get it out and add this number to your contacts. Memorize it too. If you ever need my help, I'm a phone call away."

Penny didn't know when she'd ever need the older man's help, yet she followed his instructions, both memorizing the number and adding it to her contacts under Xander's hardheaded uncle. She put her phone away, and Dimitri tucked the card into his pocket moments before Xander returned.

"Let me guess…my uncle enthralled you with the time I got locked in Macy's overnight. In my defense, I was seven and wanted to prove to my friends Santa kept a secret workshop there," Xander said when he sat back down, his hands in the air in mock surrender.

The light returned to Dimitri's eyes as if it had never left. He stood and pulled Xander into a hug. "You caught me. I'm glad I got to see you, even for a short time. She's special, son." Dimitri pivoted back to Penny. "I hope we'll meet again. Take care," he said, squeezing her hand.

Penny defaulted to polite neutrality. "Thank you for your hospitality, Dimitri." There was a lot she needed to unpack, but she lacked the energy to try. What she wanted – no, what she needed - was to give her control over to someone else.

She'd give almost anything for Xander to take over....

"Enjoy the rest of your time here," Dimitri said, bringing Penny back to the present.

"Thanks again."

"Ready to explore and shop?"

Penny suppressed a shudder at the way Xander leaned in close to her. The low rumble of his voice played havoc with her desire. "Yes, please."

Xander grabbed her forgotten ball cap off the table and pulled the brim low over her face. Penny was thankful for a way to hide the heat of her cheeks when he placed his hand at the small of her back and escorted her out of the diner.

Hours later, after her successful yet torturous shopping expedition, Penny slipped away from Xander, desperate and needy to rub one out, yet she didn't act on it, edging herself by waiting for the tub to fill. She squeezed her thighs together, glimpsing her flushed features in the bathroom mirror before it fogged with the steam rising from her bath.

Penny settled beneath the fragrant water, her fingers teasing back and forth over the rugged peaks of her nipples, wanting to keep herself on the precipice, but not go over. No... she wanted Xander to make her come.

"Wow." Penny stared at her reflection, not quite believing who looked back. The dark wig and red lips, combined with her natural porcelain skin, gave her a Snow White-like appearance. Funny, she always found the evil queen more alluring. Maybe it's because she secretly desired to be wicked.

Penny went with a smoky shadow, using shades of mauve and charcoal to make her eyes look like shimmering pools of amber. Not bad for doing it herself. With the addition of the masks they'd wear tonight, no one will recognize her.

All she needed was to convince Xander.

Penny imagined his hands in place of hers, sliding over the material covering her breasts. She cupped them, squeezing her flesh. What will it be like to have Xander suckle her nipples and take as much of her breast into his mouth as he could?

Oh, how she longed to find out.

Her eyes traveled over the rest of her reflection in the full-length mirror. Her dress ended at her feet with two slits running up the front of each leg, stopping below the juncture of her thighs, keeping the tiny pair of lace panties she wore out of sight.

Penny told Xander earlier she wanted to go out for dinner, knowing he'd have a place in mind. Her stomach twisted. Food's the last thing on her mind. She hungered for what he could give her.

Penny took a fortifying breath and stepped into the main room. Xander sat on the couch, facing the window. He'd left his suit jacket unbuttoned, and his elbows rested on his knees while he looked at something on his phone.

Xander twisted his strawberry-blond hair into a loose knot instead of his usual tight braid, and despite his standard attire of a fitted black-on-black suit, he was the most relaxed she'd seen him.

"You ready...," Xander's words trailed off when his gaze lifted from his phone to her. Penny had this sudden urge for him to look at her like that for the rest of their lives.

While her head filled with fantasies, Xander moved toward her, circling her like prey. His gaze raked over her from head to toe. When he spoke, Xander caught her off guard with his question. "Is this part of your plan?"

"I don't know what you're talking about." Penny lifted her chin and met his gaze with what she hoped was a defiant one.

He stepped further into her personal space. "You sure about that, Princess?" Xander asked, fingering a lock of the silky black wig.

"Okay. You got me." She drew her shoulders back, hoping against hope that Xander would agree to what she wanted. "I want you to take me to Club Decadent."

Xander's fingers froze, wrapped in the strands of her wig, while his silvery-blue gaze searched hers. "How do you know about Decadent?"

He held up his hand. "Wait, I know. Taylor." Maybe Penny needed to stop charming Taylor into helping her out. She's going to get the guy in trouble.

"Penelope, it's time you told me the real reason we came to New York."

"I need you to stop being my bodyguard and pretend for one night."

Xander kept his voice low and, dare she believe, seductive? “If something other than protecting is going to happen, it won’t be pretend.”

Wait. Does Xander want this too?

Penny gathered her courage and laid it all out. “I want you to give me a night of passion and discovery. I’d like to explore some things with you. Then, I want you to fuck me. Can you do that while still protecting me?”

Xander chuckled at her bold statement. The rumble climbing from the center of his chest held a dark promise. “Is that all you want?”

His question sent a shiver down her spine and scorching heat to her core. Penny realized that if she told Xander everything she wanted, he might give it to her. “I want to submit.”

Penny swore she’d hear a pin drop in the silence following her confession. With the dam now breached, she can’t stop the flow of words.

“I want... I want to experience what the woman did when she fell apart in your arms, between you and her husband.”

Penny wanted to cover her face and cool the flames Xander’s sharp intake of breath caused after spilling such a secret, yet she kept her hands at her sides and met his gaze.

Xander didn’t mince words. “I knew you were there. I heard you gasp.”

“Did you know I witnessed all of it?”

“No.” Xander looked confused. “You attended the opera with Taylor that night.”

"I claimed a headache, and we turned the car around. It was supposed to be you who took me. I like Taylor, but it's not the same. When I got back, I dismissed Taylor and went looking for you."

Xander's scowl deepened.

Well, this is going well. Why stop now?

"I saw everything from the moment you ran into each other to how they looked at you, and you, at them."

"You don't know what you're asking for, Penelope."

Penny gave him a scowl of her own when he used her full name again. A futile attempt for Xander to keep a professional distance. They're way past that.

"I know what I want. I want to experience what you gave that couple. More even. If tonight's all I get before I'm forced to marry a stranger, then I want to experience everything."

"You want to be pleasured by two men? Taken over by two men when you've never-?"

"It's the fact you know I've never fucked someone that's embarrassing enough."

Xander stopped his pacing and faced her. "Language, Princess," he admonished, and Penny found the chastisement arousing. "Besides, you told me."

"No. You listened in on a private conversation."

"With yourself," Xander said, beyond exasperated.

"Not the point. I may not have your kind of experience." Penny poked the center of his chest, driving her point home. "What I have is access to the internet. Plus, you've seen the type of books I read."

Xander grabbed her finger, preventing Penny from making another jab, though it didn't stop her momentum. "I also have several toys and a vivid imagination. Just because there isn't a revolving door of men doesn't mean I don't know what I want."

Xander's eyes darkened to the shade of an impending storm, the only outward sign of his internal struggle to process everything she revealed. *She knows she's a lot. Some may even consider her too much.*

"Anyone who thinks that is a piece of shit, and if I ever hear someone say something like that to you, it will be the last words they ever speak."

Holy shit, that's hot.

Xander smirked.

Penny read enough to know that honesty and trust are requirements when exploring anything in a dominant and submissive dynamic. She already trusted Xander with her life, and she wanted to give him more.

"Take me to the club." She pleaded, giving it one last shot. "I want what only you can give me. The control. The domination. Your desire to share ...."

Xander's jaw flexed. "Princess, it'll take one hell of a man for me to share you with anyone."

"But you do share?"

"Yes," he snapped. "Does it bother you knowing I enjoy having both men and women at the mercy of my pleasure? How I like to be in control of their every need and desire?"

If he meant bothered, like hot and bothered, then, oh yeah. Penny knew what he was referring to. "No, it doesn't bother me."

Penny didn't want him to doubt it. "Oh, fuck. It excites me and turns me on." She seldom cursed, yet she knew Xander liked it when she did.

"Over the past three years, you became my world, whether you'll admit it. Now, my world is about to change despite my desire that it not. If everything's going to be different, I want one night to experience all I can, and I want it with you."

Penny dared to reach up and stroke his beard, the coarse hair soft against her fingertips. "Please, Xander." Then she dared a little more and trailed her fingers down his corded neck until they rested at the collar of his shirt.

"Alone in my bed, I'd picture the night I saw you." Penny shifted closer, and the heat from him seeped into her skin.

"Except," she whispered, tilting her head back to meet his penetrating gaze. "When I pictured it, I'm the one who comes apart between you."

Chapter Five

Xander

His cock hardened the moment he caught sight of Penny's seductive disguise. Xander didn't have any fight left. Call him selfish, but he needed these memories as much as Penny did.

Either he's going to kill Taylor for being a gossip or-

Xander let his gaze travel over her. From the top of her wig to the tips of her stilettos, she enjoyed every inch of his perusal.

-or he's giving Taylor a bottle of his favorite scotch to thank him for his meddling.

Penny's floral scent filled his senses the closer he got. It's one he'd recognize anywhere as hers and hers alone. Xander remembered catching a hint of it the night in the hall. He'd known she lurked in the shadows. He just didn't know how much she saw until now.

Six months into his job, Xander had already reached his breaking point with Penny. He'd pawned off the night at the opera to Taylor because he'd been afraid he'd act on the desires he could no longer keep in check. The moment he growled Penny's name against the other woman's neck brought an awkward end to his efforts to distract himself from wanting a woman he couldn't have.

From then on, he kept any other entanglements far away from Penny. The few partners he'd taken the edge off with became fewer the longer he remained her protector. Xander had fucked nothing other than his hand for the last year. Everything's a poor substitute for his Princess, and tonight, he's going to make Penny, Daddy's dirty girl.

"Alright, Princess. If we do this, two things are going to happen. One. Your submission is mine. If tonight's all we have… well, I want these memories, too." Xander cupped her face between his palms, not letting her look anywhere else.

Penny nodded.

"I need your words."

"Yes."

"You're going to need a safe word. We'll keep it simple and use the traffic light system. Green lets me know you're ready, and yellow means you need to slow things down. And red will stop everything immediately. Questions?"

Penny's response was quick. "No."

Xander wanted to ensure Penny understood. “You can ask me anything, or stop this with one word. Never forget, while I control your pleasure, my beautiful siren, you hold all the power.”

Lost in the liquid amber of her eyes. It took Xander a moment to realize Penny had asked him a question. “Hmm?”

“You said two things. What’s the other one?”

“We’re not leaving this suite until I make you come. The first time you orgasm for me will not be at Decadent.”

“Xander, please. I need you.”

He needed her to understand the effect she has on him. Xander pressed his thickening cock against the juncture of Penny’s thighs. “The way the word please falls from your lips,” he whispered, his thumb grazing her bottom lip, careful not to ruin her lipstick. Yet.

He rocked his hips against hers. “I can’t wait to listen to you beg me to let you come.”

Penny gasped, and Xander witnessed her amber eyes turn molten with desire when she asked, “What are you waiting for, then?”

“You asked for it, Princess.” Xander gripped the slender length of her throat, and her pupils dilated from his hold. His thumb grazed her jawline, and he tilted her head further back to capture her mouth.

“Open for me,” Xander demanded, his lips brushing against hers with each word.

Then he crashed his mouth onto hers, sliding his tongue past her parted lips. He explored her, and she met his tongue stroke for stroke.

Penny moaned and tugged on the collar of his jacket, trying to pull him closer. His hands spanned her lower back, one slipping lower to grip her ass and pull her flush against him.

Xander broke their kiss and let go of her to undo the knot of his tie, letting it hang around his collar. He reached for the top buttons of his shirt and worked the first few open.

He almost laughed. His sweet Penny is in for a shock. She gasped, taking in the tattoos covering his upper body from his collarbone to his hip and from his shoulders to his wrists.

"How did I not know you're covered in ink?" Penny asked, trying to pry a few more buttons open to get a better look.

"It's not like I parade around you half-naked." His amusement turned into a groan when Penny dipped her fingers beneath his open collar and traced the line of dark ink he revealed. Her gentle touch sent a shock of desire through his system.

"I wish you did. We might've gotten here a hell of a lot sooner."

Chapter Six

Penny

"Penny...."

"I'm more than aware we cannot dwell on what-ifs." More than aware, dwelling helped no one, and Xander's tattoos are the perfect distraction.

How did she not know?

And then Penny realized that all these years, she'd never caught Xander with a button of his shirt undone. Let alone in a t-shirt. Why did it never occur to her to ask Xander why he never wore short sleeves?

His full lips, the ones she may have an addiction to, turned up at the corners in a sexy smirk while he undid a few more buttons, revealing more black and grey ink.

"Are they everywhere?" Her question came out all breathy, yet Penny didn't care. She wanted to explore each shaded line with her fingers, followed by her mouth. Tattoos fascinated her. She didn't have any, though she always wanted one.

Xander allowed her to take over unbuttoning his shirt. Her patience having left the building a long time ago, and Xander taking his sweet time, didn't help.

"Just my upper body," he said.

With his shirt open, Penny placed her palms against his stomach. His muscles flexed, and when her fingers circled his nipples, Xander captured her wrists, pressing her hands flat against his chest, ending her exploration.

Penny whimpered. *Whimp-purred.*

Her fingers flexed within his grasp. She wanted to explore more while Xander held her hands captive.

"Can I look at the rest?"

"I wish we had time. I'd demand you explore every inch of my body."

Their limited time is not something Penny wanted to dwell on. When she tried to put some space between them, Xander stopped her, placing his index finger beneath her chin. The slight pressure forced Penny to meet his gaze.

"There isn't enough time for everything, little one."

"Xander, I'm five-eleven. Little isn't a word ever used to describe me." It bothered her in her younger years, like when she grew a head taller than every guy she met. Now Penny embraced her height and wore stilettos to stand even taller. Yet next to Xander… Penny appeared delicate and petite.

She needed to look up to meet his gaze despite the added height her shoes provided. With his lips close to hers, he said, "Sweetheart, when you're six-six, ninety percent of the population falls into the little category, plus it suits you."

One of Penny's favorite fantasies is being with someone strong enough to hold her up with a hand around her throat and his hips between her thighs. For the past several years, Xander's features filled the formerly blurry face.

Penny knew Xander was the person thanks to their intense workout sessions. He lifted her as if she weighed nothing. Tossed her over his shoulder like a rag doll. Even when he overpowered her, Penny knew he'd never hurt her.

If she'd found the confidence to confront him about what simmered between them sooner, perhaps things would have turned out differently. Agony filled her. How will she cope with the reality of Xander being her bodyguard and walking down the aisle with another man?

To be honest, at least with herself, Xander has always been more than just her bodyguard.

"Hey, where'd you go?" Xander asked.

Chapter Seven

Xander

Penny's troubles played across her beautiful face, and Xander vowed then and there to make them disappear, at least for tonight. He clasped her hand and stepped back, turning Penny in a slow display to take in every inch of her.

"Forgive me for not telling you how stunning you look this evening, Princess. You stole all my common sense the moment you walked in the room."

Xander turned Penny until she faced the bedroom door. His hand dropped to her hip, and he guided her until her hand wrapped around the door-knob. "Open it unless you prefer to use the bed I slept in."

"No, I want you where I sleep." Her shoulders rose with the intake of a deep breath, then she opened the door and moved to stand beside the bed, facing him. Penny's fingers twitched nervously at her sides.

Xander studied her. He wanted to give Penny endless memories. "I don't want to damage your beautiful dress. Take it off."

Penny reached behind her and undid the clasp holding her dress in place. Xander waited, the anticipation like nothing he's ever experienced. Then she stepped out of the dress, leaving her clad in a black lace thong and those sexy-as-fuck stilettos.

"Allow me." Xander took her dress and laid it on the bench at the end of the bed, careful not to wrinkle it. She didn't hide her body when he faced her. Penny straightened her spine, pulling her shoulders back. She widened her stance and pressed her palms against her thighs. The position displayed her beauty.

Fuck. Xander wanted Penny's scent in his beard, her taste on his tongue.

"Lose the underwear too." Without hesitation, Penny slid the bit of lace down her legs and used her right foot to kick her underwear away. The bit of lace landed at his feet.

"You're such a brave, confident, and beautiful woman." Xander didn't miss the way she basked in his praise. "Your praise kink will receive a lot of attention tonight, Princess. Do you also have a degradation kink?"

Penny's nose scrunched. "What do you mean?"

"Do you want an example?"

"Yes...please," Penny said after a moment's hesitation.

"Is my dirty little whore wet for me?" Xander didn't have to wait long for Penny's reaction.

A flush spread from her cheeks down the length of her throat, and she let out a gasp before biting her lip to silence it.

"Well?" he demanded.

"Y-yes."

Xander wanted specifics. "Yes, you like the added degradation, or yes, you're wet for me?"

"Both," Penny moaned. "It's both. Your dirty whore is wet for you."

Xander grunted. "Noted. I'll give you a bit of degradation, too." He snagged her panties from the floor, bringing the damp fabric to his nose, inhaling her scent. "Fuck, you're intoxicating."

Penny let out another gasp when he tucked the delicious scrap of lace into his pocket. He arched his brow and gave her a stern look. "What? You won't be needing them."

Penny licked her lips and didn't protest any further.

"Good girl."

Xander shrugged out of his suit jacket and tossed it onto the chair in the corner. His shirt and tie followed. Penny's gaze raked over him. Her eyes on him felt like a physical caress.

He skimmed his knuckles along her cheek, relishing the softness of her skin. Then he did something he'd longed to do for years, brushing his lips against hers in a tender kiss. Xander wanted to wreck her, yet he needed to show Penny how much he cared.

Xander pressed his forehead to hers; his warm breath teased her damp lips when he said, "You're breathtaking." He gave in to the urge to explore Penny, touching her neck, stroking a finger along her collarbone to the peaks of her breasts, committing every curve to memory. She sucked in a sharp breath when he pinched her nipples.

"So fucking beautiful." Xander twisted them between his fingers, and Penny cried his name.

"Please, I need more," she begged.

His thumbs teased her rosy tips. "Get on the bed."

"What are you going to do to me?"

"Does my Princess like dirty talk?"

Penny gave him a seductive look over her shoulder while she crawled to the center of the bed. "What do you think?"

Xander's brain short-circuited with Penny on all fours, and her peach of an ass in the air, wiggling like an invitation. It took a moment for him to come to his senses. When he did, Xander captured her ankle and flipped her over. "Far enough, Princess."

He removed her shoes, setting them on the floor beside him. Then he placed her feet on the edge of the mattress, never once taking his eyes off hers.

Xander loomed over her, something no other man had done, and he battled a possessive desire to keep it that way, but deep down, Xander knew that wasn't true. Penny expressed an interest in being shared, and he wanted to control someone else making her come.

"Remember to use your safeword if any of this becomes too much." Xander nipped her throat, then growled in her ear, "I'm going to soak my beard in your cum, Princess."

"Oh," Penny moaned and squirmed beneath him. Her voice sounded raspy with desire, turned on by his filthy words, and he wished for the time to explore how to make her come from his words alone.

"I want you to soak my beard so I can wear your scent and breathe you in until it's all I can smell."

"Oh, fuck. Please." Her plea was a whimper as her hips rocked, eager for him to get between her thighs.

"I can smell how aroused you are, and it's driving me wild. I need to fucking taste you."

Xander pushed off the bed to stand over her once more. "Up on your elbows and hook your hands under your thighs. I want you to pull your knees toward your chest. Yes..." he groaned. "Show me how wet you are."

Chapter Eight

Penny

H-o-l-y fuck, this is happening.

Of course, the literal puddle of arousal forming beneath Penny told her it was. Dirty talk. Who knew how much she'd love it? Is it possible to orgasm from words alone?

"Don't make me ask you again," Xander growled, making Penny shiver. The second thing his growl did was make her body obey. She shifted onto her elbows and grabbed the backs of her knees. Then she pulled her legs toward her chest, exposing her pussy to his gaze.

"Fuck. You're beautiful, Princess."

Penny basked in the warmth of his praise and arched her hips to offer him everything.

"Look how wet you are for me. I haven't even touched you."

She blushed and lowered her gaze.

"Don't take your eyes off me," Xander commanded, making her gaze snap to his. "I want to see the moment you explode on my tongue."

"Oh...." Her breath came out in a whoosh, and her core spasmed. Penny swore she experienced a mini-orgasm.

Xander loomed over her and dragged his hand down the center of her body until his fingers dipped between her folds and circled her clit with utter precision. "Anyone else ever touch you like this, Princess?"

"You already know the answer to this." Penny's hips moved of their own volition, and she rocked against his hand.

"I do, though I want to hear you say it." Xander shook his head. "No. I need to hear you say it." He kept his touch feather-light, and Penny groaned with frustration.

"Fine. Other than myself and my gynecologist, you are the first person to touch my pussy. Everything you're going to do to me tonight will be a first."

"Fuck...." Xander's jaw clenched, and his gaze dropped to between her thighs, taking in the way he pleasured her.

Penny reached up and tugged his beard, directing his gaze from his hand back to her face. She said nothing, just traced her finger along his bottom lip. Xander's hand stilled between her thighs, waiting.

She pulled him closer until her lips grazed his. She kept her gaze locked with his and said, “Thank you. Thank you for everything.”

“I’ve yet to do anything worth thanking me for.”

“Yes, you have. You do more than just protect me. You make me brave enough to offer you my submission.”

The air grew heavy with too much left unsaid, and it’s the last thing Penny wanted. “Please...Xander. I need you.”

“Do you?” Xander dipped a finger inside her and teased her clit with his thumb. Penny arched into his touch, seeking more. Needing more. “Beg for what you want.”

“Please, Xander. I-I want your mouth on my cunt. I want you to make me come. Please let me be your dirty girl.”

“Keep saying such filthy things, and I’ll fill your mouth with my cum.”

Xander dropped to his haunches, his massive shoulders forcing her legs wider when he pulled his finger from her core, slick with her juices. Then he sucked it past his lips and licked it clean. “Mm...fuck, you taste amazing.”

“Please....”

Xander gave her a wicked look and licked his lips. He didn’t make her wait any longer and wrapped his lips around her clit, flicking his tongue against the bundle of nerves.

"Oh, fuck, Xander." The man devoured her, nipping her with his teeth, tonguing her from her clit to her asshole, and driving her to a literal out-of-body experience.

His nose rubbed against her clit, and Xander tongue-fucked her core. His beard even tickled her inner thighs in his unrelenting need to consume her.

"Please, I'm going to...."

Xander slipped his hands over her stomach to cup her breasts, twisting and teasing her nipples, adding to the overwhelming sensations.

She gripped the bedsheets beneath her as a wave of ecstasy crashed over her. Penny cried out Xander's name, falling back against the pillow until Xander growled against her core, "Don't make me punish you for disobeying me."

Her gaze jumped back to his, the threat of punishment leaving her on the precipice of the biggest orgasm of her life.

"Want to come?" Xander asked between licks of her clit.

"Yes, oh god, yes. I'm right there." Penny arched her hips up, begging him with both her words and body.

"As you wish."

Did he just Princess Bride her?

With no time to find out, her brain short-circuited, and she tumbled over the edge, chanting his name like a prayer. Her wetness flooded his tongue, and he groaned his appreciation, lapping her juices while she rode the waves of endless release.

“Oh god, Xander.”

Xander swiped his tongue along her slit, making Penny shudder with an aftershock. He lifted his head from between her thighs with the most satisfied smile on his glistening lips. Then he climbed over her and kissed her, giving her a taste of her desire.

“We’re nowhere near done,” he growled next to her ear. Then Xander flipped onto his back in the middle of the king-size bed and said, “You’re going to ride my face, Princess.”

Penny almost choked. There’s a lot of her to giddy on up. “I don’t know if I can-”

“You can, and you will. That orgasm was the first of many. I promised I’d wreck you, Princess, and I’m a man of my word. Now get up here and sit on my face.”

Penny swung her leg over his torso and straddled his chest, then froze. How did she do this? Xander’s shoulders are so broad. How’s she supposed to climb over them? Penny gasped, and her spiral came to an abrupt halt when Xander’s hand gripped her throat.

“I wish for the time to unlock every one of your desires, but I promise to give you everything I can tonight. Enough memories to last a lifetime because I need them, too.”

Xander's confession gave Penny the courage to make one of her own. "You're mine, Xander. I don't care how unfair it is. You'll always be mine."

"Penny...." Xander used his grip on her throat to pull her to him for a hard kiss.

She wanted to be this perfect, sexy submissive, but she'd done nothing like this, and no matter how confident she was, putting all your weight on someone's face is a little intimidating. "Erm, how do we...?"

"Lean forward and get a good grip on the headboard." When she did it, he said, "Now, pull yourself up here until your sweet pussy is over my face. And Penny?" She tipped her chin and met his gaze between her thighs. "I meant what I said. I want you to drown me in your sweet scent."

Oh. Fuck.

Penny forgot about being self-conscious. Xander's filthy words empowered her. Penny hovered over his face, and he gave her more. "Cover me with your cum. Mark me, the way I'll mark you. Anyone I allow close will know who I belong to."

"Yes, Xander. I belong to you," she cried.

"Good girl. Now, ride my face." Xander grabbed her thighs and yanked her right onto his face. Leaving no doubt, when he said "sit," he meant his ability to breathe would be optional.

With his encouragement, Penny held the headboard tighter and used Xander's face from his nose to his bearded chin like a sex toy.

He groaned the moment his tongue speared her folds. The vibrations took her to the edge of a second release. She screamed, and her thighs locked around his head, holding his face to her pussy. Penny panicked and tried to move. Xander kept her in place.

"Do you want to die of suffocation?"

"You're not getting off my face until you've come." Her pussy muffled his words, and she felt them more than she heard them.

"Oh, erm, okay." She'll just come quickly to avoid killing him.

Xander gripped her thighs harder, holding her to him. His lips, teeth, and his tongue... *oh my god, his tongue,* worked her sensitive flesh until her orgasm slammed into her. Penny screamed his name, her pussy spasmed, and her arousal flooded his mouth.

Penny's grip on Xander's head slackened, and he let go of her thighs. She shifted on shaky legs when he lapped at her oversensitive clit. Xander squeezed her ass cheeks, and with one last kiss to her pussy, he dropped his head onto the mattress.

She collapsed beside him on the bed, trying to recover from the best orgasm of her life. Xander rolled to his side and kissed her. She palmed his erection, straining behind his zipper, wanting to taste him, too. "Can I return the favor?"

"You will, Princess. Not this time, though." He said no, yet he undid his pants and pulled out the biggest cock Penny's ever seen. Even the dicks she saw in porn didn't compare. Precum pooled at his tip, and Penny licked her lips with anticipation. Xander levered himself above her, straddled her hips, and stroked his thick length.

"Look at me, and I'll show you what you do to me."

Penny became mesmerized by the slide of his hand up and down his dick. She gripped his hips, digging her nails into his flesh.

Xander gritted his teeth. "Fuck yes. Dig those little claws into me. You fucking own me, Princess." He grunted, and the first rope of cum splashed against her stomach. The next hit her mound, and by the time he finished, it reached the undersides of her breasts.

Penny's fingers swirled in his cum, rubbing his essence into her skin. Xander didn't take his eyes off her while he righted his pants and tucked his spent cock away.

"Can I ask you something personal?"

Xander grunted. "Aren't we past the point of worrying about anything being too personal?"

"True enough." Penny glided her coated fingertips over the tips of her breasts, coating them in his cooling seed. "Do you have a cum kink?" Xander's gaze followed her fingers to her mouth.

"I have to have a taste," she whispered when he remained silent. Captivated by what she's doing.

When Penny sucked her fingers past her lips, Xander's salty cum exploded on her tongue. They both moaned.

Xander leaned over and rubbed the rest of his cum into her skin, marking her like he promised. Then she almost orgasmed again when he licked his fingers clean.

"Yeah, Princess. I enjoy sharing cum and spit. Lucky for me, it looks like you do too." Then Xander leaned over and captured her mouth. When his chest grazed her tender nipples, Penny groaned into his mouth.

All too soon, he pulled away. "Don't move." Xander went into the adjoining bathroom. She heard the water running, but didn't have the energy to move, even if Xander hadn't told her to stay put.

What else will she discover about Xander? What else will she find out about herself?

Xander pulled Penny from her musings when he pressed a warm cloth between her thighs. Her brow wrinkled in confusion. "What are you doing? Don't wipe your cum away." She pleaded, her arousal turning to upset.

Xander stilled her. "Shhh, Princess. I have no intention of wiping my cum off you. I wanted to clean up the stickiness between your thighs to keep your skin from chafing."

"Oh, um, okay." Penny relaxed, and Xander rubbed the warm cloth over her pussy. When he finished, he kissed her sex.

"You smell fucking amazing, covered in my cum." He finished cleaning between her thighs and pressed another lingering kiss to her hip, making her squirm. "You good, Princess?"

"Aye, thank you."

"Always." Xander looked her over. "I didn't mess you up too much." He tugged on the strands of her wig. "Excellent test to make sure this stays in place," he said with a smirk. "Come on, let's freshen up and dress."

Penny almost said, 'To hell with going to the club.' This lone experience with Xander tempted her to stay in this bed with him for the rest of the night, but she craved something more and believed he did, too. "Yes, let's."

Xander helped Penny up and gave her a few minutes in the bathroom before helping her dress. She hated when Freya tried to dress her, but the way Xander caressed each part of her body as he covered it up, sending her temperature rising. She wanted him to do this for her every day.

Xander kissed the back of her neck when he did up the clasp holding her dress on. Then, he met her gaze in the bathroom mirror. "Ready?"

Penny smiled. Ready for anything. "Yes."

"Let's go then." Xander stopped on their way through the main room. "Wait, we're going to need masks."

"I know. I purchased one for each of us. The masks are in the box on the table. I told you I did my research."

"Fucking Taylor," Xander muttered, making her giggle. Penny's easy camaraderie with his partner sure came in handy for her.

Chapter Nine

Penny

Their driver dropped them off at a nondescript warehouse, and they climbed a set of stairs to where a stern-looking security guard waited. Xander removed a card from his wallet and handed it to the man. His eyes widened before handing it back. "It's good to have you back, Mr. Ward. Did you want me to let Mr. Jones know you're here?"

"I'm sure Jasper's busy. If I run into him inside, I'll say hello then. Thank you, Tony," Xander replied. Tony opened the door for them, and Xander pressed a hand to her lower back, ushering her inside.

They entered an elegant lobby, where Xander pointed out some features, such as the lounge and changing areas, while they waited in line to check in.

Penny stole glances at others arriving for a night of pleasure, catching people shedding their outerwear and transforming into their authentic selves. All masked, of course, since she and Xander came on masquerade night.

Xander cupped the back of her neck. “Are you alright, Princess?”

Penny lifted her gaze to meet his. “Yes, Sir.”

The possessive hand at the back of her neck tightened, and Xander made a primal sound next to her ear while his other hand got busy with a handful of her ass. Her gasp filled the air between them.

“Why do you honor me?” Xander kept his voice low, his words for her alone.

“Because you respect me. Sir.” There’s the sound again, and it might be Penny’s new favorite thing to hear.

“I do, Princess. I respect you so fucking much.” Xander checked them in, then pulled Penny out of the way of the others. Once they checked in, he held up two yellow bands. “These are for us to wear.” He hesitated for a second, then explained. “They have a color system here, and it lets other patrons know if you’re open to accepting offers to play.”

Xander slipped it around her left wrist, then did the same for himself. Penny looked at the bracelet and asked, “What does the yellow one represent?”

“It’s like the traffic light safeword system. Red means do not approach. Green means all offers are welcome.” Xander fingered the band he secured to her wrist. “Yellow means someone can approach us to inquire if we are open to company.”

"I see."

"Do you?"

"Yes." Penny understood loud and clear. "The option to play with someone is there, but you have the final say whether they do."

Xander shook his head. "No, Princess. You have the final say. I'm just the one who relays the message. Are you ready?" he asked, offering her his arm.

Penny took a deep breath and smiled, gripping the crook of his elbow. "I'm ready."

The music grew louder as they walked down a short hall opening onto a platform overlooking the belly of the club. "This is the Overlook bar. What do you think?"

Penny went to the glass railing surrounding the upper floor, taking in everything going on below. "First impression? The name of the club fits. Everything about this place is decadent," she said, leaning close to him to be heard.

"Let me take you somewhere quieter." Xander led her down the grand staircase, past writhing bodies on the dance floor, to the stage where Penny stopped them, captivated by what was taking place on the dais.

"Oh."

A naked woman cuffed to a large, leather-padded wooden cross drew her attention. The man at her side wore loose black pants, his chest coated in a fine sheen of sweat from wielding the leather flogger in his hand.

Xander pulled her against him, his palm splaying across her stomach in a possessive hold. Penny pushed her ass against his groin and shifted her hips, teasing him while the erotic scene played out.

He gripped her hip and squeezed, stilling her movements. "Keep teasing me," he growled next to her ear. "And you'll find yourself strapped to the cross next."

Penny gasped, stilling her movements.

"Good girl."

The man on stage landed a sharp blow across his partner's thighs. She jerked within her binds, letting out a long moan. He then dropped the flogger and grabbed a handful of her hair. Pulling her head back, he wrapped his other hand around her throat. The tender way he looked at the woman while he held her in such a fierce grip showed the depth of their connection.

It made Penny long for something she didn't know what to call.

"Seen enough?"

Penny lifted her shoulders, then nodded.

Xander stared into her eyes for a moment. "I understand your curiosity, Princess, but I don't want to overwhelm you. How about we head to the bar at the back, get a drink, and talk?"

"Okay." Xander steered Penny out of the growing crowd with a hand at the base of her spine. It was then that she'd realized the difference since they'd arrived in New York.

Xander touched her.

How will she deal with him going back to his professional distance after this?

Xander led her toward a set of red velvet curtains held open for them to walk through, and it was like they'd entered another club. Done in brass tones and dark wood, it's like a modern-day speakeasy, albeit a kinky one, going by the BDSM-themed furniture.

People used the couches in the center of the space. They set their drinks on top of the tables, which caged their pets beneath. "Oh, my."

A shiver of desire skated down her spine, and it's from more than what she's experienced so far. Someone watched them, but when she darted her gaze around, she didn't meet anyone's gaze.

"Everything okay?" Xander asked, sensing her sudden tension.

"I'm good, I promise." Penny reached up and tugged on Xander's beard, and he returned her smile.

They turned to take in the erotic portraits lining the walls. Each one more breathtaking than the last. "These are beautiful."

"Mm... they're from Jasper's private collection."

"Who's Jasper?"

"Jasper's the majority owner of Decadent and the former captain of our unit."

"You've never told me about your military service. Is talking about it off-limits?"

"No, it's not off-limits, though I can't discuss anything classified."

"What was your rank?"

"I was our squad's major general."

Penny knew that a rank like that meant Xander was top dog. "Why doesn't it surprise me you were the boss?"

Xander laughed and pulled Penny closer to him. "The eight of us worked together like a well-oiled machine, but as far as official ranks go, yeah, I was in charge."

"The rest of the team holds five percent stakes in this place. Well, except for Grey, he has ten percent, plus he works here."

Xander led her to the two open seats at the end of the bar. "There's a two-drink limit," he warned.

"No biggie." Penny wanted all her faculties for whatever's coming tonight.

Chapter Ten

Lex

Lex sipped his whisky, relishing the burn as the alcohol made its way down his throat. He leaned against a wall, giving off a 'do not approach' vibe, and except for a few lingering stares, no one disturbed his solitude.

Which is counterproductive for why he'd come to a sex club.

Lex expected a lot out of one night. Fuck, he needed it, though. A night to explore something he never allowed himself, giving him a memory to look back on while being coerced into something he wanted no part of.

Again, lurking in a dark corner didn't help.

Opulence and sex surrounded Lex. Thick enough to taste, yet no one interested him enough to cause more than a lingering gaze, let alone spark a desire to have a conversation. When he grabbed a drink from the bar, this corner seemed like an excellent place to observe and dwell on things to come.

Today's the last day Lex controlled the company he created from the ground up. This morning, he signed over the majority interest to the new CEO.

Lex never expected his father to ask him to leave everything and fulfill such an outrageous family duty. Yet, here he was, obliging. Now, the man who got him in here tonight is the new owner of the company he created.

Lex felt his expression turn bitter while he stared into the depths of his glass. Who the fuck is he kidding? He didn't want to give it all up. He didn't have a choice.

To hell with tonight.

He'll finish his drink and head back to his hotel. His future, even one night of it, isn't here. Lex tossed back the rest of his whisky, then set his empty glass on the tray of a passing server.

About to leave the safety of the shadows, he stumbled and used the wall to keep himself standing. He even forgot how to breathe until the burn in his lungs reminded him to.

Them. They are what Xander needed tonight.

The tall, voluptuous, black-haired beauty caught Lex's attention first. Her eyes, visible beneath the mask she wore, glanced everywhere, as if she didn't know where to look first. If Lex gambled, he'd put money on it being her first time in a place like this.

She's stunning.

Her heels amplified her height, and the slits in the skirt of her dress allowed every tantalizing inch of her long, toned legs to show.

A smile lit the lower half of her face, and Lex swallowed, his mouth dry despite the drink he'd just finished. When the man at her side leaned in, whispering something in her ear, Lex studied him.

Fanculo-Fuck. He's big, muscular, and tall. They made a striking couple.

They turned away from him to look at the erotic art lining the wall. It gave Lex a view of her bare back. Her creamy skin enticed him, and he envisioned what it'd be like to trail his nose along her spine, making her shiver with desire while he breathed in her scent.

When his gaze reached the base of her spine, where the golden skin of the man's large hand struck a beautiful contrast, his mind conjured the image of that same hand wrapped around his throat.

Lex sucked in a sharp breath when he saw the colored band sticking out from beneath the man's shirt cuff. He glanced down at his own yellow wristband. When Lex searched the woman's wrist, he found she wore the same.

Both are open to the right offer, like him. Still, he hesitated. It was then that he heard a throat clear beside him.

Lex didn't want to tear his gaze away from the couple, worried he might lose track of them if he didn't keep them in his sights. He also didn't want to offend the person at his side and reluctantly tore his gaze away to find a ruggedly gorgeous man with auburn hair and beard in a three-piece suit standing beside him.

Oh, hello.

The man smirked. “Hello.” He turned his head to find out who or what held Lex so captivated.

Warmth highlighted the timber of his voice when his gaze landed on the couple, and the man said, “I see.” Those two words filled Lex with irrational jealousy.

“Easy, boy. I’m not after your spoils.”

Was Lex that obvious?

“I’ve never met the woman, though I know the man you can’t take your eyes off, and I believe it’s in your best interest to introduce yourself.”

“Huh?” *Who did this guy think he was*?

The man held out his hand to shake as if he’d read Lex’s mind. “Jasper Jones. I own Decadent. Well, I’m one owner, anyway.”

When Lex let go, Jasper shoved his hands into his pockets. “If you say hello, I believe you’ll thank me if we ever run into each other again.” Jasper moved past him and said, “I hope you have a good night, now.”

Lex turned back to the couple, watching them lean close to one another and talk. He felt this pull toward them and moved a few steps away from the corner he’d hidden himself in.

With everything about to change for him, Lex wanted to forget his responsibilities and his father's expectations. Tonight, more than anything, he wanted to give himself something to remember in his darkest hours. When the couple made their way to the bar, Lex followed.

Chapter Eleven

Xander

Xander helped Penny onto the seat next to the wall, taking the one on her other side to put himself between her and everyone else in the place.

No one will recognize Penny here with her mask and auburn hair tucked under the dark wig. Xander still assessed everyone who came near. *Protecting Penny is his top priority, no matter what happens tonight.*

He liked and loathed the club's masquerade night. The masks kept everyone's identities hidden. It also kept Xander from knowing who might approach them, leaving him unsettled. He loathed not being in complete control.

The bartender approached with a smile. "Good evening. What can I get you to drink?"

Penny studied the drink menu, then looked up and returned the man's smile. "Hi there. May I have a cosmopolitan, please?"

Xander loved the way Penny treated everyone with respect and kindness. Wait. *Loved*? He needed to put words like love under lock and key. Beyond tonight, Penny didn't belong to him, and Xander must remember that.

The bartender turned to Xander and asked, "And for you, sir?" Grateful for the distraction, Xander's gaze darted to the top shelf and smiled when he spotted a familiar bottle. It's like Jasper left it there for him, which he likely did. "I'll take a Glenmorangie 18 neat."

"Excellent choice. I'll return in a moment with your drinks." Xander nodded, and the young man moved down the bar to make Penny's Cosmo. She squeezed his forearm, and his focus returned to her.

"You need something, Princess?"

Xander's gaze landed on her full, soft lips. The way Penny's mouth felt against his now played on a permanent loop in the back of his mind, and he wanted more.

Watching Penny repair the damage she did to her lipstick gave him an overwhelming urge to continue corrupting her. Xander wanted to mess it up again, smear her lipstick while mascara tears tracked down her cheeks from choking on his cock.

Xander leaned in to capture her mouth when their efficient bartender returned with their drinks. "Stay right there, Princess."

He reached for his wallet when a smooth voice with a hint of an Italian accent sounded beside him. "Please. Allow me."

Long, tanned fingers held a black AMEX toward the bartender from his other side. Xander tracked those perfect, long, tanned fingers to the cuff of a white dress shirt partially hiding a gold Rolex.

Wait...perfect?

Xander spun and faced the man, blocking Penny from view with his upper body, and the automatic rebuff died on his lips. Tall, yet several inches shorter than him, with jet-black hair, a square jaw, and full, sexy lips.

Fuck. Don't focus on his lips.

Xander's gaze trailed over the rest of him. His physique looked lean and muscular, and the charcoal suit he wore fit him like it was made for him. This man screamed wealth and privilege.

There's something familiar about him. Xander tracked the bartender, handing the card back to...?

"*Grazie.*"

Xander met the glittering green eyes behind the black mask. Distracting yet familiar jade-colored eyes...recognition tickled the back of Xander's mind, and then the realization hit him like a bullet in the back.

No. Fucking. Way.

Chapter Twelve

Penny

Penny met the gaze of the stranger over Xander's shoulder, and something akin to lust fluttered in her stomach. For years, she'd obsessed over Xander. Aware of his desire for more than one sexual companion, yet never coming across someone she might consider sharing him with.

Until now.

The man's gaze shifted back to Xander, who remained oddly still. To break the sudden tension, Penny leaned forward on the bar top and raised her martini in a toast to their generous new friend.

"Thank you for the drinks. You'll have to excuse Xander. He's more of the silent and broody type."

Xander looked at Penny over his shoulder. Silent and broody didn't cover the turmoil she saw in his eyes. He blinked, and it was gone, making her almost believe she'd imagined it.

Almost.

Penny's attention became riveted when he lifted his full, sensual lips into a sexy smirk, and she let out a small gasp when the light caught his intense, jade-green eyes, and he shifted his gaze between her and Xander, taking a sip from his drink.

The dark-haired, green-eyed stranger with a chiselled jaw and lean physique ran the tip of his tongue along his lower lip, then he tried to shock her...with his brattiness when he said, "Lucky for me, I like silent and broody." He winked, and Penny couldn't stop the bubble of laughter.

The man switched his drink to his other hand, slid his palm past Xander, and offered it to her. "My friends call me Lex. What's your name, *Dolcezza Mia*?"

Xander moved faster than she did, wrapping his hand around the other man's. Then Penny's jaw dropped at Xander's response. "I'd appreciate it if you didn't call her your sweetness until our second date."

Of course, he speaks Italian. Wait...what?

The sudden silence between them broke when Lex tilted his head back and laughed deeply, his hand still clasped in Xander's.

Lex took another sip of his drink, then held up his glass. The lights behind the bar make the amber liquid shimmer. "You have exquisite taste." Even though he implied the alcohol, the way Lex's gaze swept over her, he was not referring to the booze.

Penny's gaze shifted between Xander and Lex. She'd dealt with the simmering, unattainable heat between her and Xander for years, yet this man, Lex, added more flames to their fire in mere minutes.

This is her night to take chances, to seize every opportunity she can. Penny decided she wanted them both, and she needed to let Xander know. Though if she's reading him right, Lex sparked his interest, too.

Can it be this easy?

"While I enjoy it, you need to put a pin in your alpha behavior and let me shake his hand. I'd like to introduce myself to the man who quenched my thirst."

It did the trick. Xander kept his eyes on Lex and directed his question to Penny. "You want to get to know him, little one?"

Xander will never allow this to go any further without her explicit consent.

"Aye." Xander turned to face her then. His piercing gaze now focused on her, searching for and confirming the truth in her eyes. Penny wanted this. She wanted them.

Xander turned, doing something he'd consider an unnecessary risk, and turned his back toward Lex. "Things are happening fast here, Princess. Are you sure?"

Penny swallowed, then spoke her truth. "When it feels right, it doesn't matter how fast we go."

Chapter Thirteen

Xander

The urge to agree fought with the desire to grab Penny and run. Fate's messing with his head, and Xander needed to know. Is the man beside them, Alexandre Ricci, Penny's future husband?

Those jade-green eyes are unmistakable.

Xander needed to get a look at him without the mask to be sure, and the way to do that was to get the three of them alone in a room.

Penny gripped his waist, her fingers digging into his flesh to get his attention. Xander lowered his head closer to hers, and she whispered, "You feel it, too, don't you?"

Xander can't lie to Penny. Not about this. He pressed his forehead to hers, and his confession ripped from him. "Yes."

He turned to face Lex. Consequences be damned. "Care to join us in one of the private rooms upstairs?"

It took Lex seconds to answer, and when he did, Xander wanted to paddle his ass. "Wasn't I already?" Lex asked with a wink. His blatant brattiness turned Xander on.

Xander wanted to put Lex on his knees and turn his ass a delicious shade of red, but there were more important things to discover and discuss. "We have rules. To be more specific, I have rules."

"I'm listening."

"Penny's pleasure and safety are top priority." Her hand squeezed his side, and he stepped back to include her in their conversation.

"You'll do nothing to harm her, and if she utters the word red, whatever is happening between us ends. That goes for any of us." Safe, sane, and consensual is how Xander played, and he expected anyone he invited to his bed to follow the same rules.

"I'll do nothing to offend or hurt the lady or you."

"Good." Xander leaned over the bar and signaled the bartender.

"Yes, sir?"

"I reserved a private room. Let the DM know I am ready for it."

The bartender gave Xander a brisk nod, stepping away to pick up the phone behind the bar.

"When did you reserve a room?" Penny asked.

"When we got here."

The bartender reappeared. "Room Eight is ready for your use, sir. Master M is the DM on duty this evening. He will let you in. Can I do anything else for you, sir?"

Xander's gaze dipped to the lapel of the fitted black vest and read his name tag. "Thank you, Kevin. That'll be all."

"Enjoy your night." He moved away to serve another customer.

Xander helped Penny out of her seat and gestured to Lex to precede them. "Shall we?"

When they reached the top of the stairs, Grayson Matthews, or Master M as he's referred to here, waited behind a podium. Xander felt a twinge of guilt. It's been far too long since he's seen the youngest member of their military squad.

Bare-chested, except for a leather harness and leather pants to match, Gray's gaze leveled on the three of them. When he met Xander's eyes, his expression softened into genuine welcome, and immediate recognition, despite his mask, and he clapped Xander on the back in a classic bro hug.

"How are you, Gray?"

"The minute Kari finished checking you in, she called my desk phone, and I told her I'd believe it when I saw you for myself. Damn, it's good to have you back."

Xander smiled and returned the hug. "The rumor is true. For tonight, anyway."

"Quick trip? Did you visit Dimitri? I need to pop into the diner again soon."

"Yeah, we stopped in for breakfast this morning. I know Dimitri would enjoy a visit. I wish we had more time, but we head out tomorrow night."

"We, eh?" Xander winced when Gray tipped his head around him to look at his company.

"Mind your business. My guests are private people."

"You know the club rules. I've gotta check in with them. Is everyone here with consent?"

"Yes," Lex and Penny promptly replied, and Xander had to resist the urge to praise his pets.

Gray eyed them both, then nodded, satisfied with Lex and Penny's eager responses. "We can catch up another time."

Xander squeezed his shoulder and gave him a thankful smile. Gray offered a knowing, sexy smirk, making Xander laugh. The beautiful, smug bastard. He's like a baby brother, but goddamn, he's a handsome fucker.

He unlocked door number eight and said, Gray showed them to a room down the hall, unlocking the door for them. "You know the rules, and you know where to find me if you need anything. Enjoy your night."

When the door shut behind them, Xander leveled Lex with a look. "Stay there. Back pressed to the wall. You're not to speak or move until I tell you to."

Xander waited. Positive, no one has ever spoken to him this way, and he didn't conceal his satisfied smirk when Lex clenched his fists and pressed his back to the wall without protest.

"Good boy," Xander praised, testing the waters and finding Lex more than agreeable when he groaned and tipped his head against the wall. Lex is going to learn right now. In a room like this, one person made the rules. Him.

With Lex subdued for the moment, Xander turned his attention to Penny. He took her hand and led her to an oversized leather chair.

Xander cupped her chin, keeping her gaze on him. "Do you trust me?" he asked. Her answer meant everything to him.

"Always."

Xander let go of her and undid his tie, sliding it free from his collar. "I'm going to sit you in this chair and blindfold you. I won't restrain you, but whatever is happening stops if you get up from your seat without my permission. Do you understand?"

"Yes."

"Yes, what?" Xander asked with a growl, gripping Penny's chin. Xander knew his broad shoulders blocked Lex's view, making this a private moment between them.

"Yes, Sir." He didn't miss the sparkle in her eyes or the way her deft tongue swiped the tip of his thumb.

Penny's submission tonight is a gift. Her daring desire even more so, and it touched the deepest parts of his soul. For three years, he protected her, never once stepping over the line. Tonight, it all changed.

"Good girl," he said, kissing her lips.

Xander let go of her chin, and Penny sat in the chair. He covered the eyeholes of her mask with his tie and secured it behind her head. Then he dropped onto his haunches and clasped her hands in his. "Color?"

Penny licked her lips and replied, "Green, Sir."

"Mm, perfect." Xander guided her hands to her lap, gathering the front of her dress and exposing her long legs.

"You have permission to touch yourself."

Xander stepped back, and Penny's fingers dipped beneath the hem of her dress, hands at the juncture of her thighs. "Eager, darling? I need to go have a word with our new friend, then we'll start the show."

"Wait. How will I see when I'm blindfolded?"

Xander brought his mouth to her ear. "Use your imagination, little girl. Remember, touch yourself all you want. No coming until I say so."

Penny licked her lips, making Xander want to bite them. "Yes, Sir."

"Good girl."

With Penny situated, Xander returned to the surprisingly obedient man pressed against the wall. He didn't hesitate to invade Lex's personal space, standing toe to toe. His hands went to the wall on either side of his head, caging him in.

Damn those beautiful jade-green eyes.

Xander wanted to get lost in them, and the last thing he needed was to complicate things further. He needed to know. Xander put his lips next to Lex's ear, his words for Lex alone. "Show me," he demanded.

"Show you what?"

"If you want to play with us tonight." Xander wrapped his right hand around the base of Lex's throat, teasing his thumb over his racing pulse while he swallowed beneath his palm. "You heard me. Show me who's under this mask." He fingered the velvet material that kept his suspicions from being confirmed.

"Her safety is my number one priority. I need to know if you want to play with us tonight, or if you'd rather choose the door next to you. Make your choice. Now."

Chapter Fourteen

Lex

Lex suppressed the urge to push back against Xander, needing to play by the other man's rules if he wanted anything to happen between the three of them.

Who the fuck is this guy?

Xander chuckled. "Hm...that's such a loaded question. I'm the man who can give you everything you desire tonight." Xander sounded like a sexy genie, ready to grant all of Lex's wishes.

Great, now Lex is picturing this giant, sexy-as-fuck, muscular man in nothing more than flowy silk pants with his hair in loose waves around his shoulders. He wanted to... fuck.

Lex shuddered while Xander assaulted his senses. The man's soft lips and trimmed beard skimmed Lex's jaw, and a musky, unnameable scent filled his nostrils, intoxicating him like a fine whisky.

"Can you smell her sweet scent? I bet you're imagining just how sweet she tastes. If you want to sample her yourself, you need to show me."

Lex's eyes widened. Xander wore Penny's cum like a badge of honor, and he breathed deeply until the urge to suck her essence from his lips almost overwhelmed him. He didn't even realize he gripped Xander's hip, rocking against the thigh now wedged between his legs.

"What's it going to be?" Xander asked when Lex didn't answer.

Lex tipped his chin up and met the intense blue eyes a few inches from his, and he swore the intensity he saw in their depths touched his soul. "There's only one choice."

It's them. Lex knew he'd regret it for the rest of his life if he didn't explore this pull between the three of them. He didn't look away when he pulled the mask off and didn't miss the tiny flair of recognition.

How? The software Lex created for his company ensured that if an image of him appeared online, it would be visible for thirty seconds. Did Xander have dealings with his company? His family?

When it came down to it, how Xander recognized him didn't matter. It'll matter a hell of a lot when he dwells on this later, yet in this moment, Lex knew Xander would not betray him. He'd keep him safe like he did Penny.

For the first time since the night a soldier who looked like a god returned his brother home after being kidnapped, Lex wanted to get on his knees for another man.

Now, Lex wanted his curiosity appeased.

“Your turn,” Lex dared to command him. Desperate to take in Xander’s features without the obscurity of his mask.

Disappointment filled him when Xander gave a firm shake of his head. “You’re not the one calling the shots, but I promise you’re safe with me.”

Then Xander flipped Lex to face the wall, pressing his cheek to the smooth concrete. His broad chest pressed against his back, and he shuddered when Xander nestled his thick cock against the crease of his ass. “It’s time to play.”

Chapter Fifteen

Xander

Xander bent his head, touching his forehead to Lex's shoulder. Then he took a deep breath and tried to calm his racing heart, needing a moment to collect himself. A moment where those green eyes weren't trying to peer into his soul.

Fuck. Fuck. Fuck.

How did Xander process being pressed against Penny's future husband and being attracted to him, too?

Fuck. Fuck. Fuck.

He should've shouted red, but he didn't. His mouth remained shut, and he pressed closer to Lex. His hips rocked in a slow, sensual rhythm.

A twist of fate put them on the same path, and Xander wanted nothing to happen to this tenuous connection between the three of them.

He never said he wasn't a selfish fucking bastard, and there's an even deeper history between him and Lex.

The last mission he and his team took part in, a rescue mission, involved Lex's older brother Roberto, and while they returned Roberto to his family unharmed, and while no one died, thank fuck. His team didn't fare as well. Their last mission changed the trajectory of all their lives.

Xander returned Roberto to his family personally, considering it his duty to see the young man home, and despite being overwhelmed by his parents' gratitude, Xander's eyes lingered on Roberto's younger brother. The lanky young man with striking jade-colored eyes.

Alexandre Ricci is in his arms. Fuck.

What are the odds of the three of them coming together like this? Almost impossible. Despite the reasons to stop this, Xander refused, ready to accept the fallout of his actions to have this night with Penny and Lex.

Xander set all of it aside for consequences he'd deal with later. "Penny and I have already established a safeword. You now have one, too. We'll use the traffic light system for now. Color?"

"*Fanculo*-fuck. I'm not a submissive," Lex sputtered. Despite his pushback, Lex followed Xander's lead, keeping his voice low and the conversation between them. He sensed Lex kept buried an inner bratty submissive desperate to come out to play.

Xander ground his cock harder against his ass while he growled in his ear. "Lie to me again, and I'll take your apology from your mouth with my cock. Now answer me."

Xander knew he'd struck the right nerve when Lex gasped, "Green. So fucking green."

"Put the mask back on," Xander commanded.

"Why am I too hideous to look at?" Lex sassed yet followed Xander's direction.

"No," Xander grunted. "The opposite. You're too distracting, and at the heart of tonight, everything that transpires is one hundred percent for Penny's benefit and pleasure."

"Then why's your hand working my belt loose?"

Xander chuckled. "I promised her a night fulfilling explicit desires, and I never break my promises. You and I are going to give Penny a show." His smirk disappeared. "Don't forget you can say your safeword anytime if you want to stop."

"I know, but-" Lex stuttered when Xander lowered his zipper, "She's blindfolded. How's she going to see what we're doing?"

Xander palmed Lex through his briefs. "Imagination is a powerful thing, and Penny's going to use hers while she absorbs every gasp, moan, and curse falling from your lips."

"Fuck." Lex groaned. "Why not let her see?"

Xander flipped Lex back around, and his hand gripped Lex's throat. The man who will have Penny for the rest of his life.

Fuck. Fuck. Fuck.

"Now, where is the fun in that?" he asked, shoving the stab of jealousy aside.

Then Xander did something he'd wanted to do since Lex first approached them. He pressed his mouth to his full lips, licking the seam and demanding entry. When Lex submitted, Xander wanted to howl from the rooftop, though he's too busy exploring Lex's mouth in a dominating kiss.

"Can you still taste her on my tongue? Imagine how Penny rode my face, covering me in her juices as she came."

"Oh god," Lex cried, grabbing Xander tighter. His grip became needy and desperate as he searched for every trace of her.

Chapter Sixteen

Penny

Penny strained to hear Xander and Lex over the low thump of bass permeating the room. She picked up the rumble of their voices and realized there was a conversation taking place not meant for her.

She smiled to herself, knowing Xander was giving Lex a rundown of the rules. Specifically, his rules. Then Penny heard a sharp intake of breath, followed by a low, throaty moan.

Are they...?

Xander's command drifted across the room. "Suck my tongue. Show me how well you'd suck my dick."

Oh, my God.

Penny's mind conjured image after image of what Xander and Lex were doing. Each vision filthier than the last. Lex is on his knees for Xander. Or

Xander holding Lex by his throat while fondling his hard cock through his slacks and kissing him with total control.

Penny gripped the material of her skirt tighter. The desire to rip Xander's tie from her eyes became a visceral thing, yet she resisted because Xander wanted to give her this experience.

When another moan filled the air, Penny clenched her legs together, feeling a fresh rush of arousal dampening her thighs. No longer able to resist the urge to touch herself, she cried out when her fingers delved between her pussy lips and circled the swollen bud of her clit.

A grunt floated in the air. The distinct sound of a belt being undone followed Xander's deep, silky voice. "Mm...sounds like our girl is enjoying the show."

Our girl?

The words settled deep in her soul with such rightness. She is theirs. Tonight, they will own her completely.

"Is this okay with you?" Xander asks Lex.

"Your hand on my dick? God, yes, it feels fucking amazing and makes me wonder what your mouth will be like."

Penny fingered herself, focusing on her needy clit. Images of Xander stroking Lex's cock danced across her closed lids. Their salacious words fueled the need inside her.

"Such a bratty mouth," Xander said to Lex. "If I didn't already have plans to taste you, I'd punish your throat with my cock." Penny's imagination wrestled with the images of each of them on their knees, taking turns.

Penny moved her other hand between her thighs, inserting two fingers into her slick pussy. She curled them to rub her G-spot while quickening the strokes over her clit.

"Oh...," Penny moaned. Her head fell back against the chair. Xander and Lex's lustful sounds and dirty words filled her mind with such explicit images. It's like the blindfold disappeared.

"I can see how wet she is from here. Let her come, *per favore*-please," Lex begged on her behalf.

The wet, sucking sounds stopped, and Xander asked, "Are you close, little one?"

"Y-yes." Penny pumped her fingers faster. "I'm close. Please"

"How many orgasms have you already had tonight?"

"Two, Sir."

The sound of Xander's chuckle was wicked and possessive. "Does my greedy little slut want more?"

"Yes." Her cunt clenched around her fingers. So close. "Please, Sir, I want all the orgasms you can give me."

"Tell Lex how I made you come earlier."

Penny heard the sadistic joy in Xander's voice, dragging out her pleasure. Yet she answered him in the hope he'd have mercy on her. "All over your face, Sir."

"Do you want to come all over Lex's face now?"

Did she? Aye, she did.

"Please," Penny begged him. "Please let me come."

She slowed her eager fingers, not wanting to go off until Lex put his mouth on her. Penny almost became a lost cause when Xander said, "Don't stop. Edge yourself a little longer, sweetheart. I need one more taste of Lex's magnificent cock."

A strangled noise came from Lex, and Xander commanded, "Tell her what I'm doing to you."

"*Fanculo*-fuck, okay. He's stroking my balls and taking my cock to the back of his throat. Yes, suck me," Lex groaned.

Penny's legs shook, and she rocked her ass against the chair seat. "Please, I need to come, please."

"She is breathtaking when she begs," Lex said, and Penny basked in his praise.

"So are you," Xander growled. "Now, tuck yourself back in your pants. And Princess?"

"Yes?" Penny said with a gasp.

"Hands off your pretty pussy."

Chapter Seventeen

Xander

With Lex close behind, Xander crossed the room to Penny and gave a wicked smirk to Lex when he found her hands still between her thighs. "Naughty girl," he chided, pulling her fingers from her needy cunt.

Penny whimpered, sticking her lower lip out in a perfect imitation of a bratty sub, though she kept her hands at her sides.

Xander turned to Lex and stripped him of his jacket and shirt. Unable to resist, Xander ran his hands over Lex's smooth, flawless skin. "No tattoos?"

"No."

Will Xander's tattoos be a turnoff for Lex, or will he like them? Worried, he asked, "Do you find people with ink attractive?"

"Fuck yes," Lex said, scanning the parts of Xander without clothes, looking for the tattoos hidden beneath. "Do you have any?"

Xander grunted in response, not answering Lex either way, though he savored the strange sense of relief at his answer. Xander directed Lex to stand between Penny's thighs, adjusting his toys like he wanted them. "Spread your legs wider for him, sweet girl."

He turned to Lex. "On your knees, pretty boy. It's time for your treat."

Lex eagerly dropped to his knees between Penny's spread thighs. Xander stilled Lex with a hand on his shoulder, needing to check in with them. "Before we go further, I wanted to check in with you both. Give me your color?"

Xander relaxed when they both replied, "Green."

Xander pressed a firm hand to Lex's back. "Taste her." Lex shuffled forward on his knees, then lifted Penny's legs over his shoulders, getting closer to his prize.

Penny whimpered when Lex dragged his nose along the juncture of her thigh, taking in more of her intoxicating scent, when he said, "Even if I spent a lifetime with my head between your thighs, I'll never get enough."

Unaware of how close Lex is to having Penny for the rest of his life makes Xander's gut clench. *Damn it. Not now.* He'd dwell on the fallout of his actions another day. Right now, he's too deep to care.

Xander stepped behind Penny and teased the edges of her makeshift blindfold, then he placed his lips next to her ear. "Want to watch Lex make you come?"

"Yes, please. Please let me," Penny whimpered, biting down on her bottom lip. Her legs hooked around Lex's back, desperate to pull him to her.

Xander loosened his tie and dragged it away from her eyes. "What are you waiting for, pretty boy? Make our girl come." In this moment, he never wanted to stop referring to Penny as their girl.

Lex dove in, rutting his face against her core, smearing her arousal on his chin and cheeks, wanting to mark himself in her scent like Xander did.

Penny whimpered and rocked in her seat. Xander slid his hands beneath the front of her dress, squeezing her breasts and pinching her nipples, adding to the sensations Lex provided between her legs.

Penny grasped Lex's dark hair, holding him there while she rocked against his mouth. Then Penny did something unexpected, catching Xander off guard when she wrapped her fingers around his wrist, connecting the three of them.

Xander expelled a shuddering breath and nipped at her ear. "Come, Penny. Come for us now." She followed his command and tumbled into an intense release, and Xander almost came in his pants at the sight.

Lex groaned against her center, dragging out the intensity of Penny's release. He lapped at her, licking her clean and bringing her down from the high of her orgasm. When she loosened her grip on his hair, Lex sat back with a satisfied grin on his shiny lips.

Xander tipped his chin and said, "Help her out of her shoes." Lex slipped them from her feet, and Xander offered his hand, helping Penny to stand on unsteady legs.

He cupped her face and kissed her lips, giving them a nip. "You looked fucking beautiful coming on his tongue." Xander turned Penny to face Lex. "Thank him for your orgasm, sweetheart."

Penny wrapped her arms around Lex's neck and leaned forward, with Xander staying against her back. "Can I taste myself on your lips?" she asked him, and Xander grit his teeth, doing his best to stave off his orgasm.

"Si, dolcezza." Penny sucked on Lex's bottom lip, tasting her cream. Xander encouraged her with his body to deepen the kiss, crowding closer and cocooning Penny between him and Lex.

The way she fit between them is something Xander will remember for the rest of his life. And he needed… more. Leaving one hand on Penny's hip, he grabbed Lex at the waist with the other. This time, it was Xander who connected the three of them.

Xander kissed his way up her throat until he joined his mouth with theirs. A menage of lips, teeth, and tongues. "Mm." Xander moved his hand from Penny's hip to her throat and gripped Lex's hair.

He released their lips but kept his hold on them. "It's your night. What do you want to happen next?" Xander asked, grinding his erection against her backside while Lex rotated his hips against her front.

"Fuck me. I want you to fuck me. Both of you." Penny turned her head within the confines of his grip, raising her eyes to meet his. Xander's heart stopped when she whispered, "You first."

He stroked his thumb back and forth over her racing pulse, not sure what to do with his torn feeling about her gifting him her cherry. "As you wish."

This will come back to kick him in the balls, but like he decided earlier, the consequences are for another day.

Xander tugged on Lex's hair, pulling him in close. "Get rid of the rest of your clothes," he demanded, moving to undo the clasps holding Penny's dress in place.

Lex didn't waste any time, toeing off his shoes, then he removed his pants, and his briefs, pushing them down his corded legs. Lex captivated him and Penny. They couldn't look away as he revealed his athletic frame under all that warm, tanned skin.

"He's beautiful, isn't he?"

Penny nodded.

Broad shoulders and a smooth chest led to a narrow waist where a happy trail of silky, dark hair marked the way to the man's gorgeous cock. It pressed against his abdomen, and Xander let out a growled protest when Lex dared to stroke his cock.

"Do you want to taste him?" Xander asked Penny, playing with her breasts with one hand while his other slipped between her pussy lips. "Do you want to get down on your knees for our companion? Have the luxury of licking the precum from the tip of his cock as he feeds it to you?"

"Please, Xander...let me taste him." Xander let go of her breast and gripped the back of her neck, guiding her in front of Lex, his fingers never leaving her clit.

Xander removed his fingers from between her legs and shoved them past Lex's parted lips, pressing Penny to her knees, controlling each of them like a master puppeteer.

"Suck," Xander commanded them both. One word encompassed their tasks.

Lex groaned around Xander's fingers, and Penny moaned, lapping at Lex's cock.

"Yes, Princess. Play with his balls while you suck his cock. Just how he likes it," Xander praised, and Lex's lips went lax, Xander's fingers slipping from his mouth.

"Don't you dare come," Xander warned him. "Not until you're deep inside her pussy."

Lex grunted. "Then I'm going to need Penny to stop because I'm about to lose it down her throat. And you're wearing too many clothes for where this is going. *Sir.*"

Xander laughed at Lex's blatant brattiness, though he undid the buttons of his shirt as Lex helped Penny to her feet.

Her lips looked swollen and used, and she'd left a red ring around the base of Lex's dick from her lipstick. Fuck, he liked the way she marked the other man.

"Get on the bed and keep touching one another. Keep your eyes on me."

"Yes, Sir," Penny said, crawling up the bed. Her hips swayed as her knees slid across the waterproof sheets.

Lex cleared his throat and nodded, giving Xander a more subdued compliance as he joined Penny on the bed.

Xander pulled his shirt from his pants and shrugged it off, draping it over the back of the chair Penny had occupied earlier.

He enjoyed Lex's eyes widened when he took in the full scope of his ink. "Wow. Now I get why you asked me about liking tattoos. Let me reiterate, I. Really. Fucking. Do. *Cazzo sei sexy*-Fuck, you're sexy."

A prideful blush warmed Xander's cheeks. He worked hard on his body, and he chose the ink adorning it with careful consideration. Though he seldom had the chance to show it off like this anymore.

Xander pulled the elastic from his hair, letting it fall in loose waves around his shoulders, and he moved to the side of the bed.

Penny straddled Lex to reach Xander. Her eyes roved over him, trying to take in everything at once. Then she did something that almost made Xander's knees buckle. She sank her fingers into his hair and dragged her nails over his scalp.

He loved it when someone played with his hair; it was one reason he grew it out after leaving the military. It's been too long since anyone's done it. Xander closed the distance between them and kissed Penny.

Her nipples brushed his chest when their kiss intensified, and Lex gripped his thigh. "You're beautiful," Lex said, and Xander wasn't sure if he was referring to him or Penny. Though he confirmed it a second later. “The two of you are fucking beautiful together.”

Xander put enough space between them to undo his belt, followed by the button and zipper of his pants. Then Lex shucked them down his thighs, and Xander broke the kiss with Penny to send a glare his way.

“I already told you, you’ve got too many clothes on for where this is going. Merely things along.” Lex winked, and Penny giggled.

“I wish we had time to explore this bratty side of yours, but this stunning siren between us wants to be fucked. Don’t you, sweetheart?”

“Yes, please.”

Xander kicked his pants away, letting Penny and Lex get a good look at what Xander offered, stroking his cock and putting on a show. They licked their lips in anticipation of having a taste. Xander slipped further into his dominant role and issued some more commands.

“Lex, get comfortable. Penny, I want you on your hands and knees over him with your ass high in the air.”

Xander smacked her right cheek when she wiggled in his direction, smacking her hard enough to leave a blooming imprint of his palm. Penny moaned and wiggled her ass a little more, begging him to do the same to the other cheek, which he did.

Xander grabbed two condoms from the bowl on the table and tossed them beside Lex’s thigh, then he got on the bed and kneeled behind Penny. He rubbed her ass where he’d reddened it, sliding his hands up her back. He pushed her down, putting her chest to chest with Lex. "When I said ass up, I meant ass up."

Xander met Lex's gaze over her shoulder, the man giving him a nod. Good with whatever they're about to do, but Xander needed to hear it from Penny. "Ready?" he asked.

"Aye, Xander. Fuck me, please." Her lilting accent thickened with her growing desire.

"With pleasure."

Xander grabbed the condoms, sheathing himself first, then he rolled the latex over Lex's cock, making him pant and moan. Penny's moans joined his when he ran his tongue through her drenched folds to flick her clit.

She'd come several times already tonight, and Xander wanted to know how many more Penny could give them. "Come all you want, sweetheart." To Lex, he said, "Your job's making sure she does."

"Yes, Sir," Lex said, surprising Xander with the lack of sass.

Xander pressed the head of his cock to her entrance. The heat of her core surrounded his tip, making him eager to press inside her, but he kept his hips still. "Ready, Princess?"

"God, yes."

Lex kissed Penny and played with her breasts. Then Lex reached between them and caressed her folds and the head of Xander's dick in his search for Penny's clit.

The combination of Lex's fingers and the heat of Penny's opening became too much, and he almost came. Xander grunted, desperate to regain his control, and Lex gave him a wink. The brat knew what he was doing. Lucky for Xander, Lex didn't push him further, sliding his fingers upward to circle Penny's clit.

These two people are his, for tonight at least, and Xander will carry this night with him for the rest of his life. He pushed forward and slid into his own version of Heaven's gate.

Chapter Eighteen

Penny

Penny writhed between the two men. Lex's busy hands teased her nipples and circled her clit while his mouth plundered hers, overwhelming her senses. Then, the head of Xander's cock notched at her opening. His thick crown stretched her in preparation to take the rest of his impressive length.

She'd read enough spicy romances to have groaned over the lines. *'Oh, my God. It's so...big. Is it going to fit?'* Yet in this moment, Penny asked herself if it would.

She's about to have sex for the first time with one man while draped over another. *How is this her life?* Her anticipation battled it out with her nerves. Anticipation won by a smidge. Penny wanted this. She wanted both men, and she's going to have them.

Penny lifted her lips from Lex's and stared into his eyes. He cupped her face, holding her still when Xander asked, "Color?"

Without breaking Lex's captivating stare, they answered, "Green."

"Take a deep breath and relax for me, Princess. I don't want to hurt you, but this might sting." Xander pushed his cock inside her, and Penny expelled the breath she held on a whoosh across Lex's parted lips as Xander filled her like no other man ever had.

Penny arched her back, crying out when the man she'd loved for three years claimed her virginity. She wanted no one else to be her first. Lex caressed her cheek, bringing her focus to the man who'd fill her next. "You're taking his cock so well, dolcezza," Lex praised.

Her stomach brushed Lex's cock, and it left a trail of precum behind, marking her skin, the way she feared he'd leave his mark on her heart. Penny kissed him again, wanting his lips to make her forget the pain she'd face later.

"Princess...," Xander groaned. "The way your sweet pussy is taking me...." The awe in Xander's voice made her fly, yet his firm grip on her hips kept her grounded between him and Lex.

Penny wanted to move. Wanted Xander to move. "Mm, I'm so full."

Lex teased her clit. The rough pad of his finger made her whimper, and still no one moved.

"Xander, please fuck me. I need you to move. I might die if you don't move."

Lex chuckled. "We can't have that. Better move, Xander."

Xander growled and rocked his hips, the force of his thrust grinding her body against Lex, who moaned in response. "No topping from the bottom, brat."

"Yes, Sir," Lex said, sounding chastised, though Penny doubted it when he winked at her.

"Are you okay, Princess?"

"Yes," she gasped. "So good."

Xander took that for the permission it was, sliding his dick out of her, then plunging back inside. Not holding back, filling her, he owned her pussy.

Penny reached between them and wrapped her fingers around Lex's cock, stroking him while pushing her hips back to meet each of Xander's demanding thrusts.

"Fuck, you feel good, baby. Your pussy is gripping me like a vise. I need you to come for me. Then it's Lex's turn."

"Mm... touch me, please. Circle my clit. Yes. Just. Like. That." Penny cried out when Lex followed her direction with such precision, and she spasmed around Xander's cock, gifting him with the orgasm he demanded from her.

Xander shocked Penny when he pulled free from her core while her pussy still fluttered around him. He didn't come, and didn't leave her empty for long, taking Lex's cock in hand, Xander guided him to her opening, lowering her onto his shaft. "Take Lex's cock for me now, Princess."

"Ohh...."

The moment his cock slipped inside her, Lex took over, gripping her thighs and thrusting in and out of her pussy. She didn't even realize Xander had left to dispose of his condom until he stood next to the bed and cupped the back of her head.

Xander held the base of his cock in his other hand and tapped the tip of his dick against her lips, smearing precum along her bottom lip. Penny licked her lips and moaned when she tasted him.

"Open," Xander commanded.

Penny parted her lips, taking his crown into her mouth, sucking his salty flavor from his slit. She took him deeper into her mouth until he pushed into her throat, and she gagged.

Xander pulled back, letting Penny catch her breath, and gripped her chin. "When my cock's at your throat, swallow and breathe through your nose," he instructed.

"Okay." Her voice sounded raw when she answered.

Xander put the head of his cock against her lips and pressed back inside. "Take me. I know you can. Yes...that's it, baby."

His praise encouraged her, and she doubled down on her efforts while Lex thrust beneath her. Her tender clit rubbed against his pelvis, bringing her closer to another orgasm.

If this is what it's like to be with two men... Penny didn't know how she'd ever be okay with just one. She wanted to experience this for the rest of her life.

"Please let me...let me come," Lex begged. His plea was full of breathless desperation. Then his head dipped next to hers, and he sucked one of Xander's testicles into his mouth, desperate to push the man in control over the edge.

Oh...wow, that's hot.

Xander grunted and issued the command. "Come."

The heat of Lex's orgasm filled the condom, separating them when he thrust one last time, holding himself still inside her, pouring his release into her while he groaned their names.

"Time for your treat, Princess." Xander's salty release flooded her mouth. Penny moaned, sucking and lapping up every drop.

Their orgasms triggered another for Penny. One more powerful than the last. She swallowed every drop of Xander's cum and milked the last of Lex's release with her pussy.

Xander pulled free of her mouth and smeared the last drops over her swollen lips. Then Lex licked those drops from her in a messy kiss.

Lex carefully withdrew from her body, holding the base of his cock to keep the condom from slipping. Then he shifted off the bed to dispose of it.

Xander sat on the edge and pulled her into his arms. "You're perfect, Princess. Was this everything you wanted?" he asked, his lips next to her ear, the question just for her.

"More." Never being more honest.

Lex must have handed Xander a water when he held the cool liquid to her lips and told her to drink. "Drink, baby. Let me take care of you and get you hydrated."

Penny panicked at the softness of Xander's voice. "Please don't tell me this is over. I'm not ready for it to end. Take me back to the hotel so we can be alone." Her words came in a jumble; heck, she wasn't even sure what she said. Penny nestled her head beneath Xander's chin, breathing in his familiar, comforting scent.

Penny didn't notice the silent look shared between the two men or how Lex's eyes filled with disappointment and Xander's regret.

Chapter Nineteen

Lex

There's his cue to leave. Of course, Xander and Penny didn't ask him to go, but Lex understood this to be a special night for them, and his role in it had ended.

He's not bitter. Lex needed to chalk this up for what it was. A fantasy-filled, pleasurable night between three people.

Lex picked up his discarded pants and briefs and stepped into them. He threw on his shirt and jacket next, not wanting to prolong his exit or make things any more awkward.

He finished tucking his shirt into his pants when Penny said, "Lex, wait. Please don't go yet. Come here, please?"

He looked at her over his shoulder and saw Penny holding out her hand, beckoning him. When Xander took a deep breath and did the same, Lex closed the distance between them. Unable to resist them both.

Penny shivered and used her other arm to cover her breasts. Lex picked up her dress and Xander's shirt on his way to them. He didn't like the power imbalance of him dressed and them not. Penny gave him a tender smile, taking her dress from him, doing a reverse striptease, making Lex want her just as much with her clothes on as when she had them off.

Xander tugged his shirt back on, covering all the delicious ink Lex wanted to explore with his hands, lips, and tongue. Pity their time's up, preventing him from doing so.

Penny turned, giving Lex her back, a silent request to help with the clasps of her dress, which he happily obliged. When done, Lex trailed his hands down her arms and placed a reverent kiss at the base of her throat, his eyes on Xander the entire time, who stared back with equal intensity.

Penny broke the silence. When she turned and said, "I-" She glanced at Xander and amended. "Thank you for joining us tonight. You helped bring one of my deepest desires to life, and I'll cherish our time together."

Xander came to stand behind Penny, offering his silent support. Then he stunned Lex when he reached around her and gripped his arms, encircling Penny between them, and said, "I'll never forget this either."

Lex sensed Xander's words carried an even heavier weight and swallowed around the sudden lump in his throat. In just a few hours, the three of them formed a deep connection, and he'll forever be thankful they let him be a part of what they shared.

Lex did his best to convey what tonight meant to him. "Thank you for allowing me to join you. You both let me embrace every part of myself, and I'll never forget it."

He felt his cheeks heat. It's the closest he's come to voicing his bisexuality to someone. Well, two people in this case.

"Aye, we'll never forget it either."

Lex cupped Penny's cheek and placed a tender kiss on her lips, then stepped back, putting space between him and the couple he already regretted walking away from.

"*In un altro tempo, in un'altra vita*-In another time, in another life." He backed toward the door, wanting to keep them in his sight. "It was an honor to share my time with you. Take care. Both of you."

"Did you want to leave through the back exit with us? We have a car waiting and can drop you where you need." Xander said, surprising Lex with the offer. Almost like he didn't want their time to end yet, either.

He needed to get away before he started having impossible ideas about the future. "Thank you, no. I have a car waiting out front and a morning flight."

He raised Penny's hand to his lips and kissed her knuckles. "Goodnight, dolcezza." He tipped his chin toward Xander. "Sir."

When he stepped outside the room, Lex leaned against the closed door for a moment. He breathed in through his nose and out through his mouth to calm his racing heart. He might've forgotten his family obligations altogether if he'd stayed a minute longer.

Lex gave his head a shake. Xander and Penny are not his future, no matter how much he now wishes them to be. Hell, for all Lex knew, Xander and Penny weren't even their real names.

Chapter Twenty

Xander

Xander tucked his jacket around Penny's shoulders, helping her slip her arms into the sleeves. She'd worn nothing over her dress when they left earlier, and the late hour brought a chill to the night.

He surveyed the room, ensuring they left nothing behind. Then he ushered Penny out the door and around the corner to the staircase monitored by a security guard.

The man gave Xander a nod and opened the door for them. Less than a minute later, they sat in the backseat of the hired car. He kept Penny nestled against his side on the short drive back to the hotel.

Xander's palm rested low on Penny's hip. Energy buzzed between them in the silence on the elevator ride to their floor. Neither of them wanted to talk until they reached the privacy of their suite.

He locked the door behind them and did a sweep of the room. Satisfied there's nothing wrong, he turned and faced Penny. "Come here, Princess."

They'd removed their masks in the car, and now alone in the suite, Xander cupped her face and traced her delicate cheekbones, losing himself in the sweet taste of her mouth.

Their kiss deepened when Penny pulled his hair free of his elastic and drove her fingers into the strands, tugging him closer. Like her, Xander didn't want this night to end. Not yet. "Shower with me?"

She nodded, and Xander laced their fingers together, guiding her through the bedroom and into the ensuite. Xander placed her in front of him at the vanity. "I want to take care of you. Will you let me pamper you, sweet girl?"

"I'd like that." Penny guided him to each pin, holding her wig in place. They made a pinging sound in the quiet bathroom as he dropped each one into the sink. Penny sighed when he set the wig on the counter and unbraided her hair.

Xander kissed the top of her shoulder and met her gaze in the mirror. "Give me a second," he said, turning on the shower to let it heat. He removed his shirt on his way back to her, tossing it aside to deal with later.

Penny grabbed one of her cosmetic wipes to take care of the rest of her makeup, and Xander snatched it from her hand and tsked. "I'm taking care of you. Remember?"

"Aye." Her cheeks flushed a rosy shade of red, and when he tipped her chin up, Penny's eyelids fluttered closed, and he wiped the makeup from her face.

"You're beautiful," he whispered, wanting to count the freckles dotted across her nose he'd revealed.

"I don't want tonight to end," Penny said a moment later.

"Neither do I. Yet the sun will rise in a few hours."

"It isn't here yet."

"No, Princess. Not yet. Let me help you with your dress." Xander undid the clasps and helped her out of it. Then she reached for his belt.

He didn't protest when she fell to her knees and tugged his pants and briefs down his legs. How could he when he lost his ability to speak? The thick length of his cock slapped his abdomen, eager to say hello. Xander shuddered when Penny placed a reverent kiss against his tip.

"Fuuuck," he groaned. With his hand in her hair, Xander pulled Penny to her feet. Kissing her, he walked them both into the shower and under the warm spray.

Xander took great care, washing Penny from head to toe. Then, with her tucked against his side, he washed himself and rinsed them both clean, shutting off the water a few minutes later. He wrapped a towel around Penny and dried her off.

Two hotel robes hung next to the door, and Xander knew there was not a chance in hell he'd fit into the one meant for him. He secured his towel around his hips and grabbed the other robe for Penny. With her seated at the vanity, Xander brushed the tangles from her hair and dried it.

"Mm... feels amazing, thank you." Her little moans excited him, and Xander's dick grew hard beneath his towel. He sucked in a breath, surprised when she cupped him through the terry cloth, and met his eyes in the mirror. "Take me to bed. Please?"

After tonight, Xander didn't know how he'd ever say no to her again. "As you wish."

Penny's hands moved to his hips when she turned to face him. "Do you know what it does to me when you quote The Princess Bride?"

Of course, he knew. It's Penny's favorite movie, and he smirked when he replied, "Why do you think I said it? I know anything *Wesley* says makes you swoon." Xander scooped her up in his arms, making her giggle, and carried her into the bedroom.

Xander kneeled on the bed, laying Penny out beneath him. He hovered above her, tracing his fingers along the side of her face, sweeping wayward strands of her hair back while he trailed kisses along her cheek to her lips.

His damp hair fell in a curtain around them, and he groaned when Penny sank her fingers into it, tugging it the way he liked.

Xander deepened their kiss, licking Penny's lips until she parted them and met his tongue with exuberant strokes. "Spread your legs for me, Princess," Xander whispered against her lips. When she did, Xander settled between her thighs, lowering his weight onto her, making sure he didn't crush her by staying balanced on his forearms. "Is this okay?"

"God yes, Xander. Give me more."

Xander yanked the top half of her robe open, freeing her luscious breasts. He squeezed her breast, teasing her nipple with the rough pad of his thumb. Penny writhed beneath him, and her hands went to his hips, tugging at his towel. He lifted his hips, and she flung the material to the floor.

Penny met his gaze and wrapped her hand around his dick, guiding him to her dripping core. He hated to break this moment. He wanted to sink into Penny and feel every bit of her heat with nothing between them, but he'd fucked no one bare. "Wait. Let me grab a condom."

Penny stopped him, wrapping her legs around his waist to keep him there. She met his gaze head-on. "I have no desire for children at this point in my life. I don't have any STDs and have a contraceptive implant. Oh, and Xander?"

He didn't dare hope when he asked, "What, Princess?"

"I want nothing between us. I want your cum dripping from my pussy. To know what we shared was real. If we just have tonight...I want you to make me yours in every way."

Even if this ripped his heart out, there's no way Xander can say no to that kind of plea. He wanted to tell Penny he could be hers forever; instead, he said, "Tonight, I'm yours." She dipped her eyes and blushed. "Don't look away, Princess. I want to see the moment I fill you."

Xander pressed inside Penny, sinking his cock to the hilt. The sensation of wet heat surrounded him, testing his resilience. "Fuck, you're tight. The way you grip me... fuck, I need to move. Are you ready, Princess?"

Penny rocked her hips, desperate for him to move, and her demanding cry confirmed it. "Yes. Please, Xander. Fuck me. Fill me with your cum and make me yours."

Xander gripped her leg, pulling it to her chest, allowing him to hook his arm beneath when he finally moved, fucking her even deeper at this angle.

"Fuck yes. Your perfect pussy is going to make me come, so I need you to come first."

He coaxed two more orgasms from her tender pussy. The way she clenched around him with each release sent Xander into a primal rut. "Penny, I-" He couldn't hold back any longer and pushed himself deep, muscles tensed until he broke, unloading inside her and filling Penny with his cum.

Chapter Twenty-One

Penny

The sun's warmth, filtering through the parted curtains, stirred Penny from her tumultuous dreams. As she slid her hand across the mattress, she already knew she'd find the other side empty. Xander left hours ago.

"Fill me with your cum and make me yours...."

Penny's plea from last night echoed in her mind, ensuring she wouldn't be going back to sleep. Last night was...*intense*? *Unbelievable*? "Everything...," she whispered.

She stretched beneath the sheets, and a pleasurable ache radiated from her center to every muscle in her body. The sticky remnants of Xander's cum coating her thighs, a definitive confirmation of what happened between them...happened. She had sex. Lex's captivating green eyes filled her mind, and Penny shot up in bed, more than wide awake now.

Oh, my God. She had sex with two men last night.

Penny gazed around her empty room, panic threatening to take over when she took a deep breath, one after another, trying to calm her racing heart. Lex isn't here, so she can't worry about what he might think right now.

She knew things would be different in the light of day. Penny fucked two perfect men last night, giving more orgasms than she'd ever given herself. They worshiped her like she was the Princess Xander insists on calling her.

How will she settle for an awkward marriage bed with a stranger? Worse, how did she go back to Xander being just her bodyguard? What if he quit? Penny rubbed the center of her chest to stave off the pain. It's a question she never wanted to contemplate.

A firm knock on her bedroom door signaled the end of any reprieve she might've had.

Xander didn't open the door, remaining on the other side, until she granted him entry. Penny rolled her eyes. So, it's going to be like this. "After everything?" she asked loud enough to be heard through the door.

"It's the way it has to be," came his muffled response from the other side of the thick wood, though she understood him loud and clear. What happened between them last night will not continue into today.

Of course, Xander is doing the responsible thing. Why did it have to hurt so fucking much? And did the ice out have to happen while they're in another country? Penny sighed, resolving to play her part. After all, one night is all he promised.

Penny made sure her robe covered everything and opened the door. The tender and controlling Daddy Dom from last night's gone, and in his place, the stoic bodyguard remained. "Good morning, Pene-"

Penny stopped him mid-greeting and plucked the coffee he made for her from his hands. "No need to make this more uncomfortable. I knew the rules going in."

The perfect brew soured on her tongue, and Penny decided she didn't want to spend any more time here. Why drag out the inevitable if Xander's already shut her out? A Broadway show wasn't enough incentive to stay.

He stood in her doorway, catching the myriad of emotions crossing her face.

"We're supposed to leave this evening, but I'd like to leave now. Can you make the arrangements, please? I'm going to pack and get ready."

She raised her cup in a one-sided cheer. "Thank you for the coffee. Give me an hour, and we can head out."

She closed the door on him, not letting him get a word in, and headed into the bathroom. Let him stew. Penny held back her tears until the hot water from the shower hit her face. Never hearing Xander's whispered, *As you wish*, while she sobbed beneath the spray.

Chapter Twenty-Two

Xander

Xander tugged on his beard and cursed. His heavy stride and the scowl he wore ensured everyone stayed out of his path as he made his way to the office he shared with Taylor. The guilt made his head pound, and the regrets he had about their time in New York rivaled the ones he didn't.

He fucked up. Big time.

When Penny and Lex learn the truth about each other... well, Xander hoped they'd forgive him. The reality of it is, he didn't deserve to be forgiven.

Their return flight happened in silence. Penny stayed in the bedroom except during takeoff and landing. She didn't say a word to him beyond a polite acknowledgment, and the moment they stepped inside her home, Penny uttered a firm good night and went to her room.

In less than two weeks, Penny's father will announce her engagement to Alexandre Ricci, and Xander knew the moment they laid eyes on each other…well, let's say he will deserve every bit of Penny's anger.

Xander got little sleep, and without coffee, he wasn't ready for the interrogation that met him when he opened his office door and found Taylor already there. Xander side-stepped him and headed right for the coffee machine.

"So?" Taylor dragged the one word out like the loaded question it was.

Xander kept his back to Taylor, taking his sweet time to fix his black coffee. "Penelope enjoyed an uneventful time in New York filled with shopping, dinners out, and Broadway shows."

Lies, lies, and more lies.

Xander turned and leaned against the wall, several beats of silence passing between them until Taylor said, "Sounds… fun?"

"What do you mean?"

Taylor set his mug down and crossed his arms. He may not have Xander's size, but he knew how to intimidate when he wanted.

"Let me spell it out for you. We all have memberships at Decadent."

Xander needed to rage, and Taylor became an easy target. "For fuck's sake, you're the one who told Penny about the club. If you hadn't blabbed, I might not be in," Xander cut himself off, almost revealing what Taylor already guessed.

“Might not what? You know how persuasive Penny is.” Taylor chuckled. “Hell, she’d make an excellent interrogator.”

Taylor dragged a hand through his hair, and his amusement fled. “Look, I should’ve known she’d convince you to take her there. How it wouldn’t take much for you to give in. I know it’s something both of you have fought against yet wanted since the day you met. I have eyes. But Xander, if her father ever found out-”

Xander lurched, gripping Taylor by the shirt. “You think I don’t know the risks?” He gritted out, letting him go as quickly. “Sorry.”

Tayler didn’t even blink at his manhandling. He straightened his tie and met Xander’s gaze head-on. “I get it. I suppose it also doesn’t help when Gray outs you in the group chat.”

“Grayson has a big fucking mouth.”

“It’s part of his charm. He also has nothing to do with what’s going on between you and Penny.”

Xander turned away. “Nothing’s going on between me and Penny.”

“Now there’s a load of bullshit. At least Gray didn’t know you brought your current assignment with you. Look, maybe no one else has noticed the ridiculous chemistry between you and Pen, but I have. You’ve fought the attraction from the get-go, but it’s a battle you were always going to lose. The club? Of all places...?”

This made Xander face him, pointing a finger toward his chest. "How can you stand there and give me shit about taking Penny to Decadent when you're the asshole who told her about the place?"

"Want to tell me about the other person who joined you instead?"

"Fuck, no. Goddamn it, Grayson. For someone whose job involves a high level of discretion, he gossips worse than a teenage girl. He's going to get his ass kicked the next time I see him."

Taylor struck a nerve. It isn't just Penny fucking with his head. A bratty, green-eyed Italian is creating equal havoc. Xander knew Taylor would lose his shit if he found out who their third was. He might also fall on his ass laughing at the whole fucked-up situation.

With Taylor, it's a toss-up.

"On that note, if there are no security issues to discuss, I'll relay an update to Penny's father."

Taylor went from relaxed and joking to alert, and Xander knew he wouldn't like what he had to say. "Uh, yeah...James held a meeting here with some powerful and dangerous men while you and Penny were in New York."

Now Xander found himself on high alert, and the need to get to Penny and ensure her safety almost had him tearing open the door and taking off down the hall. It was his extensive military training that kept him in place.

He and Taylor painstakingly worked to gather intel on the extent of Penny's father's dealings with the European mob. For years, they found nothing. James kept whatever he'd gotten involved in away from Penny. Six months ago, that changed, and they didn't understand why.

"Who all was here?"

Taylor ran his hand through his short brown hair and huffed out a breath. "The heads of all five families." Before he could ask any more questions, Taylor filled him in. "They arrived the morning after you left. Sequestered themselves in James' boardroom for four hours. They departed the same way they'd come. Together."

"Did you get any details about the meeting?"

"Not the meeting itself. You know James keeps his office and boardroom bug-free. Hell, I had to do a perfunctory bug sweep for him before their arrival. It's what I saw when they left."

Xander caught Taylor shifting on his feet, a tell that he's uncomfortable with what he's about to say. "Just fucking tell me, man."

"They all deferred to James, kissing the ring he wears on his pinky on their way out. There's only one reason a mob syndicate would do that...and with Penny being his heir...." Taylor shook his head. "I don't know, man, this is pretty damning."

Xander knew how fucking damning it was. Yet he said, "It's still not enough to know for sure."

"Xander...."

“Enough, Taylor. Give Jonathan a call and have him send us everything on Marco Ricci. After all, he’s the one who recommended us for Penny’s detail. We need to connect all the dots.”

“I’ll do what I can.”

Xander rinsed out his coffee cup, then he stopped in front of Taylor to say one more thing. “The truth has a way of coming out. Please don’t assume things until we know for sure.”

Taylor slapped Xander’s shoulder. “Funny. I wanted to say something similar to you.”

“Believe me, I already know,” he muttered and walked out the door.

Chapter Twenty-Three

Penny

Penny raised the glass of champagne to her lips. "Happy birthday to me," she sang before taking a sip. Her twenty-fifth birthday arrived with the speed of a freight train.

Soon her father will announce her engagement to those gathering in the ballroom below. Penny expelled an unladylike snort. "That's right, everyone," she told her empty room. "I live in a castle with an honest-to-fucking-god ballroom. Like, how is this my life?" she asked the bubbles tickling her nose.

With the effects of the champagne becoming apparent, Penny set the flute aside, softening her anxiety to a more manageable level. She did her best to accept the decision her father made for her.

In his eyes, marrying someone like Alexandre Ricci is another way to protect her, though Penny liked the word stifle better. She didn't believe her father knew her. To be honest, she didn't know him either. Her mother died, leaving her father broken-hearted and bitter over never having had a son.

Not for the first time, she wished for a different outcome. To make choices for herself. She wanted Xander, and she wanted more time with Lex, too. Neither is possible.

Xander returned to his staunch professionalism, acting like nothing had happened. *"I'm sorry. This is how it must be."* His words replayed on a loop in her mind. After half a dozen attempts, she stopped asking.

There are limits to a girl's humiliation.

Now Penny sat in front of her vanity, waiting for Freya to do her hair, and she tried not to think about how Freya would help her into the gorgeous burgundy dress hanging from the closet door when all she could picture was Xander meeting her gaze in the mirror as he pulled the zipper up.

While she waited, Penny grabbed her phone and Googled her future spouse like she'd done since her father told her his name. And like every other time, she produced zip. Zilch. Zero. Except for one meaningless bio on a corporate website. No socials. No online presence at all. Like, who lives like that? "Apparently, the guy I'm going to marry does."

She considered asking Xander about him, then changed her mind. Back and forth she went until here she sat, and it was too late to do anything about it. Or was it?

Freya knocked on her door.

"One moment, please," Penny called out. She reread the single paragraph for what seemed like the millionth time. It mentioned when he founded his tech company and the charities he supported, with no other details given.

She left the page and opened her contacts, her thumb hovering over Xander's name. Xander will know more... jade-green eyes, dark hair, and a wicked smile.

Xander could also find Lex.

One night. They agreed on one night, and Lex was an unexpected bonus. Both men gave her an experience she'll never forget. Which is what she asked for, but....

Freya's next round of insistent knocking startled Penny from her unattainable thoughts. It's time to let those frivolous ideas go. "Coming!" Penny shouted, not wanting Freya to bang down the door.

Chapter Twenty-Four

Lex

"*Dovresti essere eccitato*-You're supposed to be excited," his father said, nudging Lex with his elbow when they walked through the massive doors at the entrance to Castle Fergus.

"*Faccio del mio meglio, Padre*-I'm trying my best, Father."

"*Prova piu forte*-Try harder," he said between clenched teeth.

A serious-looking man in a black suit ushered them down a hall beneath a massive stone archway. Lex must admit, his future home is stunning, and security is tight, too, glancing at more folks in suits spaced out along the hall. All of them are quite serious-looking.

"James takes all precautions with his daughter," his father said, switching to English. "Get used to having a shadow son. Soon, you will have more power than your brother, Roberto."

Lex didn't want to go through with this engagement any more than he wanted the power that came with marrying this woman. "Roberto is welcome to take my place."

His father turned his sharp gaze on him, pinning him with a look any other man would wilt under. "You know Roberto is taking over my endeavours. With you both having a seat at the table, think of the power our family will have."

"And you know, I wanted nothing to do with this."

"*Basta con queste sciocchezze*-Enough with this foolishness. You had your fun with your little company; now it's time for you to do what's best for us."

Lex bit his tongue. No point in reminding his father, *his little company*, the one he'd built from the ground up, was worth billions when his father demanded he walk away. He's a tech geek at heart and longs to go back to the company he founded, not step deeper into the family fold.

His father nudged him again. "Try to look like you're enjoying yourself, Alexandre. It's not like you're headed to the guillotine. You're meeting your future bride, and I know you'll find her pleasing."

"I said, I will try."

"See that you do."

They walked into the softly lit ballroom, and Lex looked around. Somewhere in the crowd is his future bride. Dread settled deep in his belly.

Perhaps it's a little like heading to the guillotine, after all. Especially when there are two people in New York, Lex can't get off his mind.

Penelope Anne Fergusson.

Lex imagined her to be as pretentious as her name implied. His father gave him an honest-to-God information packet during the flight here. Filled with stale facts and her educational history, which Lex admitted was impressive.

His father neglected to include any photos of his bride-to-be, and when he asked why, his father smirked and told Lex to get on his fancy computer and look for himself if he wanted to know. Except he didn't search the internet for anything he could find on Penelope. He's an ethical hacker, and despite his skills, he refused to investigate her.

His mind drifted to Xander and Penny, and not for the first time, Lex considered whether they'd given him their real names. Lex sighed. He'd never experienced such an instant connection, and not for the first time, he wished for more time to explore the spark he knew they all felt.

Another strong elbow from his father hit his ribs, and with a grimace, Lex's gaze rose to meet a set of familiar amber eyes. Those that haunted his every waking moment for the past two weeks.

Lex blinked, sure he imagined them, except her shocked expression must match his own.

The sleek midnight hair is gone. In its place, what Lex assumed were Penelope's natural auburn locks cascading down her back like an autumn fire. The shade suited her better.

A movement behind her made Lex shift his gaze over her shoulder, and the other individual he dreamed of stood behind her like a stoic protector. His stony face gave nothing away.

Questions swirled in Lex's mind, and he didn't know how he remained upright. *How is this possible? Is he her bodyguard? Are they together? Is this arranged marriage keeping them apart?*

Looking at them both, Lex wanted to have his cake and eat it, too.

Without the masks to impede his perusal. Lex trailed his eyes over the visible scar. It went from Xander's temple and disappeared beneath his beard. Without the facial hair, Lex knew it ended at his jaw.

How did he know this?

Ten years ago, on the night of his brother's rescue, overcome with relief, Roberto came home alive. Confusion wracked him when his eyes fell upon the tall, muscular man with blue eyes and a deep cut that needed tending from his temple to his jawline.

The soldier and the man he submitted to two weeks ago are the same. Years of training kept their expressions set to polite blandness, but they're shocked like him. Penelope, or Penny, he believed she preferred, extended her hand for him to take. "It's a pleasure to meet you."

Lex didn't miss the tremble in Penny's fingers when she placed them in his palm. When he brought her knuckles to his lips, her familiar flowery scent filled his lungs, and something came over him, and he teased her with a nip of his teeth, making her gasp.

No one noticed except the man standing behind Penny. When Lex raised his head, he caught Xander's silvery gaze. He swore the man mouthed the word *brat,* and if that didn't turn him on....

His father pushed him aside to take hold of Penny's hand. "Happy birthday, my dear. We haven't seen one another since you were a child, but I'm happy to welcome you into our family. Like your father has welcomed Alexandre into yours."

"Thank you for the kind words. It's wonderful to see you again."

When Marco's gaze landed on Xander, he called him over. "Xander. Come, say hello." Lex's breath caught when he approached, and his father slapped Xander's shoulder with great affection. "Always good to see you."

"It's good to see you, too, sir."

"Roberto sends his regards. He wished to be here for his brother's engagement, but couldn't get away. He'll be here for the wedding."

Penny's father stepped in and put an end to their conversation. "Let's get on with the announcement, shall we? Make things official."

"Right, right," Marco said, squeezing Xander's arm. "You know, it's funny how the world works. You saved Roberto's life. I recommend your services to keep Penelope safe, and now, with Alexandre marrying her, you'll keep them both safe."

Lex bounced his gaze from Penny's to Xander's and noted the other man didn't blink at his father's observations. Did Xander already know about the arrangement?

Xander recognized him. Knew who Lex was before....

Why didn't Xander speak up?

Lex wanted to corner the man and demand an answer, and it pissed him off because he couldn't. He wanted answers, and he wanted them now.

Moments later, their fathers stood on the raised platform at one end of the large room, garnering everyone's attention. Holy shit. This is really happening. Until moments ago, Lex believed he'd be getting engaged to a stranger, not the woman whom he'd connected with on such a visceral level; he hadn't been able to get her out of his mind.

And the man who affected him just as much stood steps away, staring at them both.

An electric current flowed along Lex's arm the moment he took Penny's hand and helped her up the step. The next thing Lex knew, they made the announcement, and he placed the ring, burning a hole in his pocket, on her finger.

Lex didn't hear a word of what his or Penny's father said. The white noise of his rushing blood drowned out their words.

The quartet in the corner played, and Lex escorted Penny to a space in the middle of the room cleared for dancing. He bowed, and she curtsied, then Lex guided her around the floor in an effortless waltz.

Penny trembled in his arms.

Lex brought his lips near her ear. "The three of us need to talk."

Penny moved her head back enough to meet his gaze, and for a moment, he forgot to breathe. My god, she's even more beautiful than he remembered.

A blush warmed Penny's cheeks, and Lex realized he'd said it aloud. He owed her an apology for his forwardness, but Penny spoke first. "You're right. We need to talk," she snapped with quiet intent, and Lex realized just how angry Penny was.

Penny didn't shiver with nerves. She vibrated with rage.

Chapter Twenty-Five

Penny

She waited three hours to get them alone. Penny's cheeks ached from the effort to maintain her smile, and if she uttered one more, 'It's nice to see you. Thank you for coming,' she'd scream. She marched ahead of Lex and Xander toward the library, eager for the answers to the questions swirling in her head.

"Penny, I-" Xander almost sounded... pleading, and Penny squared her shoulders and hardened her heart against the hurt that threatened to overwhelm her.

"Don't you dare," she said, turning to face the source of her disbelief and anger while Lex took a seat off to the side, his expression devoid of any emotion.

"How long have you known?"

He released a deep breath and voiced what she'd put together. "About Lex being Alexandre?"

She nodded.

Xander looked away and tugged on his beard. "From the moment I met his gaze, I couldn't shake the feeling of familiarity. I knew for sure when he removed his mask."

"You removed his mask while you left me blindfolded? Why didn't you say something? Is this all a fucking game to you?" Her whispered question echoed in the room's silence.

Xander's shoulders sagged under the weight of her accusation. "No. Not true. I-"

"When you figured it out, why didn't you stop everything?"

"I don't know," he said, his voice rising.

Frustrated, Penny threw her hands in the air and exclaimed, "That's not an answer."

"You're right. I fucked up. I'm sorry, Princess." Xander took a step toward her, and she stepped back, and he stopped. The look on his face was one of remorse, weakening her resolve.

"I said nothing when Xander recognized me, but our safeword never even crossed my mind. I wanted what happened between us. To keep our little fantasy bubble intact," Lex said, speaking for the first time since they entered the library.

Penny looked over to find Lex leaning forward in the chair, his elbows resting on his splayed knees while he studied the glass of liquor in his hand.

How can he look so sexy when she's pissed at him? Then Lex's piercing gaze landed on hers, and the next thing he said made her tremble.

"We all went there for something we needed. I didn't want to take it away from us, and I believe your man here came to the same conclusion. What we shared was for all of us to cherish, and while I can't speak for Xander, I assume he didn't know how to tell you because our meeting again was inevitable."

Xander cleared his throat. "Princess?" Penny stood between them, Xander in front and Lex at her back. Penny swallowed when she met Xander's gaze, his blue eyes stormy with emotion. "I was wrong not to warn you."

The full extent of what they did sank in. "Xander." Her voice sounded louder than she expected, and her gaze shot to the closed door. The last thing they needed was for someone to overhear this conversation.

"The room's secure. No matter how loud it gets, it'll remain between us. You're safe to express yourself however you want."

It didn't lessen her anger. "Oh, aye. How's this for expressing myself? Unbeknownst to me, my first sexual experience occurred while straddling my future husband. I believe I may need more than a minute to deal with this kind of mindfuck."

Then, almost of its own volition, Penny's hand shot out, and she slapped him across the face.

Xander flinched, and Penny saw her handprint blooming on his cheek. She gasped with instant regret, reaching for him with an apology on the tip of her tongue when Xander's low voice stopped her.

"Don't you dare apologize. It's the least I deserve. Tell me, do you regret what happened between us?"

Penny wanted to tell him no. She regretted nothing except her not knowing all the details. It's not what she said to Xander. "I don't want to talk anymore. I'm going to my room."

Chapter Twenty-Six

Lex

The door hadn't even closed behind Penny, and Xander was on his phone. "You got eyes on her? Good. I don't like how many people are roaming the place. Stand guard outside her door, and I'll relieve you in a bit," he said, meeting Lex's gaze when he ended the call.

"So...," Lex said into the silence falling between them. He stood, shoving his hands into his pants pockets to keep himself from reaching out and touching Xander. "This is a fucked-up situation we've found ourselves in."

Xander didn't respond, and Lex winced a little, eyeing the defined handprint still visible along his cheekbone. *Who knew the gentle Princess packed a wallop? Perhaps she's anything but delicate.* The idea turned him on... everything about them turned him on. Fuck, this is messy.

"It looks like it hurts."

Xander shrugged. "I deserved it."

"I can't argue with that," Lex said with a derisive chuckle. "You must know her hurt runs far deeper. She's in love with you, and I don't believe it's one-sided. I spent time with you for a few hours, and even I saw it."

Perhaps pointing out another man being in love with the woman he's supposed to marry is unexpected, yet there's no jealousy. Quite the opposite. If there's a chance Lex might have more…time with them both, he wants to seize it.

"How did you know?" Xander asked, not bothering to deny his or Penny's feelings.

Lex moved closer. "You knew much more than Penny and me."

"Pretty sure you're both up to speed now." Xander's words sounded gruff, yet he looked contrite.

"Well, not quite." Lex didn't know what had come over him. This sudden urge to poke Xander. To test him. "Penny doesn't know how you feel."

Xander gave him a stunned look, making a gesture that encompassed all of Lex. "You want me to tell Penny I'm…that I have feelings for her? You're getting married in four weeks. You must fucking hate me."

"Hate is not an emotion I'd ever use with you, Xander," Lex said, coming to stand toe to toe with the powerful man. He kept his hands in his pockets not to reach for what's turning out to be a powerful temptation.

"I'm aware if Penny had a say in this over-the-top arrangement our fathers made, you'd be marrying her, not me." Lex shook his head. "The funny thing is, that night in New York was inevitable. I don't know how else to explain it."

Xander did his damnedest to ignore those declarations. "I know it's fucked up how it happened, but Penny wanted-"

"I'm not jealous, nor do I begrudge Penny wanting something for herself." Lex gazed into Xander's stormy blue eyes, ensuring he didn't miss the truth behind his words.

"The only regret I have is that we didn't have more time together. I went to the club looking for something... extraordinary, too. How amazing to experience it with the two of you? Penny may be angry now; she has every right to be. She is going to forgive you." Lex couldn't stop a smug smirk from spreading across his face. "Which means she'll forgive me by association. You just need to do a bit of grovelling."

The tops of Xander's cheeks reddened. "I've never groveled."

Lex gave in to the urge to touch him and pulled his right hand from his pocket, setting it on Xander's shoulder. "You'd better learn fast." He tried to offer a comforting squeeze, though he likened it to squeezing granite. "Fuck, you're hard."

Xander choked out a surprised laugh. "You're such a fucking brat."

Lex didn't know what it looked like for a thirty-year-old man to feign innocence; all he knew was Xander didn't buy it. The air crackled between them until Xander shifted, putting space between them.

Right. Now's not the time or place. If there ever is one again.

Lex shifted past Xander to the door. "Have you gotten her out of your mind for over a minute since our night together?" Xander asked, stopping Lex in his tracks.

He kept his back to Xander, not willing to show him the emotion behind his answer. "I haven't stopped. I also don't have years of history with her." Lex dared a glance, and what he saw in Xander's eyes made his breath catch.

"You need to understand something, Mr. Ward. Penny isn't the only one I can't get out of my head. I never forgot you, soldier." Then Lex opened the door and walked out.

Chapter Twenty-Seven

Penny

Penny wiped a wayward tear away with her finger, praying her makeup remained intact when she approached her father's study. All too aware of Taylor trailing behind her at a respectful distance.

She gave the door a soft tap. When she heard her father's summons, Penny looked to find Taylor standing at the end of the hall. He gave her a nod, and Penny took it as encouragement. Then she stepped into the room.

Her father stood by the window, sparing her the briefest glance before his gaze returned to the darkness beyond, letting the condemnation in his words make a direct hit. "You stepped out of your party. Did you not enjoy the celebration I hosted in your honor?"

"Yes." Besides being blindsided by the man from New York, the same man she's supposed to marry, Penny's managing this crisis like any other. "I am sorry, Father. Things became overwhelming, and I needed a few minutes to speak to Le-to my new fiancé. He's...nice."

Nice? How about charming, funny, gorgeous, sexy…well, maybe not those last two. No, she'll keep the description nice. There's no need to scandalize her father or humiliate herself for life.

"I chose well for you, didn't I? He will handle things, and you won't have to worry. Neither will I," her father said, pulling Penny from her thoughts.

Taken aback, Penny wondered how many drinks her father had consumed this evening. "Yes, like I said, Alexandre seems nice. As for him taking care of everything… are you sure I can't take over for you? It's the reason I pursued the education I did."

Her father turned to face her. Anger mottled his face. "You will marry Alexandre Ricci. Your union is the right decision for this family."

What about what's right for me? She wanted to scream. Penny bit her bottom lip to prevent the words from escaping. Instead, she pursued the idea that took shape the moment she left the library.

"The problem is, I don't know him. It's what I wanted to speak to you about. I'd like to use the island home for the next three weeks. To get to know Alexandre with no distractions."

The private home on the Isles of Scilly will offer the seclusion she wanted. Her father purchased it for her mother and stopped going there when her mother died.

Penny knew the names of the couple her father hired to keep up the place, and a simple phone call ensured it'd be ready for their arrival. She'll be safe, and no one will disrupt them there.

It's a tremendous request, given the wedding's scheduled for a week after their return. Penny took the chance that her father would agree. "It's an excellent opportunity for us to become closer," she added with one last attempt at swaying him.

"Granted," he said, waving her off. Penny's eyes widened at the ease with which her father agreed.

"Thank you, Father. I thought I'd need to argue my case."

James grunted. "It's something Alexandre's father insisted upon. If you'd read the terms of your marriage contract like I told you, you'd already know this."

"I'm sorry I wasted your time, then."

He turned to face her. "You come back ready to marry Alexandre and secure the future of this family, and I don't care what you do leading up to it. The staff has already taken care of the plans for your wedding," he said, turning his back to her again, dismissing her like a bothersome burden.

Penny let loose words she'd clung to for far too long. "I know things changed after my mother died. I understand you coped with your grief the best you could, but you stopped being there for me. You sent me away to boarding school every year thereafter. I accept the fact that we aren't close. Father... you've become cold these last few years, like you...like you hate me."

She backed toward the door, unable to stand another moment of her father's presence, and, while tears blurred her vision, she held them at bay.

"I'll come back ready to marry Alexandre because I am your ever dutiful heir. When I return, though, things are going to be different. I'll no longer avoid the council meetings or remain in the dark."

Her father kept his back to her and said nothing, staring out the window.

"See you in three weeks, Father." Penny fled, slamming the door behind her.

Chapter Twenty-Eight

Xander

Xander sent Taylor on his way the moment he reached Penny's door. He hesitated, unsure if he should disturb her, yet he didn't want to leave things the way they were in the library and hoped she'd be able to forgive him.

He let out a deep breath and knocked, unsure if Penny would even answer. When the door cracked open, the relief he felt was short-lived when he caught sight of her tear-stained face.

He followed her retreat into her bedroom and closed the door behind them. Then he dropped to his knees in front of her. "Penny, I am so sorry I've caused you such pain."

"Xander, please." Penny offered him her hand, then pulled him to his feet. "This...," she waved her hand in front of her face, "isn't because of you."

"Who did this, Princess?" Xander shoved his hands into his pockets to hide his clenched fists.

"It doesn't matter. Besides, it won't change anything."

"If not me, then who? Did Lex do this?" Taylor would've told him if Alexandre had come to Penny's room.

"My father, okay?" Then, she did something unexpected. Penny screamed and flung her arms across her desk, sending everything to the floor. "My fucking cold-hearted father."

Xander worried. He understood her anger and frustration, but this can't be Penny's outlet. She'll hurt herself, and he can't allow her to do that.

He wrapped his arms around Penny, grabbing her wrists and holding them in one of his hands. "Shhh, I've got you," he whispered. "You've gone through a lot, Princess. I understand you have this pent-up rage and are looking for a way to escape, but I can't let you injure yourself."

Xander sighed, ruffling tendrils of her hair with his breath. "I can help, but you'll have to trust me, and it's the last thing I deserve."

Penny's movements stilled. His words pierced her rage, stripping the fight from her. When she slumped against him, Penny said something that made his heart soar. "I trust you, Xander. I'm furious with you right now and don't forgive you, but I never stopped trusting you. Please help me."

"Princess...." His words trailed off when he met her gaze. The look in her eyes decided it for him, and he pulled her toward the bed. He sat on the edge, looking at her tear-stained face, knowing he'd made the right decision.

Penny released a startled gasp when he tugged her across his lap. Her hands landed on the mattress to stop her forward momentum. "Xander?"

"Shhh...Daddy's going to make it all better."

Penny moaned.

"Do you like the idea of calling me, Daddy?"

"Yes...Daddy."

"Fuck, you're perfect, princess." He flipped the dressing gown she wore over her hips and groaned, finding her naked beneath. "No panties?"

"I-I was about to shower when you knocked." He traced his hand over her creamy skin with reverence. Then he placed his other hand at the base of her spine and trapped her squirming legs between his thighs.

"Color, Penny?"

The past two weeks disappeared when she answered, "Green, Sir."

"Good girl. Now, I'm going to give you what you need."

Xander landed the first smack on the fleshiest part of her cheek. Easy. This isn't a punishment, more a release. Penny sucked in a breath and moaned. Xander knew the sharp sting sent heat radiating through her.

"You're being a perfect girl for me, Penny. Do you feel it?" Xander landed another smack, this time on her left cheek. "Let the heat take your pain away."

"Y-yes, Sir."

Xander moved in a steady rhythm, never hitting the same spot.

Smack.

Smack.

Smack.

Over and over, Xander's palm struck her bum and the backs of her thighs. Penny's tears flowed, no longer from upset but from a cathartic release.

"Let it out. I got you." Xander gave her a few more smacks, slowing down until he caressed and soothed her tender flesh. When her tears slowed, Xander righted her dressing gown and helped her to sit up beside him.

He wiped her tears away while she peered at him from beneath her damp lashes. "I forgive you," she whispered.

Xander stiffened and pulled away. "Princess, this isn't any kind of apology. I have every intention of begging for your forgiveness. I want-"

"Stop. Enough, please. It doesn't matter how it happened anymore. You knew what I needed. You always do."

"I am sorry, Penny." Xander closed his eyes and leaned into her touch when she caressed the cheek she'd slapped, replacing the pain with tenderness.

"I'm sorry too," she replied. "Thank you for coming to check on me. There's something I need to talk to you about." She shifted, wiggling her tender behind, trying to find a comfortable position, and it made Xander's cock hard. Then her words stopped his arousal dead in its tracks.

"I'm planning to go to the island in the morning. My father gave his permission. No... that's not quite true. I've three weeks to get to know Alexandre - Lex," she amended. "His father included the stipulation in our wedding contract. He's hoping for love to bloom between us."

Xander did his best to keep the pain slicing through his chest from showing on his face. "Give me a few hours, and I'll have everything ready. You can leave then."

Penny met his gaze. "Security arrangements will be minimal since you're coming with us."

"What?"

Chapter Twenty-Nine

Penny

Xander flew them to the island on the family's Piper Cherokee and arrived after lunch. Penny was pleased to find out the caretakers had uncovered the furniture, aired out the rooms, and stocked the kitchen with everything they needed for their stay.

Lex did his best to lighten the mood, dubbing this their island adventure, while Xander did his best to keep a stubborn distance between them, despite how he'd helped her last night. Penny's derrière still felt tender from the spanking he'd given her.

When Xander left them in the house, using the excuse of sweeping the perimeter to make his escape, Penny couldn't stand it anymore.

"Give me a moment, please," she said to Lex, following Xander down the hall, catching up to him in the kitchen.

"Xander, wait."

"Did you need something?"

Penny stepped in front of Xander, beyond ready for this confrontation. "Why are you behaving like this?" she asked, over all this hot and cold, back-and-forth bullcrap.

He didn't meet her gaze when he said, "I'm ensuring you and your fiancé are safe. I'm doing my job."

"Bullshit. You've never treated me with such indifference."

Xander yanked his beard in frustration. "None of this is fair. This trip is for you to get to know your future husband. Why don't you go find him and do what you came here to do?"

"I never figured you for a fool, Xander. This trip is so much more than getting to know Lex."

"Oh, yeah? What's it about then, Princess?"

"The three of us. Whatever's between us isn't over. For the next three weeks, we have the opportunity and privacy to explore anything and everything."

"What will that do? All we're doing is dragging out the inevitable." Xander's gaze shifted past her shoulder, and Penny didn't have to look to know Lex stood behind her. She and Xander weren't quiet.

Xander gestured to the open patio door. "I need to take care of this." Then he turned and walked away.

"The three of us are alone in this house with no prying eyes and a freedom we won't have anywhere else," Penny called after him. The way his head dipped, she knew he heard.

"Hm. Xander's a stubborn one, eh? Let him figure things out." Penny turned to face her other problem, and Lex smiled at her like he didn't have a care in the world.

How can he be infuriating and endearing at the same time?

"It's a gift."

Penny blushed. She really needed a better filter between her mind and mouth.

"Come, Bella. I'll drop your suitcases in your room on the way to mine. We can settle in, open a bottle of wine, and enjoy the sunset. Perhaps we can get to know each other better, like you say." Lex winked, then turned to go.

Penny didn't move. She stood frozen, her indecision holding her in place. Is Xander right? Is she delaying the inevitable, only to be hurt worse in the end?

When Lex realized she wasn't behind him, he returned to her side. Close enough to touch, though he didn't. Oh, how she wanted him too.

"Penny, I know this trip will give us a chance to explore... whatever this is." Lex looked away from her and toward the open patio door. "The night the three of us spent together is the most real I've ever been. With anyone, including myself."

He reached out and tucked a stray curl behind her ear. His fingers lingered, tracing a path from her temple to her neck. "I guess what I'm trying to say is you may not know me well, but you and Xander know me better than anyone else."

Lex's soul-baring words and gentle touch made Penny shiver.

She closed her eyes, relishing his touch while avoiding the intensity of his gaze when she said, "Lex, what if I said the night at Decadent is the most real any of us has been?"

He tugged at her hair. "Look at me, Penny." When she opened her eyes, he told her, "I'd want to know how we get more of it."

"It's all I've thought about since that night."

Lex's warm smile grew wicked. "We ought to work together and convince Xander of this, too."

"How?"

Chapter Thirty

Lex

"Hear me out. I know you want Xander. I also know despite how little we know each other, you're attracted to me, too. And I won't deny I have feelings for both of you. Look, Penelope-"

Lex held up his hand and corrected himself. "Sorry, I mean Penny. I promise to be honest with you and never hurt you, to the best of my ability. What our fathers are forcing us into is archaic, and I wish for things to be different." He reached out, yearning to touch her, then paused. "May I?"

"Yes," Penny said without hesitation, and Lex traced his fingers along her jaw, trailing his thumb over her cheek and her full bottom lip.

"Your skin's so soft." Lex palmed her throat and stroked her racing pulse. Fuck, he wanted to kiss her.

"You know what? We're getting off track. Why don't we settle into our rooms, then meet back here, and share a bottle of wine? I don't know about you, but after the last couple of weeks, I could use a drink."

"Alright. I'd like to wash the travel off me and change into something fresh. We have a fully stocked wine cellar. I trust you'll choose well." Penny gestured to the hallway. "Lead the way."

Lex retraced their steps to the front of the house to retrieve their bags, but they weren't there.

"I took care of those for you, sir," said the woman coming down the stairs.

"Hello, Leana," Penny said, greeting the woman.

Leana smiled and dipped her chin. "I put your cases in the primary suite, ma'am. I didn't know where the gentlemen's bags would go, so they're on the landing upstairs."

"Thank you. I'm glad I caught you. We have dinner covered tonight."

"You won't be needing us then?"

"Actually, for the next three weeks, I'd like you to consider the house and the grounds taken care of. I want you and your husband to enjoy some time off."

"But, madam-"

"No, we insist. We want privacy to get to know one another."

"But Mr. Ward is-"

Penny stepped closer to the other woman, and Lex caught his breath when she said, "Mr. Ward is the only exception we want to make."

"Yes, ma'am. I will go tell Kenneth now." She gave Penny a hesitant smile. "We have some home projects we've put off. If you need anything, we're a phone call away."

"Thank you, Leana."

Lex waited until the other woman left in search of her husband. "*Mr. Ward* is going to be pissed you didn't run this by him first."

Penny turned to face him and put her arms around his neck. She drew Lex closer. Her mouth a breath from his. "*Mr. Ward* needs to realize that where there's a will, there's a way." Then she kissed his lips and whispered, "I want to ensure the way is free of every obstacle."

"I admire how calculating you are, dolcezza, though your biggest obstacle is the muscled giant himself."

"I know," Penny said, and kissed him again. Lex matched her passion, demanding entrance past her lips, and stroking her tongue in a heated dance of give and take.

Lex groaned against her lips, not wanting their interlude to end. He needed a shower and to change into something more suited to relaxation. With one more peck to her lips, he pulled back. "Meet me in the kitchen in thirty minutes. I'll invade the wine cellar, and you locate the glasses and opener."

"Deal."

Twenty-five minutes later, showered and dressed in a pair of linen slacks and a V-neck shirt, Lex entered the kitchen with two dusty bottles of wine. Pleased to find Penny already there.

Penny wore black cotton leggings, slouchy socks, and a soft sweater. She looked adorable and sexy. Lex smiled, and she waved the bottle opener in the air.

"Uh, wow, you have quite an extensive wine collection."

"Really?" she asked. Lex resisted the urge to smooth out the furrow between her brows. "I figured there might be a few bottles since my father hasn't used the place since my mother passed ten years ago. I hope they haven't turned to vinegar."

Ah, yes, something else in common. Lex and Penny both lost their mothers to cancer.

"Sorry for your loss. To lose your mother at such a young age. Does the grief ever get easier?"

Her eyes filled with sadness. "I'm sorry too." Penny fidgeted with the hem of her sweater. "Erm, I'm not sure if easier is the right word. You deal. Somehow, you get through the days, and you keep living. Your mom passed away last year, right? My father attended her funeral. He didn't allow me to attend."

"With the state I was in that day, I don't recall more than a couple of people there. The service and everything remain a blur."

Lex took the bottle opener from her hand, busying himself to avoid Penny's inquisitive gaze. "This requires alcohol. Let's find out if this wine's still drinkable. They diagnosed her cancer in March, and she passed in July of the same year."

"I'm sorry."

"Please, no more apologies. We spent my mother's remaining time together and shared many deep conversations. She had little pain, but-" Lex sighed. "Fanculo il cancro."

"Aye, fuck cancer."

Lex sniffed the open bottle. "Smells alright."

Penny held out their glasses, and Lex poured them each a healthy amount. She met his eyes with a look of sympathy and understanding, raising her glass. Penny encouraged him to do the same. "A toast. To our moms."

Lex clinked his glass with hers and sipped the bold red wine. "My mother would've liked you."

Penny took a sip of her own, contemplating his confession. "Even if she knew what we're doing here?"

Lex leaned closer, her warmth drawing him in. "And what are we doing here, Princess?" He enjoyed the heat blooming on her cheeks at the use of Xander's nickname for her.

"I believe we're trying to figure out if going against what everyone expects from us, against what society deems acceptable." They drifted closer, leaning across the kitchen island toward one another. Penny sighed and met his eyes. "If it's worth the repercussions, we'll face them."

Lex plucked the glass from her hand and set both their drinks aside, twining their hands together.

"My mother and I talked a lot. Unlike doing anything physical, talking didn't drain her energy. I spent hours at her bedside when my father or brother couldn't, and one day she asked me if I planned to settle down. I told her I didn't believe I would." Lex chuckled. "Little did I know."

His laughter faded, and he told her more. "My mother knew I desired something separate from what being a member of our family entailed. I moved to London and built my tech company and a charity to fund programs for children to have access to technology and a place to learn how to code."

"Do you still run the company? What am I saying? Of course, you don't."

He wanted no more lies between them and gave her blunt honesty instead. "It's true. I signed my company away the day we met in New York. It's not that I wanted to. There wasn't a choice."

"Huh. You'd think the organization would find your company useful."

"Oh, they do. My father just didn't want me running it anymore. Said it'd be too distracting. I wish I still worked there. I enjoyed creating and coding new software. What's done is done, though, I guess."

"Aye."

Lex passed her glass back to Penny, taking a drink of his own. Not used to talking this much about himself. "I regret nothing because it brought me to this moment and this place with you."

Movement from the corner of his eye caught Lex's attention, and over Penny's shoulder. He saw a looming shadow near the patio door and decided on a whim to stir a bit of trouble.

"Can you cook?" he asked. "Since you've sent Leana and Kenneth away, we'll have to feed ourselves."

"What do you mean, can I cook? Can you?"

"Is this your way of saying you can't?"

"Ugh. I get why Xander calls you a brat."

"You still haven't answered the question, Princess," Lex said with a laugh.

"Neither have you."

Xander's shadow moved a little closer. *There we go, big guy. No more eavesdropping. It's time to come inside.* "You ready to talk now?" Lex called. "We appear to be hapless fools in the kitchen, unable to even boil water. We fear starvation unless you have some decent culinary skills."

Chapter Thirty-One

Xander

Xander walked the perimeter. Twice. Finding nothing to distract him from the two people he wanted... no, craved. They drew him like magnets, and he approached the house with quiet steps, catching the tail end of their conversation.

Penny and Lex sounded... comfortable with one another. When Xander peered around the side of the house, he found them with their heads close and their hands entwined. Their soft laughter filled the air. Fuck, they looked beautiful together.

Xander leaned against the wall, rubbing his chest; the rapid beat determined to tell him something. It's not jealousy or anger. Quite the opposite. He longed to join them.

While he made sure everything was secure, Xander also processed the situation he found himself in. He, Penny, and Lex will be alone for the next three weeks. Is he going to spend it fighting his attraction to them, or will he give in and do what he believes all three of them want?

It's time Xander took control. Though he also needed to protect his heart, because at the end of this, when he had to go back to being Penny's bodyguard, he was afraid he'd be leaving his heart in their hands.

"You ready to talk now?" Lex called, pulling Xander from his thoughts. "We appear to be hapless fools in the kitchen, unable to even boil water. We fear starvation unless you have some decent culinary skills."

Knowing there's no sense pretending he wasn't lurking, Xander stepped through the doorway and headed right for the fridge. Lex and Penny played silent observers while he took out ingredients for grilled chicken and Greek salad, raiding the pantry for rice and bread. Once Xander set everything on the counter, he turned to face them.

"I have rules."

Xander's fingers twitched with the urge to put her over his knee when Penny rolled her eyes and mumbled, "He always has rules."

Lex clapped his hands and smiled. "You're in then? With us?"

Xander didn't plan on denying the inevitable. "Yes, I am, and despite what's already happened between us, we need to take it slow." Xander held up his hand, stopping the protest already forming on Penny's lips.

"These three weeks are about the two of you getting to know one another. No matter what else takes place here, it's what must happen. Now, I know you both want to explore this further, and I won't lie, the pull between us is intense, but when our time here ends, we must, too."

"Xander-"

"Penelope, you and Alexandre are getting married at the end of this month." Despite the seriousness of his words, Xander almost laughed at the matching pouty expressions they wore when he used their full names. They might not like it, but Xander craved that bit of professional separation while having this conversation, needing to reinforce the protective wall around his heart.

"Things are going to change, and I won't risk you being hurt if someone were to catch us."

"What if we do everything in our power not to get caught?"

"No, Lex, I won't risk it. Second rule. I'm in charge. If you want this, you'll have to follow my rules. If you want to stop this, use your safeword. I will always honor it. I promise to check in with you and make sure you're safe. You're my priority. You both are."

Penny's eyes shimmered with unshed tears.

Xander couldn't allow Penny's emotions to sway him. "Please, Princess, I need you to give me this. If you do, I'll give you and Lex all of me."

"Okay." Penny rounded the kitchen island and pressed herself against him, twining her arms around his neck. She stood on her tiptoes, her fingers gripping his hair to pull him closer, and when she met his gaze, she made a demand of her own. "Kiss me."

Xander's gaze shifted behind her to Lex, who leaned against the counter, saluting Xander with his glass of wine. Lex's stare, full of lust, stayed glued to them. "Please kiss her."

Well, he didn't need any further encouragement. Xander cupped Penny's cheek, his thumb tracing the delicate bone as her amber eyes darkened with desire. He pressed his mouth to hers, keeping the kiss soft because he meant what he said; he didn't want to rush this.

Lex moved closer, yet he didn't invade their space, and Xander let go of Penny, not wanting to get carried away. "Can you two chop the vegetables while I cook the chicken and rice?"

"We aren't hopeless. Come on, Penny," Lex said, breaking the tension. He handed her the cutting board from beside Xander, and she grabbed a knife. When Penny settled on a stool at the island, Lex stayed beside him, staring at him... more specifically, at Xander's mouth.

"Something you want, brat?"

"Do I get one too?"

"Rule number three. I'll do my best to keep things fair, though it makes me hard when you ask for what you want." Xander caged Lex against the counter and grazed the other man's lips. He nipped until Lex groaned, and Xander smiled against his mouth. "Now, go wash the vegetables."

"*Ma voglio di piu*-But I want more." Lex whined. His disgruntled expression made Xander laugh.

"Maybe I'll give you another after dinner. If you behave." Xander smacked him on the ass to get moving, and Lex arched back, seeking more. "Later," he growled.

Cooking with Penny and Lex turned out to be domestic bliss. *How is something unremarkable and exceptional at the same time?* Xander shrugged and put the pan on the stove for the chicken and a pot on another burner for the rice.

Penny grabbed her phone, loaded a favorite playlist, and soon soft music came from the Bluetooth speaker.

Xander listened to them talk about their favorite music while they prepped the salad. He kept busy, letting them do most of the talking, content to listen to their accents thicken with the more wine they consumed.

Chapter Thirty-Two

Penny

One week into their stay, and Penny has reached peak levels of bliss and frustration.

Xander ditched his suits, wearing shorts, t-shirts, or lounge pants – sweet, cock-hugging lounge pants. He showed off his incredible body and sexy tattoos, allowing Penny and Lex to explore his body at their leisure.

And boy, did they.

Xander kept to his word; they were taking things slow – way too slow in Penny's opinion. This house has turned into a sanctuary and private paradise for them, where they can be in each other's presence.

Their bubble of privacy grew smaller every day. Time was going by too fast; no matter how much they tried to savor it, their perfect bubble would burst, and Penny didn't know what to do. Xander said nothing more about this continuing when they returned home.

She pushed the intrusive thoughts to the back of her mind. Penny needed to be in the moment, where she could enjoy them both. Her two Alexs snuggled with her on a circular lounger on the back deck when she suddenly did an unladylike snort-giggle.

"What are you laughing about?" Xander asked.

She tried and failed to wipe the smirk from her face when Xander shifted to his side and loomed over her, making her feel protected and hunted at once.

"Yes, dolcezza. Do share. What do you find so amusing?" Lex said from her other side, tracing a finger over her hip to the tie of her white bikini bottoms.

Penny squirmed between them, enjoying their wandering fingers. "You both have the same name, yet have different nicknames."

"You just realized now?" Xander leaned in, nuzzling her neck, and she giggled at the way his beard tickled her.

"Well, no. It popped into my head that you're my two Alexs, and it made me laugh. I've known you share the same first name since they introduced you to me on my birthday."

"Well, we'd share it if he spelled his right," Xander said with a smirk.

"What?" Occupied with untying her bikini bottoms, Xander's comment distracted Lex from his task.

Xander leaned over her, trying to kiss the miffed expression off Lex's face. When it didn't work, he teased him some more. "Everyone knows the proper spelling is with an *er*." Xander winked and fell back on the pillow beside her, bursting with laughter.

Penny had never seen Xander this...relaxed. Ever. When he opened his eyes, he caught her staring, and his laughter simmered to a chuckle. "What?"

"You have the most carefree laugh. I wish I got to hear it more often."

"Keeping you safe is a serious job, Princess," he said, brushing her hair back from her face, and she yearned for more of the lightheartedness he shared a moment ago.

Lex snorted behind her. "Yeah, when she's heir to the European mafia throne, keeping her safe is a serious job."

Xander stiffened, and silence settled around them. Xander knew who her father was, didn't he?

He used his index finger to raise her chin until she met his gaze. "When your father first reached out for my services, he used our mutual connection to Lex's father to persuade me, and I turned him down."

"I'd no idea."

"My security firm runs out of New York, and a long-term gig in a small Scottish village didn't seem doable."

Penny tried to read his inscrutable gaze and couldn't. "What made you change your mind?" she finally asked.

"You."

"Oh." Penny bit her bottom lip. *She changed his mind?* When she tried to look away, Xander wouldn't let her.

"James sent me your picture-" Xander hesitated, and swallowed, taking a deep breath before saying more. "The moment I looked at your photo, I knew I couldn't walk away."

"Taylor agreed to come with me. Your father told us he was an aristocratic, powerful business person with too many enemies. We believed him at first, but as time passed, Taylor and I grew suspicious and looked into things. Lex's comment confirmed what we suspected."

"Yet you stayed even after you knew the truth?"

Xander caressed her face, and Penny leaned into his touch. "Oh, Princess. You had your hooks in me real deep by then. I go where you go, and I will always keep you safe."

Lex looked up from his phone. "Huh. It's neither of our spellings. According to Google, Alexandros is the original spelling, and, according to this article, it is superior. Meh, what does a Times columnist know, anyway?" Lex demanded, tossing his phone aside, apparently oblivious to the conversation she and Xander had.

"Hm... I remember my uncle calling me Alexandros as a kid," Xander murmured, good with returning to their lighter conversation. "He hasn't done it for years, though."

Xander glanced at his watch and turned to look at her and Lex. "Speaking of time, you've got a date to get ready for, and I'm going to walk the perimeter and take the boat across the bay. Want me to bring anything back?"

"Oh." The idea of those delicious pastries from the market made her mouth water. "Please stop by Nella's. Her pastries are to die for."

"Already on the list." He sat up and pulled on his t-shirt, covering all that delicious ink. "I'll see you both later."

Xander leaned over, placing a hand on either side of them. He'd left his hair down, and it curtained her and Lex when he caged them in. "You two enjoy yourselves." Then he pressed a kiss to Lex's mouth.

Desire bloomed deep in Penny's core. Having a front-row seat to the way Xander took control and Lex submitted filled her with an undeniable thirst to watch him take Lex for the first time.

Soon his mouth hovered over hers, and Penny ran the tip of her tongue along her bottom lip to entice him. Xander lowered his head and chased her tongue into her mouth.

All too soon, he left for the boat dock.

She and Lex stared after him, unable to help themselves. After all, the man's a walking billboard of muscled, tattooed perfection.

Lex held out his hand. "Come on. Xander's right, and we agreed to abide by his rules. Besides, I have a special date planned for us this evening."

"Oh?" Smiling, Penny took his offered hand. Since they stayed in and around the house, they'd gotten creative about their dates. "What should I wear?"

"Select something... comfortable." He said, tugging her along. Why did it feel like he wanted her to select something he could get her out of fast? The idea made her shiver with anticipation.

Where Lex liked Penny to choose what she wore for him, Xander liked to hand-pick what he wanted her to wear. Both ways made her heart race.

Lex stopped them outside the sliding glass door and cupped her face in his hands. He searched her gaze, finding everything she tried to hide.

"I hope this isn't too soon, which is weird to say when we're getting married in such a short time... *mi sto innamorando di te*-I'm falling for you, *amour mio*-my love." Lex wrapped his arms around her, pulling her into a tender kiss.

"What about Xander?" Penny needed to know if something beyond this island is possible for the three of them.

Lex's sigh ghosted her lips. "You won't be upset with my honesty?"

"What? No, we're in this together, and none of this will work without complete honesty."

"Well, when I picture us and our future, Xander's there. Not just as a bodyguard. He's...with us in every part of our lives." Lex shook his head. "I hope you're dragging this confession from because you envision the same."

"Aye. Xander's become ingrained in my life. We've eviscerated the lines between bodyguard and client despite his misgivings and what he believes the rest of the world will say. The three of us make sense."

Lex's gaze trailed over her like a caress, and his words sent a shock of arousal to her core. "I'm going to fuck you tonight, dolcezza."

Penny's inner sex fiend did a happy dance on her happy parts. She clenched her thighs, trying to offer her needy clit some relief.

Since the night of Xander's rules, they have fooled around a lot. Penny knew what they looked like naked and how it felt to be sandwiched between them, to kiss and caress them. But they hadn't fucked. Not her mouth, her pussy, or even her ass. Not since their night in New York.

She wanted to be with Lex. To know what it's like to be with him, like she experienced with Xander. Their days and nights here are slipping away, and Penny wanted to make the most of their time left.

"Please, Lex... I want it, I want you. Please, fuck me."

"*Cazzo, ci*-fuck yes." Lex kissed her again, harder this time. Slanting his head for better access, he licked past her parted lips, stroking into her mouth with his tongue, mimicking how he'd fuck her pussy.

Damn, the man can kiss.

He groaned, pulling away. "You need to get ready. I'll be at your bedroom door in two hours."

Lex gave her ass a playful squeeze when she walked past him into the house. Then he brazenly palmed his thickening length through his pants, letting her know how much she affected him. "Two hours, Princess."

Penny needed to shower and shave. Everything.

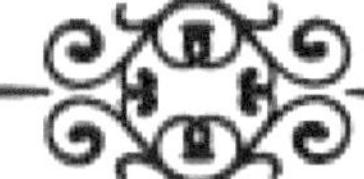

She picked out a matching white bra and panty set and pulled the pale-yellow sundress over them. She kept her makeup light and natural, putting her hair into a side braid that draped against her collarbone. Penny slipped her feet into her sandals just as Lex knocked.

Her breath caught when she opened the door. Lex wore a white open-neck linen shirt and matching pants, highlighting his golden skin. "Bellissima," he said, taking her hand and kissing her knuckles.

A blush heated her cheeks. "Thank you. You look handsome, too."

"Grazie, dolcezza. Ready?" Lex asked, offering his arm.

"Yes." Penny tucked her hand in the crook of his elbow. "Where are we going?"

"Well, it's secluded," he told her, leading her down the stairs. "There's a crackling fire, excellent wine, delicious food, and good company."

"Mm, sounds wonderful."

Lex guided her past the living room toward the back of the house, and Penny realized a moment later that he was taking her to the library. The one her mother created.

"I've found you with a book more often than not over the past few days and know you love to read. Do you ever listen to audiobooks?"

A memory of listening to the deep, sexy voice of a narrator growl *Good girl* in her ear is an immersive experience she planned to have again. "Uh, I've listened to a book or two."

"Well, tonight I'd like to be your book narrator."

"You want to read to me? But my mother filled this library with romance novels."

Lex chuckled. "Oh, I know. I had this idea for our date when I explored it the other day."

"My father used to tease her and call it her obsession. This is my favorite room in the house. When I was little, I believed it was magical."

He opened the door and stepped aside for Penny to precede him, and she let out an audible gasp. "Seems pretty magical to me," he said, his lips pressed against her ear.

It's like they entered a different world. The lamps on either side of the couch kept the shadows at bay. While a fire crackled low in the hearth. Lex laid out a blanket in front of the fire with pillows piled in one corner and a basket of food in another.

And of course, the volumes of books surrounding them. All of them are romances, ranging from classic tomes to books by Johanna Lindsey. Even a collection of Harlequin romances took up two entire bookcases.

Penny held a soft spot for bodice rippers, her first introduction to giant, muscle-bound men - *thank you, Fabio*.

The last time her family came here, she remembered sneaking between the library and her room, reading as many as she could with a flashlight beneath her covers.

A pre-teen with burgeoning hormones, they were an introduction to her sexual awakening, and they filled her with fantasies of what type of man she hoped to find for herself.

Penny also knew those books gave her an equal amount of unrealistic expectations. Yet the situation she found herself in now, well...the reality surpassed any fantasy.

“This looks amazing,” she told Lex, taking everything in.

“Wine?” he asked, holding up a bottle of red.

“Mm. Yes, please.” He filled her glass and poured one for himself. Then, taking her hand, Lex guided her through the stacks of books her mother organized by genre.

“I’ve forgotten how many books she owned.” Penny mused, dragging a finger along the spines, skimming the titles while they wandered past the shelves.

"Choose something for me to read to you."

"Oh, that might take a while," Penny murmured, scanning the titles, unsure what to choose.

"Well... when I set everything up earlier, I found a book I wanted to read to you. I hear it's one of your favorites," Lex said, giving her a sinful smile.

"Oh, yeah?" Intrigued by which story he chose, Penny turned to face him. "Which one is it?"

Chapter Thirty-Three

Lex

Lex wrapped his arms around her and kissed her cheek. "As you wish."

He saw the joy on Penny's face when she looked at him over her shoulder. "Did Xander tell you it's my favorite movie?"

"He may have let it slip when I asked." Lex reached for a book on the shelf above her head, pulling down a familiar leather-bound book. "When I saw this, I wanted to read it to you. I'm sure there are... spicier books in here if you prefer, I can-"

"No. The Princess Bride is perfect. I'd love for you to read it to me." Penny tugged him toward the blanket with the mountain of pillows he arranged.

Lex settled against the pillows and beckoned Penny to join him. "Is it alright if I hold you while I read to you?"

"I'd like that."

Penny laid her head on his chest, and Lex caught the scent of the flowery shampoo she used, and he couldn't help breathing her in, committing it to memory. He bent his legs on either side of her hips, and she placed her palms on his thighs, nestling against him while he held the book in front of them and slipped his glasses into place.

Penny rested her chin on her shoulder, a smirk playing about her lips when he adjusted the frames on his face. "What?"

"Oh, I belong to this online book club, and they were posting about male characters and their slutty little glasses." Penny reached up and touched them. "Now I know what they meant." Her lips grazed his. "You look so fucking sexy."

Heat scorched Lex's cheeks, and he cleared his throat. "Uh, thanks."

Penny settled back against his chest. "How about you put those slutty little glasses to good use and read to me?"

"Yes, ma'am." Her voice, tinged with authority, did something to him he planned to unpack later.

Lex traced the raised letters on the cover and read aloud, "The Princess Bride by S. Morgenstern." He flipped the pages to the first chapter when Penny gripped his leg.

"Don't you dare skip the kissing parts."

Lex laughed, familiar with the film. "I wouldn't dream of it."

"Once upon a time...."

Four chapters in, Lex closed the book. Unable to take a second more. Since chapter two, Penny had been rocking her ass against his cock, and he'd reached his limit.

He needed to fuck her.

"Why did you stop?"

"Because, Dolcezza...." Lex set the book on the table and flipped her, making her straddle his hips when she faced him, and put what she told him earlier to the test.

Lex slowly slipped his glasses off the bridge of his nose. He held them between his fingers and smirked before he folded them and set them on the table beside the book.

"Damn those slutty little glasses," Penny whispered.

Yeah, reading time's over.

"If you rub your perfect ass against me one more time, I'll come in my pants like an eager teenager." Lex groaned, her core rubbing against his cock.

"Please, Lex." Penny wrapped her arms around his neck, and he dragged his hands from her hips to cup her face, bringing her mouth to his.

Lex devoured her soft lips, enjoying the hint of wine on her tongue. "Take me to bed, Lex. I need you inside me." Lex shifted them to their knees, guiding her to stand, never stopping their kiss.

He searched her eyes, then his gaze drifted to her swollen lips. Desperate to have them surrounding his cock.

"I'll meet you upstairs. Keep your clothes on; I want to be the one to undress you. I'll douse the fire and be right up." Unable to resist giving Penny one more kiss, Lex then sent her on her way. "Go. Or I'll take you right here on the floor."

Penny got a far-off look on her face, and he knew she pictured him doing just that. "Another time, Penny. I'm fucking you in a bed tonight."

"O-okay. I'm going. Don't be long. Please, Lex, I need you."

"I'll be right there."

Lex doused the flames and put away the rest of the food on his way upstairs. On his way to Penny's room, Lex stopped at Xander's room and went into the adjoining bathroom. After all, Lex believed it to be considerate to leave a note....

Penny disobeyed.

For the first time, Lex growled, finding Penny naked in the middle of the bed, and not clothed like he told her to be. She loosened her braid, and her hair lay across the pillow, looking like a goddess he wasn't worthy of.

She cupped her breast, teasing her nipple, and the hand working between her thighs moved quicker as he stepped into her room. "You took too long," she whimpered. Her busy hands brought Penny closer to her orgasm.

"Princess." Lex meant to sound scolding. Instead, it came out as a groan. He moved to the side of the bed, pulling his shirt off and dropping it to the floor. "I ought to punish you for such blatant disobedience."

His pants and briefs went next. His hard cock slapped against his stomach, eager to get inside Penny. Lex crawled over her and pulled her fingers from her pussy, sucking them into his mouth, moaning when Penny's tangy flavor exploded on his tongue.

Lex pinned her hands above her head and crushed his lips to hers, letting her taste herself on his tongue. When their lips parted, he said, "Though, I'd much rather fuck you."

"Yes, Lex. Fuck me now and spank me later."

He laughed and nuzzled her throat. "Careful, dolcezza, or I might never let you leave this bed."

Lex trailed kisses along her jaw and down her throat, where he licked and nipped at her sensitive skin, making her squirm beneath him. He wanted to touch and taste every inch of her and let go of her wrists to palm her breasts.

He squeezed her flesh, plucking and teasing her nipples. When he sucked one of them in his mouth, Penny's hands found their way into his hair, gripping the strands, trying to pull him up her body.

"Soon, dolcezza. Let me pleasure you. Your tight little slit needs readying for my cock," Lex said, kissing his way down her stomach.

"Please. I need to come."

"And I want to taste your release, and you're going to give it to me." Lex shifted down the bed until his mouth hovered above her sex. Penny tilted her hips towards him, begging with her body, and he answered her silent plea, sucking and licking her core.

Penny's nectar trickled past his lips, and he groaned as he drank her down. He didn't exaggerate when he told her he'd happily spend the rest of his life with his head between her legs.

Lex focused on her clit, sucking the swollen bud into his mouth. Penny shifted, and she locked her long legs around his head. With her fingers still gripping his hair, he came to terms with her suffocating a fortunate man when she cried out his name, and her orgasm flooded his lips and chin.

He didn't let up, flicking his tongue against her clit until he rolled her into the next one. When Penny slowed the rocking of her hips and her grip on his hair relaxed, Lex lapped at her swollen folds, consuming the aftershocks of her release.

Penny's legs slipped from around his head, and Lex drifted up her body, leaving cum-covered kisses in his wake. "Taste yourself on my tongue." Penny moaned and sucked his tongue into her mouth.

His cock pressed against her center. Penny lifted her hips, taking the head of his cock inside her. Her heat surrounded his tip. "Oh, fuck." Lex's orgasm built at the base of his spine.

As part of Xander's rules, the three of them discussed their options on their first night here, wanting to be on the same page with intimacy. Penny used an IUD, and with three recent negative medical screenings, they agreed they wanted nothing between them.

Lex wanted to fill her pussy with his cum, and watch it cream from between her thighs. He'd never fucked without a condom. Now, sinking into Penny with nothing between them, he never knew such completeness with anyone else.

"Please, Lex... I need you to move."

He pulled back, and Penny arched her back to meet his thrust. "Yes," she hissed against his mouth when he seated himself to the hilt inside her tight heat.

They found their rhythm, but it was not enough. Lex wanted deeper, wanted to take her harder, and Penny was right there with him, shouting, "More."

Lex pulled out and flipped her over. He lifted her hips, arching her ass in the air and pressing her chest to the mattress. "Look at you, so fucking gorgeous," he praised, slamming back into her.

"Oh god, you're deep. Fuck me harder, Lex. Please, I'm gonna come."

He reached beneath her, stroking her clit. Lex needed Penny to come around his cock. He gripped the back of her neck, holding her in place beneath him.

"Vieni per me, bella-come for me, beautiful."

"Lex," she cried out. Her cunt squeezing his cock, soaked his length in her arousal.

With the way her pussy gripped him, Lex came harder than he ever had. He held himself deep inside her, pressing his chest to her back to reach her mouth. Their kiss became sloppy and delicious.

“Mm, I’m full of your cum,” Penny moaned against his lips.

He smirked. Xander will return soon, and when he does, he’ll find the message Lex left for him.

Lex stayed inside Penny, shifting their bodies onto their sides. He wrapped his arms around her and snuggled her from behind, needing the connection. “Rest, dolcezza. I’ve got you.” Lex trailed kisses along her temple and whispered sweet words in Italian until they dozed off.

Penny stirred against his chest almost an hour later. “Xander?” Lex slid his hand up and down her arm in a soothing motion while they listened to the faint sound of the shower down the hall. “Do you think he’ll join us?”

“If he knows what’s good for him, he’ll come here when he finishes.”

“What if he doesn’t?” The uncertainty in Penny’s voice made Lex desperate to ease her worry and make her smile.

“Are two naked people running down the hall to get him enough of a hint?” The tightness surrounding his chest eased when Penny laughed. “Though, don’t worry, I left him a note. He’ll come.”

Penny rested her chin on his chest, meeting Lex’s gaze in the dim light from the hall. “I don’t want to waste the rest of our time here. I want time with you both, together, but I also want the two of you to have time alone.”

Lex saw the moment a shirtless Xander filled the doorway over Penny's shoulder, making his cock stir once again. Fuck, he's always hard around these two. Xander looked sexy-as-fuck with his arms crossed, leaning against the jamb, listening to their conversation.

"What else do you want, Pen?" Lex asked, tucking her hair behind her ear. Xander took a few steps into the room, approaching on silent feet.

"Hm... no more sleeping in separate rooms. I want you both here. I know we're not supposed to last, but if there's a way I-" The bed dipped behind her, making Penny gasp when Xander sat on the edge. He ran his fingers down her arm, and she turned toward him.

"Hey, little one." Xander cupped her chin and gave her a soft kiss.

Then Xander's gaze shifted to Lex. "I received your invitation, and I've also tallied every bratty occurrence-"

"I have a running list going if you want to compare notes in case you missed any of my... indiscretions." Lex enjoyed being a cheeky bastard and how much Xander liked it.

Xander growled. "I also got your message, brat. Now, I want my taste."

Chapter Thirty-Four

Xander

"What message?" Penny asked. Xander ran his finger over the curve of her breast as the electricity built between them.

In one swift movement, Xander yanked the sheets back, and Penny yelped in surprise when he grabbed her by the ankle and pulled her to the edge, where he now stood between her spread thighs.

The time for hesitation is over. No more holding back. It's time Xander gave them all what they craved.

Lex lounged against the pillows with his hands linked behind his head, ready to enjoy the show. His stiff cock leaking precum onto his stomach.

Xander leveled his gaze at him and said, "Don't you dare touch yourself without my permission."

"Yes, Sir."

Xander grunted. Satisfied, Lex will obey for now. Then he turned his attention to Penny and slapped her pussy with four of his fingers.

Penny squealed, dripping with fresh arousal and Lex's cum. Xander didn't take his eyes off her when he raised his hand to his mouth and licked his fingers clean.

"You want to know what the brat's note said? He told me to 'Enjoy her cum-filled pussy.' And I sure as fuck am going to."

Xander dropped to his knees and spread Penny's legs wider. "Get over here, brat, and hold our girl's legs open. I want to enjoy my feast of your fucking."

Lex jumped to do his bidding, scooting behind Penny. He lifted her head into his lap and hooked his hands behind her knees, displaying her for Xander's hungry gaze.

"Fuck." The creamy combination of them dripped from her opening, and Xander took a deep breath, dragging their essence into his lungs. "I'll never get enough of this."

"Xander, please," Penny begged.

"Yes, Princess. I won't make either of us wait any longer." Xander put his hands beneath her bum and raised her pussy to his lips. He flattened his tongue and licked her from asshole to clit, swallowing as much of them as he could.

Penny and Lex kept their gazes riveted on him while Xander lapped their cum into his mouth. The way it soaked his beard, their combined scent consumed him.

It was filthy.

It's depraved.

And it's everything Xander wanted.

CHAPTER THIRTY-FIVE

Penny

If Penny knew of a way to stop time by now, she would've done it. With every moment the three of them spent together, the ticking clock counting down their time together grew louder.

From what she and Lex understood, Xander still planned to end things once their time here ran its course, and they're so close to the end. Penny wanted to rail against what society said was proper. She didn't want to marry Lex if it meant giving up Xander. She's already fallen for them both.

Why did they have to choose?

She knew the answer. Xander didn't want to be their dirty secret. It's what it came down to, and Penny understood. Mostly. Isn't being a secret worth it when the alternative is not being together?

Penny jumped when Xander shut the door to the bedroom they now all shared.

"Where's Lex?"

He cleared his throat and shifted on the balls of his feet. "He took the boat across the bay."

Xander's...nervous.

Xander was never nervous.

"Lex reminded me I've neglected taking you on a date, and I'd like to rectify that."

"Oh? I didn't realize." Penny turned back to the clothes she'd been folding. *Lies.* They are three people who are in some version of a relationship; it was hard not to notice the snub.

With her back still to him, Penny rolled her eyes.

"Did you just roll your eyes?" Oh. Her growling daddy is back.

Totally her plan.

Penny peeked over her shoulder. "No, Sir."

"That's one, Princess." Xander's demeanor shifted again, and he grinned from ear to ear. "I'd like to take you to dinner."

Penny turned when Xander stalked closer.

"I know you and Lex have a little dating creativity competition going on, though I didn't know it included a restaurant pop-up."

Xander reached out and wrapped her ponytail around his hand, tugging her head back. "Funny. Want to make it two?"

Penny bit her bottom lip, peering up at him from beneath her lashes. "Maybe," she smirked.

"Are you trying to give Lex competition for being a brat?"

Penny went up onto the balls of her feet, her mouth reaching Xander's throat, where she nipped him. "Maybe," she whispered.

"Two." Xander's mouth captured hers, not giving Penny the chance to ask, 'Two what?' His kiss became brutally passionate, giving her a taste of what he wanted to do to her, and goddamn, she wanted more.

"I've drawn you a bath and laid out what I want you to wear in the room Lex used." He stopped when he caught the look she gave him. "What? You were in here over-analyzing everything, and I needed to get things ready for you."

"When did you get an outfit for me? It's not like there is a mall down the street-hello seclusion."

"I bought it in New York for you while you were sneaking around buying your outfit for Decadent. I saw it and knew it belonged to you," Xander confessed, making her swoon.

Damn. This. Man.

Penny pouted and teased him. "You mean I schemed to convince you to give in, and you planned to fuck me all along?"

"Oh, that's three, Princess. If I recall correctly, you convinced me to take you to the club. Not what happened between us? New York was inevitable, and Lex showing up made me fucking glad I took you to Decadent that night."

Is Xander trying to say…?

Xander's hands distracted her from her train of thought, wandering down her back to grip her ass. He pulled her to him and looked into her eyes. "Relax. I want you to take your time and enjoy your soak in the tub. Then come find me downstairs when you're ready."

Xander stopped in the doorway. His smirk grew wicked when he chuckled. "I have to say, your rising tally will make for an entertaining evening."

Penny rushed to her empty doorway. How can she have a relaxing soak in the tub when she wants to jump into Xander's arms and demand all the orgasms? Maybe she'll get off in the tub. It's not her fault if Xander wants delayed gratification. Penny can take care of herself.

Xander didn't even turn around when he said from down the hall, "Don't you dare make yourself come while you're in the tub, Princess. Your orgasms belong to me."

"A lesson in the art of anticipation, then?"

"If that's what you want to call it. Keep your hands off yourself."

Penny soaked. She relaxed, and despite the temptation, she didn't touch herself. When the water cooled, she rinsed off, got out, and lathered herself in her favorite lotion.

She dried her hair into soft waves, applied mascara to her lashes, and a clear gloss to her lips. Her time under the sun added fiery highlights to her hair and brought out the freckles across the bridge of her nose.

Penny returned to the room Lex used, putting on the outfit Xander got for her. One item. No bra. No panties. She held up the silky garment. Can she even call this a dress?

Xander chose a pale peach color that complemented her hair. She slipped the dress over her head and moaned when the soft material caressed her skin, cascading over her body like a waterfall of silk.

The top dipped low, highlighting the swell of her breasts, and Penny teased her nipples, making them even more visible through the silky material. With her bare underneath, this outfit will give him access to every part of her.

Penny found Xander in the sitting room off the kitchen, dressed in a pair of black satin lounge pants and nothing else. He left his hair loose around his shoulders, and the ink covering his torso was on full display.

Yum.

The delicious smells from the kitchen made her mouth water, and her stomach rumble. Xander turned from the window at the sound.

Xander stared at her, and the look on his face screamed *mine*. He closed the distance between them and touched her everywhere.

One of his hands roved over her body while the other gripped her hair, arching her head back. Xander teased her with the tip of his nose, trailing up the length of her throat, and making her shiver when he breathed her in.

“What I imagined is nothing compared to the reality of you in this dress,” Xander said, lifting his gaze to meet hers. “You are the most beautiful woman I’ve ever seen.”

“You’re determined to ruin me for anyone else,” Penny gasped.

“As long as Lex still stands a chance, I aim to please.”

“You and he are all I need.”

Xander kissed her. Hard. He let go of her hair and took her hand. “Come,” he commanded, tugging her outside.

Penny didn’t know where to look first. Several lanterns lit up the patio, giving it a warm glow in the dusky evening. Xander moved the outdoor furniture, leaving a table and chair.

“The cushion is for you,” he said, guiding her to it.

Xander wants her to sit at his feet? Realization made goosebumps rise on her skin. *Oh god. Xander wants her to sit at his feet.*

Penny clenched her thighs together, arousal gathering at her apex. Moisture slicked her folds as he led her to the cushion. “I want you on your knees with your legs spread. Keep your hands on your thighs unless I tell you otherwise.”

“Yes, Sir.” She lowered to her knees and relaxed into the position.

“So perfect, Princess.”

Xander kissed the top of her head. “I’ll be right back with our food.” He didn’t leave her waiting for long, returning with a chilled bottle of wine in one hand and a platter of food in the other. Once he’d arranged everything, Xander pulled out his chair and angled it to face her, sitting with his legs on either side of her.

Penny kept her eyes on him, and Xander leaned forward, bracing his elbow on his thigh. He tucked her hair behind her ear, trailing his fingers down her throat and along her collarbone.

Penny rolled her hips, trying in vain to get some friction against her clit. Xander wiggled four of his fingers. “You’re up to four, Princess.”

Penny licked her lips with anticipation, though she stilled her movements.

Xander opened the wine and poured a single glass, lowering it to her lips, offering her a drink. Penny let the crisp chardonnay dance across her tongue before she swallowed. Xander held a piece of bruschetta. “Open,” he commanded, feeding her from his hand. She grazed her teeth against his fingertips. He said nothing, popping the rest into his mouth.

She’ll have to try harder. “Is this what it’d be like?”

“Hm?” Xander lifted her chin with his index finger and rubbed his thumb along her bottom lip.

“You want to know if I’d pamper and worship you while having you at my feet? The way you’d gift me your submission until I fuck you into exhaustion every night? If you weren’t you, and I wasn’t your bodyguard?”

"Yes." Penny tried to blink the sudden onslaught of tears away, though Xander saw them anyway. How did he arouse her and break her at once?

"Princess, you're fierce and won't bow to anyone, yet you will submit to me. If things were different, with every chance I possessed, I'd have you on your knees for me."

"What about Lex?"

Xander looked off into the distance. "Yeah. I'd have your bratty future husband on his knees right beside you."

It is possible.

Penny kept the words from slipping past her lips.

"I'm not sure I can do what-ifs right now. We still have time, and I still have plans. Can we stay in the present a little longer?"

"Okay. I'll give you a little more time. We can't put off this conversation forever."

"I know. Thank you for giving me more time."

Xander fed Penny succulent bites of food he prepared for her, letting her nip and lick his fingertips until she finished eating and was so turned on, arousal dampened her thighs.

"Hm, you're up to five now, Princess. I'm not sure you can handle more." Xander warned, lifting the glass of wine to his lips.

Five? She's handled twice that from him already. She wanted more, and she figured making demands was a good way to get it.

"When are you going to punish me?" Xander took a drink, making her wait for his answer while he savored it.

"What do you mean?" His tone gave nothing away.

"You said I have five, and I want to know when you'll dole them out."

Xander chuckled and set the glass down. "Oh, I see. You believe I'm going to bend you over my knee and deliver five strikes, or however many you increase the number to, with my hand or perhaps a paddle?"

A flush traveled from Penny's chest to her cheeks while her breathing sped up. She liked the idea of a paddle. A lot.

"By the way you're reacting, I believe you'd enjoy a good paddling. That's not what's happening tonight."

Xander leaned closer, looming over her, and Penny held her breath in anticipation.

"Princess, I'm not issuing strike warnings. Five's the number of orgasms you're going to give me when you ride my face. In fact, I won't fuck you until you've given me every single one."

Penny whimpered. There's got to be a puddle of her arousal on the pillow by now. She wanted Xander to drag her upstairs and fuck her right now. Instead, he took another sip of wine, making her wait.

"Would you like dessert?" he asked.

Penny eyed the empty plate. Her weakness for something sweet and salty is no secret. "Is it in the kitchen?"

"No, it's right here," Xander said, palming his thick erection through the thin material of his pants.

Penny licked her lips, her mouth watering for a taste. "Fuck yes."

"Mm, who's my dirty girl?" He undid the tie at his waist and took his cock out. Long, thick, and veiny. Penny wanted to swallow every inch.

Xander shifted forward on the edge of the chair, stroking his length and spreading his precum down the length of his shaft. "Will you swallow every drop or share some of your dessert with me?"

"I promise to save you some."

"Such a perfect, dirty girl. Stick out your tongue for me."

Penny extended her tongue past her bottom lip, and Xander rewarded her with the tip of his cock. "Lick." And she did. Like his cock was her favorite ice cream cone.

"Fucking suck me," he demanded.

"Can I use my hands, too?" she asked, remembering that Xander told her not to move without permission.

Xander leaned in and kissed her. "You're such a good fucking girl. Please."

Penny wrapped her fingers around his base, stroking upward to meet her lips, taking him deeper with each pass until she could remove her hand and press her nose to his trimmed pubic hair.

"Fuck yes. Just like that." Xander's grip tightened in her hair, taking control. Penny grasped his thighs and kept her watery gaze on him.

"Your mouth full of my cock is a sight to behold. I'm gonna fuck your face now, Princess." Penny moaned around his girth. "Slap my thigh if you need me to stop."

Xander held her head between his palms and thrust, hitting the back of her mouth just shy of making her gag. Over and over, going a little deeper each time until the head of his cock dipped into her throat.

"Take shallow breaths through your nose. Yes, like that. I want you to take all of me." Xander hissed, and his pace quickened.

Penny blinked. The first mascara-laced tear tracked down her cheek, and Xander caught it with his thumb. "You're so fucking beautiful, Princess. I'm gonna feed you every drop of my cum."

Xander moved faster, and Penny let go, relishing the way he used her for his pleasure. Xander grunted, and the first spurts of his hot seed hit the back of her throat. Penny swallowed until he pulled back, resting the crown on her bottom lip, jerking the rest of his release onto her waiting tongue.

Penny tipped her chin up in a silent offer for him to taste. Xander groaned, and his mouth covered hers, delving his tongue inside, lapping his cum from her mouth. Filthy and oh, so fucking hot.

“Upstairs. Now,” Xander demanded, shoving his spent cock back in his pants. He scooped Penny into his arms, carrying her into the house and upstairs to the bedroom.

When they reached the bed, Xander dropped back on the mattress, taking Penny with him. With his feet braced on the floor, Xander shifted Penny to hover over his face. “Take off the dress and sit.”

Penny tore the dress over her head, and her thighs shook when she lowered her pussy over his mouth. She felt Xander’s voice vibrate against her core when he said, “Count. And you better scream every number.”

Chapter Thirty-Six

Xander

"Fuck, I need to taste you, Princess." Xander dug his fingers into Penny's hips and yanked, seating her on his face. He breathed in her heavenly scent and moaned. "You smell so fucking good."

Penny's thighs hugged his head, and he licked her from her asshole to clit, dipping his tongue into her opening. Xander lapped at her essence, ready to drown in her pleasure.

The time they spent here gave Xander a taste of what it'd be like if the right two people shared his life.

They are the right two people.

Xander did everything to ignore what his heart wouldn't stop whispering. He focused on the task at hand, which led to Penny coming multiple times. He circled her clit with the tip of his tongue, then sucked it into his mouth. She pulsed against him and screamed, "One."

With the way she surrounded him, clenching his head with her thighs, Xander could only groan in response when her arousal flooded his mouth.

By the time Penny shouted, five, her legs shook, and she whimpered when she fell off him into a sated pile by his side. “Oh my god,” she whispered, her voice hoarse from screaming.

Xander leaned on his elbow and swiped his other hand across his mouth. She soaked his beard, and he inhaled her intoxicating scent with every breath he took. “Fuckin’ amazing. Ready for more, Princess?” he asked, standing to remove his pants.

He wrapped his fingers around the base of his straining dick, giving himself a couple of strokes. Penny watched him with half-closed eyes. “I don’t know if I can come again... I need you, though. Need you to fuck me, Xander.”

She parted her thighs, and Xander looked his fill. Her gorgeous cunt looked plump and pink, wet and ready for his cock. “I need you just as much, Princess.”

Xander crawled onto the bed, and when he hovered above her, Penny hooked her legs around his hips. He lined the head of his cock with her opening, and Penny gripped his hair. He groaned when she ran her fingers through the strands, tugging with enough force to give him a nice bite of pain. Xander shifted his hips back and sank into her with a single thrust. “You feel like home and heaven rolled into one,” he groaned.

Xander wanted to come the moment he got inside her, though he held off because he wanted her to milk it from him. “You’re going to need to give me one more, baby. I need you creaming on my cock when I give you my seed."

"Xander."

"Your tight little cunt has got a vise grip on me. You've come so many times tonight, my greedy little slut. I know you can do it again." Xander pressed his thumb to her clit, and Penny whimpered, bucking beneath him, urging him deeper. "Now, give me one more."

He shifted, and the head of his cock rubbed against the front wall of her vagina. "Oh...oh my god, right there. Don't stop," Penny cried.

Her core fluttered and clenched around him. "Yes," he growled. "Milk. My. Cock."

Penny's muscles seized, and she shook with the intensity of her release. "Xander, yes...oh, god, yes."

Xander's thrusts became erratic. His orgasm barreled down his spine and into his balls. "Penny." Xander held her face between his palms and kissed her, letting her swallow his groans while he filled her with cum.

The bed shifted, alerting Xander to Lex's presence. He lifted the sheets, and Lex slipped beneath them, scooting over until Lex reached his mouth and sucked his bottom lip between his teeth. "Needy brat."

“Fuck, you’re covered in her,” he breathed, rubbing his nose against Xander’s beard.

“Mm, left it for you.” Xander grabbed the back of Lex’s head and licked into his mouth, tangling their tongues and dominating their kiss while Penny slept like the dead on his other side after he’d wrung all those orgasms from her.

“You taste like you had a good time,” Lex whispered against his lips.

Xander chuckled. “A splendid time.”

Lex peered over Xander’s side. “Is she even alive?”

“Let her sleep. She earned it. What did you get up to?”

Lex snuggled closer. “Hm, I went for a hike on the trails you recommended. Had dinner with Leana and Kenneth.” Xander grunted when Lex smacked his chest. “Did you know they’re in a D/s relationship, and Leana is the D?”

“Yes, brat. I’m aware.”

“I missed you both.”

Xander wanted to return the sentiment. Wanted to tell Lex, he and Penny have made him happier than he ever imagined he’d be. When the three of them are together, there’s a completeness he’s dreamed of. Xander didn’t say any of it, though. Tomorrow is their last full day here. Then there’s no escaping the reality of their situation.

And right now, Lex offered Xander the perfect distraction when he pressed their cocks together. "How about you wrap your big hand around us and stroke us until we both come? Turn your mind off." Lex urged, running his fingers through Xander's hair the way Penny did.

Xander groaned, sliding his hand between their bodies. He lined their dicks up, wrapped his hand around them, and stroked them from root to tip. "Hm. We need…." Xander let go of them and held his hand beneath Lex's mouth. "Spit."

Lex licked Xander's hand from palm to fingertips. The sensation ignited Xander's desire. "You're such a fucking brat."

He grasped their cocks, slicking the way with Lex's saliva. The feel of his steel length rubbing against his own cock had his balls readying to unload.

Lex kissed him. "I wish I'd turned a light on. I want to watch you make us come."

A soft hand sliding over his hip let Xander know they'd awakened their sleeping beauty. Then Penny's chin pressed against his shoulder, trying to get a look for herself.

"No, you don't need the light on. You can have a taste of what you did to me. What did you say again that night? Ah, yes, use your imagination, your other senses," Penny challenged with a snicker.

Penny rubbed up against his back like a cat in heat. Lex attacked his mouth in a passionate kiss, and Xander increased the pace of his hand. He's close, and he wanted Lex right there with him. "Come for me, Lex. Now."

He cupped Lex's balls and gave them a firm squeeze, letting him ride the edge of pleasure and pain. With one final stroke, Lex shot off like a rocket, and Xander went along for the ride. They grunted and moaned, making a mess of their hands and stomachs as they came all over one another.

"Fuck, that's hot. I vote for all the lights on next time because I need to see that happen." Penny brushed her hand over Xander's ass and squeezed. "My God, did they sculpt your arse from granite?"

The three of them burst out laughing.

When Penny's giggles settled, she groaned and crawled out of bed. "Don't move, lads. I'll be right back."

She popped into the bathroom and returned with a damp cloth. Penny flicked on the bedside lamp and gasped, taking in the copious amount of cum coating their stomachs. "Look at the mess you've made."

"Why don't you clean us up then, sweetheart?" Xander asked.

"I can do that." Penny leaned over them. She didn't use the cloth, swiping her tongue through their mess instead, making his cock stand up and take notice despite having come minutes ago.

Penny's having the same effect on Lex. She lifted her head, tracing her lips with her tongue. Only then did she use the cloth to clean the rest away.

Penny's breasts swayed close to Lex's mouth, and Xander teased her rosy peaks, coating them with the cum still on his fingers. "Made a tasty treat for you, brat. Now, clean those pretty little nipples up for me."

"My pleasure, Sir." Lex lifted his head and captured a glistening nipple in his mouth, making Penny moan with pleasure. She dropped the cloth to the floor and braced a hand against the headboard for support. Her lips parted with a sigh of ecstasy as Lex moved to her other breast.

"You missed a spot, Princess." Xander held up his hand, cum covering his knuckles.

"Did I?"

"Dirty girl. Straddle Lex and clean my fingers." She crawled over Lex, grabbed his wrist, and sucked two of his fingers past her lips. Her tongue licked between them, seeking every drop.

When she finished, Penny kissed Lex, driving her tongue past his lips and letting him enjoy their combined flavors. When it was his turn, Xander pulled her between them, deepening their kiss until she squirmed in a puddle of need.

"I know what I want to do tomorrow," Penny said, catching him off guard when he ended their kiss.

Their last day here.

This is going to hurt like a motherfucker when it's over. He'll figure it out somehow. For now, he needed to focus on fulfilling Penny's desire. "And what do you want, Princess?"

"I want what happened now and at the club, except with the lights on."

"Anything else?" Xander could see her mind was going a million miles a minute with the possibilities.

"I want both of you to fuck me. Together."

Xander met Lex's eyes and saw he wanted it, too. "All right, sweetheart. Lex and I will give you what you want. Let's get some sleep now. We're going to need our rest."

Snuggled beneath the sheets, Penny and Lex's breathing evened out, but it took a long time until Xander succumbed to slumber.

Chapter Thirty-Seven

Lex

Penny hid from them the entire morning. Lex and Xander woke to find the space between them empty, and a note on the nightstand saying she'd gone for a walk. That was three hours ago.

Lex knew she was upset about their leaving. Heck, he's pretty bummed about it, too. It's not a reason to hide from them. Or maybe it is. Xander is definitely using it to distance himself.

While Xander walked the trails near the house, Lex found Penny in the library, curled up on the couch. A blanket covered her lap, and she held a book, though it didn't look like she was reading it. "Hey," he whispered, not wanting to scare her.

Penny looked up from her book. "Hi," she said, sounding sad and defeated.

"Dolcezza, what's wrong?"

"It's embarrassing. I don't want to talk about it."

Lex moved closer, taking a seat at the other end of the couch. "This isn't about us leaving?"

"Well, it's not helping the situation," Penny snapped, then sniffled. In a huff, she tossed her book and blanket aside.

Lex tugged Penny's feet into his lap to stop her from getting up. She winced and pressed her hand against her stomach, alerting him that all was not well. "Is something wrong? Are you hurt? Let me grab my phone and text Xander. He can-"

"Wait." Penny grabbed his arm. "I don't need Xander for this, and I'm not hurt. I've ruined our plans, or at least my period has."

"You have your period?" *And the winner of stupid things men can say is Lex Ricci.*

"Yup," she replied, popping the 'p.'

Lex didn't want to upset her further and proceeded with caution. "Princess, your period didn't ruin our plans." He soothed, rubbing his hand up and down her leg. "Can I do anything for you? Heating pad? Chocolate? Ice cream? Hot shower?"

Penny groaned. "Can I have all those things? A hot, steamy shower sounds like heaven right now."

Lex set Penny's feet on the floor, then helped her to stand, hugging her tight when she sniffled into his shirt.

"So you're not grossed out? I mean, some guys are. I know sex and any scene Xander might've planned is off the table."

Lex reached his limit hearing her self-deprecating talk. Who the fuck taught Penny to believe something her body does is gross? He put his hand beneath her chin and tilted her head until Penny had no choice except to meet his gaze.

"You're not gross or any other derogatory word you used to describe something natural. I believe I speak for both Xander and me when I say there isn't a day, an hour, or a minute we don't want you. A bit of blood won't bother us, but it's your decision. If you still want everything to happen, we'll make it happen."

"Lex-"

"No, Penny. If all you want to do is snuggle, Xander and I will hold you close between us." He pressed his lips to hers.

Lex meant his kiss to be tender and reassuring. It soon turned passionate when Penny teased the seam of his lips, demanding he give her more. "Mm," she moaned. "Better already. Thank you."

"Let's get you into the shower. While you let the hot water do its work, I'll scrounge up some chocolate for you."

"Crisps too? There's nothing like something salty and sweet," Penny said with longing.

Lex chuckled, leaning in for one more kiss. "Si, Principessa. I'll make sure you get your fix of salty and sweet."

Chapter Thirty-Eight

Xander

Lex explained what had happened with Penny when Xander found him raiding the pantry, looking for crisps and chocolate for her. He told Lex to take the treats to her while he cleaned up.

With his hair still damp from his shower, Xander knocked on Penny's door. "Hey, Princess. How are you?"

Penny sat on the edge of the bed, wrapped in a plush robe, nibbling on a piece of chocolate. She refused to meet his eyes, so Xander dropped to his knees and got in her face.

"I'm all bloaty and crampy. And who wants to have sex when it's messy?"

Xander tried not to smile at her forlorn expression because he didn't want to see her upset, and he belonged to the population that had no problem having sex any time of the month. "How many times have we fucked?"

She blushed. "A lot."

"That's right, and how many of those times did we finish in pristine condition?"

"Erm, I don't recall."

"Sex is messy, Princess. And a little blood won't deter either Lex or me from making you come multiple times."

"But-"

"I promise we'll make you feel fucking good tonight." He held her hand in his. "We'd never pressure you into doing something you didn't want. Never."

Penny wiped away a wayward tear. "Sorry, hormones." She cleared her throat. "Erm, Lex may have said the same thing."

Xander cupped her face, ensuring she didn't look away from him. "Hey, don't do that. Your feelings are valid. What do you want to happen?"

Her shimmering amber eyes searched his. The breath she expelled tickled his lips, and her answer tickled everything else. "I want it all."

"Then I'll put a towel down because we're about to get messy, Princess." He pressed his mouth to hers, tasting the salty-sweet remnants of her snack.

Xander traced his fingers along the side of her face. "Lex is bringing the hot water bottle I found when the kettle boils. There's ibuprofen in the medicine cabinet, too. He also may or may not have found you more treats."

He tucked the blankets around her and asked, "Do you uh-have enough supplies because I can go-"

"If you're about to tell me, you'll buy me feminine hygiene products like it's no big deal. I'll be a sobbing mess because you're being amazing and sweet."

"It's not a big deal. I'd do anything for you."

"Anything?"

Fuck, he walked right into that.

"How about for now, you get some rest, and I'll check on you soon." Xander kissed her, silencing any protest about the words he didn't say.

Xander pulled the blankets back and tucked her in. He headed into the hall and pretended he didn't hear Penny mutter, "Coward."

Two hours later, Xander checked on Penny, finding her awake. "Feeling any better, Princess?"

"Mm...yes, thanks."

Xander closed the door behind him. "I want to apologize for earlier. I'm trying my best, Penny, I swear."

"I know you are, and I appreciate it," she said, giving him a soft smile. "Where's Lex?"

"Oh, he'll be along in a minute." Xander dropped something on the end of the bed, taking four bundles of silk rope from the bag in his hand.

Penny stared at the last item he threw on the bed. A leather paddle, and she shivered with apprehension, or maybe it was… anticipation. "Uh, I need to use the washroom."

"Of course, Princess. Take all the time you need." Xander swept his assessing gaze over her. "When you're ready, you're to return without a stitch of clothing."

A blush heated Penny's cheeks, and she bit her bottom lip. Xander cupped her cheek, tugging it free with his thumb, then sucked it into his mouth, soothing her tender flesh with his tongue. "Fuck, I can't get enough of you."

Penny pulled out of his grasp and walked toward the bathroom. Pausing in the doorway, she swept her gaze over him. "You never have to stop," she said, then shut the door.

He stared at the closed bathroom door, contemplating marching in there and laying it all on the line. Damn, Penny landed those exit-style truth bombs with lethal precision.

Xander didn't know how much time he had until Penny came back out. He flipped the comforter and top sheet down to the end of the bed and laid a large towel in the center.

"Always prepared. You a Boy Scout or something?" Lex asked from the doorway, his voice filled with amusement.

Xander glanced over his shoulder. "Or something. Being prepared is never a bad thing, my friend."

Lex winced. “Yikes, friend-zoned.”

Xander immediately stopped what he was doing. Nope. He won’t let Lex believe they’re just friends. Not for a moment. He marched over to Lex and cupped his face between his palms. “That’s not what I meant, and it’s...fuck.” Xander let go of him and ran his hands through his hair in frustration. “We’re grown-ass men. What do you want me to call you?”

Lex shoved his hands into his pockets and shrugged, pushing past him into the room. “I don’t know...lover, partner, brat? Friend seems, *non abbastanza*-not enough to describe what we are.”

“I see.”

“Do you?”

“Get naked, brat,” he growled. Not lover or partner...brat. Xander hoped the other man realized which moniker meant the most.

Lex reached behind his head, pulled his shirt off, and slid his pants to the floor. In two quick motions, he discarded every stitch of clothing. Xander had little time to take him in because the bathroom door opened, and Penny walked out naked.

Everything stopped. Xander’s breath. His heart. His soul. “Have you ever seen someone more exquisite?” Xander meant both of them, but Lex answered.

“Never.”

A flush spread from the tips of Penny's breasts and along the length of her throat.

"Kiss her. Show her how beautiful she is." Xander directed.

Lex moved closer and traced his fingers along the sides of Penny's face, sinking his fingers into her hair. "*Sei squisita, dolcezza mia*-you're exquisite, my sweetness." He kissed her then, and she melted against him.

"Play with her nipples. They look swollen and needy."

At Xander's direction, Lex let go of her hair and brought his hands to her breasts, massaging her tender flesh, making her groan and hold on to him tighter. Lex teased her nipples and whispered sweet words in Italian against her lips.

Xander loved how they fit together like intricate puzzle pieces. And the way they took his direction? There's nothing like it. He wanted to wrap his arms around them and keep them safe always .

"Enough teasing," Xander growled. "Get in the middle of the bed, Princess. It's time you got acquainted with my ropes." Turning to Lex, he said, "Don't worry, brat, I'll save a bundle for you. Take a seat while I get our girl ready."

Penny crawled to the center. "Get on your back and link your hands above your head." Xander unraveled a bundle and got on the mattress beside her.

He looped the rope around her arms, binding her from elbow to wrist.

"How did you learn Shibari?" Lex asked.

"At the beginning of my service, they stationed me in Japan for six months, and I discovered a Shibari club. They gave demonstrations and offered lessons, which helped me learn. Binding someone with ropes excites me. It's good to have willing partners."

Xander stuck a finger between the ties he'd made around Penny's wrists. "Not too tight?"

"No."

"Good." He set a pair of scissors on the nightstand. "These are here for your safety. If you use your safeword and say red, or for any reason I can't get you untied, these are here to make sure I can."

"Yes, it feels... good," she replied, sounding a little dazed. Her eyes unfocused, the pupils blown wide with desire. Penny might reach some sort of level of subspace tonight.

Xander bound the ends of the rope to the top of the headboard, tying her in place. He shifted another pillow beneath her head, not wanting her to strain her neck trying to see.

"Fuck, the way you've prepared is so sexy," Lex groaned. Xander looked over to see him palm himself.

"Hands. Off. Your. Cock. Brat. Put your hands on the arms of the chair. I'll get to you soon enough."

Xander grabbed a second bundle of rope. "I'm going to bind your legs, Princess. Bend your knees and bring your heels close to your bum. Then I want you to spread your thighs apart."

Penny giggled. "You said bum." With her Scottish lilt, it sounded adorable. He squeezed her ass cheek, and her giggles turned into a moan.

"Do you want me to use another descriptor? Perhaps arse, derriere, bottom, fanny?" He squeezed her supple flesh. "Maybe ass, peach, or backside?" Penny wiggled and whimpered when Xander squeezed again.

"Yes." Penny giggled again, apparently agreeing to them all.

If this was their last night, Xander wanted to push her limits and take her to new heights of pleasure, yet she didn't follow his order. "Color?" he asked, checking in.

"Green, Sir."

He slapped his palm where the top of her thigh met her ass. "Then why isn't my wanton little slut in position?"

"Sorry, Daddy." Then Penny moved her legs up and apart.

"Good girl."

Xander wound the rope around her right leg, making knots every few inches. The last loop secured her ankle to the back of her thigh, binding her leg in half. He pulled on the excess rope, spreading her legs wider to tie the other end of the rope to the bed frame, then doing the same to her left leg.

Xander stepped back and stood near Lex, admiring the way he displayed Penny for his and Lex's view. Her hair spread out on the pillow, her pupils blown wide with desire, and the arousal coating her pussy and thighs made him salivate, desperate to taste her.

"Fuck, you're beautiful, Princess. Isn't she beautiful, Lex?"

"*È fottutamente stupenda*-She's fucking gorgeous."

Penny tried to grind her hips, but his bindings held her in place, making her whimper with frustration.

"Soon, little one. Lex and I are going to give you the show we promised." Xander beckoned Lex from his seat and pulled him against his chest.

Xander took his shirt off, needing to feel the heat of Lex's back pressing against him. He splayed his right hand across Lex's stomach, close to where his cock strained to break free from the confinement of his pants.

"Look at your future bride. How wet and wanton she is for us," Xander rasped, his lips grazing Lex's ear. "Eager for what I'm going to do to you," Xander taunted, biting and nipping at Lex's throat.

"Please touch him, Xander," Penny moaned. "Lex is desperate for your touch."

"Is he?"

It was Lex's turn to moan. "Fuck yes."

Xander moved his hand lower until he wrapped his fingers around the other man's cock, stroking him from root to tip, keeping his grip tight.

Penny stared, her lips parted, and her breathing quicker, unable to take her eyes off what Xander was doing to Lex.

"Please take my cock out. I need to feel your touch."

Xander gave him one more squeeze, then let go of his cock. He picked up the last bundle of rope from the end of the bed. "Can you fold your arms behind your back, palms flat against your forearms?"

Lex did as he asked.

"I'm going to bind you this way. Spread your legs further. I want you good and balanced since I have nothing to secure you to."

"You're being such a good boy for me." Xander praised, wrapping and knotting the rope around Lex's biceps and wrists to form a web-like pattern. Finished, he tugged on the knots. "You good, brat?"

"Yes, Sir."

Xander rubbed his thumbs against Lex's flat nipples until they tightened beneath his fingertips, and he cried out, "*Mm cavolo, che bella sensazione*-Mm...fuck, that feels good."

Xander stepped back. "Damn it, Xander, don't stop. I need you to touch me everywhere." Lex, honest-to-god, fucking whimpered.

"Not yet. Let's talk about how many strokes from my paddle you're going to get." Xander rubbed his thumb over Lex's bottom lip. "It's a pity I won't hear you count them because your mouth is going to be occupied. Twenty sounds fair, doesn't it, brat?"

"It's very fair, Sir."

This made Xander pause. "Do you deserve more?"

Lex swallowed and licked his lips. His cock bobbed between them, precum dripping from the tip. "Maybe...maybe five more."

"Alright, twenty-five. First though, Penny gets her show."

"Please," Penny begged.

Xander dropped to his knees and sucked Lex to the back of his mouth without further warning. He teased him with his tongue, then sucked him hard, keeping his hands on his thighs to ensure he didn't fall.

Penny let out a noise full of frustration. "It's killing me not to touch myself, or either of you."

Xander grunted in response, licking and sucking Lex's balls, teasing him to the point of orgasm, then paused. Lex groaned above him, Penny screamed and writhed on the bed, and Xander relished tormenting them both.

Xander gave Lex one last swipe of his tongue up the length of his cock, then he stood, kissing Lex deeply before he said, "Our girl needs to come, and you're not allowed to. Yet. Now, it's your turn to get on your knees."

"Fuck, I get to feast on this beautiful pussy while you paddle my ass?"

Xander helped Lex kneel on the bench at the end of the bed. "I want your ass in the air and your face in her pussy." Xander put a hand on the back of Lex's neck and lowered his head between Penny's legs.

"Yes, Sir."

With his legs spread, the cleft between his cheeks was on display. Xander dragged his blunt nails along Lex's thighs, making him groan against Penny's clit. It's what took her over the edge and into the first of many orgasms.

"Beautiful girl. You're going to come so many times tonight."

Xander grabbed the paddle and rubbed circles over Lex's ass, warming his skin. His tight ring winked at him, and Xander grazed his thumb over it, making Lex shiver and double his efforts, tongue-fucking her while grinding his nose against her clit.

"You want my cock here?" Xander pressed his thumb in a firm circle, loosening the tight ring of muscle. Lex whimpered and arched his hips in response.

While Penny shouted, "Oh my god, I'm going to come again."

Xander pressed his other hand against the back of Lex's head, pushing his face into her pussy. "Like I told you, Princess, there's no holding back. Come."

"Fuck, yes. Xander, Lex." Penny ground her cunt on Lex's face, and Xander held him there until Penny's shudders eased.

"You'll need to be prepped to take me." *And we don't have the time*, Xander left unsaid.

"Besides, you have a punishment to take. If it becomes too much, let me know." He stopped teasing Lex's hole and came around to the side of the bed. Xander gripped his hair and lifted his mouth from Penny, the lower half of his face slick with her release.

Xander needed a taste and sucked on Lex's lips, slipping his tongue inside his mouth, seeking more of Penny's sweet flavor.

With a hint of copper, her tangy flavor hit his taste buds, and Xander groaned, lapping it up, moving Lex over them until they both teased her mound, making Penny cry out from the extra attention.

He broke their kiss. "So fucking tasty. Get back to eating that sweet pussy, brat. Our Princess needs to come again and again." Xander let go of his hair, and Lex worked Penny toward another orgasm.

He focused on giving his brat what he needed and covered Lex's backside with steady strikes from the paddle, turning his backside a fiery red while Penny came three more times, whimpering and begging for their cocks.

When Xander dropped the paddle and freed Lex's arms, he massaged the stiffness from them. When Lex stood, he mashed their lips together in a desperate kiss. Penny's essence swirling between them.

"I need to come. Please let me come." Lex begged.

Xander placed a finger over his lips and asked, "You with me, Penny?"

"Y-yes, Sir."

"Are you ready for us to fuck you?"

"Please, Daddy...I need you both." The reality of hearing Penny call him Daddy is better than any fantasy he's ever had.

Xander growled and directed Lex. “Get inside her. Now. You’re going to make Penny come on your cock before you fill her with your cum.”

“I-I don’t think I can,” Penny whimpered. “I’ve come so many times already.”

“You can and you will because then you’ll get to come on Daddy’s cock and take all my cum, too.”

Penny moaned when Lex thrust inside her. “Oh, fuck. You feel so fucking good, *Principessa*.”

Xander shucked his pants, stroking himself, captivated by the way Lex stretched and filled Penny with his cock.

So fucking perfect.

Lex licked the column of Penny’s throat, dipping his head to her breast and taking her nipple into his mouth. His other hand slid between them to rub her clit.

“Oh, yes, Lex. Right there. Don’t stop. Please don’t stop.”

“Fuuuck. You’re tight. The way you’re gripping me. I can’t, I can’t,” Lex chanted, coming the moment Penny did.

Lex moved to lie on the bed beside Penny, and Xander knelt between her legs. He rubbed his hands over her bound limbs, sliding his fingers beneath the ropes. “Can you last in your binds a little longer?”

“Yes. The rope doesn’t hurt. Please, I need you inside me.”

"I know, baby. Your greedy cunt is creaming Lex's cum, and daddy needs a taste." Xander lowered his head between her thighs, and Penny cried his name with the first swipe of his tongue.

"Please," she whimpered.

He lifted his head and pinned her with his gaze. "Please, what?"

"Please...Daddy."

"Such a good girl for me, Pen. And good girls get rewarded."

Xander crawled up her body and sank his cock to the hilt inside her with a single thrust. Lex kissed her lips and lavished her breasts with attention, helping Penny reach the orgasm Xander worked to wring from her.

"Come for me," he commanded, holding himself deep inside her, grinding his pelvis against her clit. Penny tightened around him, every muscle in her body going taut, and then she exploded, dragging Xander into pure bliss with her.

He didn't pull out, balancing his weight on his forearms, and keeping their cum deep inside her. *Is this how they'd get her pregnant? Coming inside her, one after the other. Or maybe they'd fuck her at the same time? Their cocks sliding inside her together, stretching her until they came.*

No, no, no. Xander didn't get that with them. He groaned, feeling the loss of Penny's tight heat the moment he pulled out of her and rolled to her other side.

"I-" Penny gasped, seeming at a loss for words.

Lex rested his head in his palm and gave them a wicked smile. "*È stata la miglior scopata della mia vita.*"

Penny arched her brow. "What did you say?"

Xander chuckled. His Italian's a little rusty, but after a moment, he pieced it together. "Yeah, man. It's the best fuck of my life, too."

"No argument here," Penny muttered.

Xander undid the ropes, releasing Penny from her binds. They'd left behind patterned indentations on her delicate skin, making her look breathtaking, covered in his marks. He glanced at the bite on Lex's throat, and those marks said one thing.

They're mine. Except Xander didn't get forever.

He concentrated on taking care of Penny while he and Lex massaged the stiffness from her limbs. Once she relaxed between them, Xander used the towel beneath her to wipe the creamy mess from between her legs.

After a quick cleanup, Xander flipped the blankets over the three of them, too exhausted to do more. His tired lovers snuggled close, their breathing already evening out.

Xander stared at the ceiling, not seeing anything in the dark except two futures, one with them and one without.

Fuck. The one without Penny and Lex is bleak. How will he ever go back to how things used to be?

The answer lunged at him in the darkness. It's simple. He can't.

Chapter Thirty-Nine

Lex

Lex woke the moment Xander attempted to sneak out of their bed, shoving his legs into the pants he'd worn earlier. Eager to get away from them despite it being the middle of the night.

"Where are you going?" His voice sounded rough with emotion. Lex sat up and shifted his feet to the floor, careful not to wake Penny.

"Go back to sleep. I need a minute." Came Xander's quiet response.

"*Fanculo*-Fuck that." Lex leaped from the bed and faced Xander, leaving mere inches between them. "Like hell you do." He whisper-yelled. "You're running away." He grabbed Xander's face with both hands. "You can't walk away after what the three of us shared. I won't let you."

"Lex...."

"Don't."

"What else can I do? This can't happen after today," Xander said, looking defeated.

"Why not?" Penny's soft voice made them freeze. She sat up, and the sheets pooled at her waist. Time stopped as Lex stared, and Xander did the same.

The moonlight from the window bathed Penny in enough light to make out the bite marks, beard burn, and fading indentations from the ropes they left behind. She'd never looked more beautiful.

Xander pulled free from Lex's grip. "If someone discovered what's going on between the three of us-"

Penny got out of bed and approached them, naked like Lex still was. His dick twitched.

Non. Il. Tempo-Not. The. Time.

"What if no one does? What if we're careful together behind closed doors or whenever we can come here? We'd have all those moments together, not apart. Isn't it worth the risk? Aren't we worth the risk?"

"Princess." The moniker was like a curse and a prayer from Xander's lips.

"Do you love us?" Lex asked. His turn to stun Penny and Xander into silence. Though Penny entwined her fingers with his, offering support as this flood of emotion poured out of him.

It's all or nothing, and Lex was damn tired of walking around what's going on between them. "I don't want to hear excuses like it's too fast or what we have is impossible. Do you love us?" he asked with more determination.

Xander tugged on his beard. And Lex knew he was about to say something monumental. "You know I do."

"Then say it," Lex demanded, determined to push Xander to break down the last of the wall he put between them.

"Goddamnit, I love you. Both of you mean everything to me. Satisfied?"

Cazzo sì-Fuck, yes!

Lex shared a look with Penny, and then, together, lowered to their knees in front of Xander. "We'd get on our knees for no one but you."

"Lex is right. There's no way we can return to the way things were. No matter how much you believe it's the right thing to do. The three of us are right because we complete each other," Penny said, letting her tears fall unchecked.

Xander stared at them both. "You're right, we do, but...."

"No more buts," Penny and Lex exclaimed. A moment later, they burst out laughing, breaking the tension.

Xander leaned forward and brushed Lex's hair back from his face, then he wiped the tears from Penny's cheeks.

"Where do we go from here?" she asked when Xander helped them to their feet.

Lex looked at them both and smirked. "Well, now that we're all in, we'll figure it out."

"Brat, you make it sound so easy," Xander grumbled, though his lips ticked up in an indulgent smile.

"Maybe it is. Not that it will be easy-easy. No relationship is. It takes hard work and communication, and we are very much still a work in progress." Lex rubbed his sternum, his heart more than ready to show Xander and Penny how much he cared for them. "I know we will figure it out."

"For the record, I love you, too. And since we're all on the same page, can we go back to bed? You two wore me out." Penny yawned, backing up her claim.

"Si, Dolcezza. Let's get some sleep." Lex led the way, helping Penny settle between him and Xander. Their breathing evened, and Lex entwined their legs, determined no one would try to go anywhere again tonight without him knowing.

Chapter Forty

Xander

They returned to Castle Fergus in the late afternoon of the following day. Less than a week remained until Lex and Penny's wedding. The moment they walked through the door, the staff swept Penny away, and Lex got pulled into meetings, leaving Xander alone and doing his best to avoid Taylor.

Over the past three weeks, Xander kept his communication with Taylor to texts. He knew his friend would piece together everything the moment he saw Xander, and he didn't need those complications right now.

The hidden passageway he went through will come in handy to avoid his best friend and keep his relationship a secret. Despite Penny and Lex's reassurances, Xander believed their discovery was imminent.

He stuck his head out from behind the bookcase in the corner, and Lex met his gaze. "Hey," Lex greeted him, and within seconds, Xander held Lex in his arms and ravaged his mouth.

"If this is the reason you wanted to meet," Lex groaned against his lips. "I approve."

"Missed you too, brat," Xander said, running his fingers through Lex's short dark hair. He tugged his lips from his. "I didn't get you here just to get my mouth on you, though it's a bonus." Unable to resist capturing Lex's mouth for one more kiss.

Unbeknownst to anyone, Xander will stay in the primary suite with them. The cluster of rooms is in its own wing, and there's the secret passageway connecting his quarters to it, though he didn't believe he'd ever sleep there again.

If Xander had his way, they'd never spend another night apart. Once he opened his heart to them, there was no turning back.

All in, is all in.

Despite his protests and threats of punishment in their private group chat on the secure app Lex installed on their phones, Xander now possessed a section of the walk-in closet. Lex and Penny's convincing argument for having clothing in the room they shared made sense.

Xander cherished how committed they were to him and to making their throuple work. What bothered him was not being a part of the ceremony, unable to touch, kiss, or celebrate with them in the way he wished to. Which is why he asked Lex to meet him.

"I wanted to talk to you about something."

Not wanting to lose his nerve, Xander pulled a folded paper out of his pocket. "I wanted to show you something I want to surprise Penny with."

He fiddled with the paper in his hand. "Maybe we can share a private moment, the three of us exchange a few words before the two of you become husband and wife."

Lex looped his arms around Xander's neck and gave him such a sweet smile. "Like our very own private commitment ceremony?"

Xander mulled it over for all of two seconds. "Yeah, I want you both to know how committed I am to you, even though on paper it's the two of you."

"I love the idea, and I know Penny will, too." Lex tugged on Xander's hair, bringing his mouth to his. "*Vorrei che fosse diverso*-I wish it could be different."

"I wish it were too, but I am beyond fucking grateful you and Penny convinced me we could work."

Lex kissed him again. "It will work."

Xander handed Lex the paper. "I'm going to Glasgow this afternoon. West's done most of my ink, and I want this to be the next one."

Lex unfolded the paper, revealing a sketch of dark flowing lines. He traced the lines reverently with his finger, and Xander caught the moment he discovered their initials hidden in the design.

"You want to get a tattoo of something that represents the three of us?"

"Yes."

"It's beautiful. Did you draw it?" Lex asked, handing it back to him.

"Yeah. I mean, West will take this rough sketch and turn it into something amazing."

"Don't sell yourself short. It seems you have many hidden talents. Where are you going to place it?"

Xander held up his right hand and tapped the center of his palm. "Here."

"Your right palm? How will you hold your gun? Uh, if you needed to use it, that is."

Xander chuckled and parted his jacket. "Ever notice my holster is under my right arm? It's because I shoot with my left. I'm ambidextrous and accurate with both, but I prefer my left."

He then held his right hand over his heart. "Anytime I do this, I hold you close to my heart. My way of saying I love you, no matter where we are or who is around us."

"Damn, Daddy, you are a fucking romantic."

Xander let out a satisfied growl and pulled Lex closer. He never realized how satisfying it would be to have the two people he cared about the most using such an honorific. He wished for the time to show Lex how much it pleased him, and then the man offered a solution.

"You know, I could use a few hours away from here. Do you mind if I come?"

"I'd love it if you came." Xander planned to show Lex the many ways he meant those words.

Then Lex asked a little quieter, "Do you think your guy might have time to ink the same design on me?"

"Your first tattoo? And you want this?"

Lex looked back at the paper. "This design of our initials that you created? Fuck yes. *Ne sarei onorato*-I'd be honored. Because you're part of the rest of my life."

Xander pressed his forehead to his. "Thank you, brat. I'll call West and make it happen. He closes the shop when I come anyway, and I'm sure he won't mind one more. In fact, he'll encourage it. You'll understand when you meet him. Though I'm not sure how I'll deal with West putting his hands on you. Any ideas of where you want it done?"

Lex tilted his head, pondering his question. Xander knew he was about to brat when a mischievous glint entered his eyes. "Hm. My shoulder? Imagine how you'd run your fingers over it or leave a bite mark beside it when you fuck my ass...."

"Goddamnit, Lex. You can't say things like that, or we'll never get out of here."

"True." Lex brushed a hand against Xander's erection. "Perhaps I can suck you off on the drive to appease your jealousy."

"Stop reading my mind, brat. I will need to mark you if another man is going near you, friend or not."

Lex's pupils blew wide with desire.

"We need to go. Now." Xander walked him to the door, opened it, and took a quick look around. "No one's about." Lex grabbed Xander's jacket and tugged him close for one more kiss.

"I'll meet you by the car," Lex said, stepping past him into the hall.

Xander used the passageway to return to his room since no one saw him enter the suite. Guests for the wedding are already arriving, and soon rooms here and in the nearby village will be full of people he didn't trust.

It put Xander on edge. He didn't like how many people would be near Penny, and now his concern included Lex. Factor in more eyes and ears in the vicinity, and it will make finding time alone almost impossible.

Penny's occupied with fittings, and Taylor's stationed outside her door. It eased some of his tension to know she'll be safe while he and Lex go to Glasgow.

Xander left his room and then took the back stairs to the garage. Eager for Lex to get his first tattoo. Xander couldn't help his wicked grin when he also looked forward to Lex sucking him off as they sped down the winding roads.

And in his excitement, he missed something vitally important.

Chapter Forty-One

Penny

The wedding's tomorrow, and apart from a stolen moment yesterday, they didn't have any time alone, and it sucked.

Penny resorted to hiding in her old room to avoid the guests arriving over the last few days. One more night, and they'd be together. She'll get ready here tomorrow and then never sleep here again. Maybe someday this will be her daughter's room...though, dreams of children are for another day, far in the future.

She busied herself with the stack of mail that Freya had left for her. Things had accumulated over the past three weeks, and she'd put off going through them. No time like the present. Penny sorted the many invitations into two piles. The yes pile remained much smaller than the no pile.

She grabbed the next envelope and froze. The plain white envelope with nothing on it caused a shiver to skitter down her spine.

Penny kept a secret.

The threats never stopped, like she'd assured Xander, choosing to convince him to take her to New York despite the danger. Worse though, she kept it all from him. The man whose job it is to keep her safe. He's going to be pissed when he finds out.

Penny reasoned it was to keep Xander from doing something drastic, like locking her within these walls. It's not something she could handle.

In fact, Xander could punish her all he wanted. She'd choose to keep it from him every single time if it meant the three of them would have what they have now.

Penny sliced open the envelope, and two photos fell out. With a slight tremor in her fingers, she picked up the one on top.

A picture of Lex and Xander standing close in the doorway of their new bedroom. She recognized the shirt Lex wore the other day. The second photo is even more damning. Their stolen moment yesterday wasn't private after all.

Penny stared at the photo. Xander and Lex held her captive between them. Lex's mouth pressed against her neck while Xander kissed her lips. Their hands frozen in time, caressing her breasts and waist.

This is Xander's worst fear. They'd grown accustomed to the privacy of the island house, and it made them reckless.

Penny's stomach bottomed out. This is far worse than she thought. Those who wanted to harm her are here in her home. Now they've set their sights on Xander and Lex, too. She picked up a scrap of paper from under the second picture. A dozen words send a chill down her spine.

A picture...or two is worth a thousand words. Isn't it, Princess?

Someone knew their secret. Knew what Xander and Lex called her. It made Penny vibrate with fury. She put everything back into the envelope and stuffed it into the desk drawer, joining the other messages she'd kept.

Penny did her best to calm herself. Once they got through tomorrow, she'd confess everything, and they'd deal with it together. Knowing how furious Xander and Lex will be, Penny expected to earn a severe punishment for this secret. One she'd deserve.

Chapter Forty-Two

Penny

Xander: Are you ready?

Lex: We're on our way!

Penny set her phone aside, and a smile spread across her face.

She devised a plan.

With over an hour until the ceremony, she wanted them to have one of their own. She may have to marry Lex on paper, but she wanted to make sure Xander knew beyond any doubt she's equally committed to him.

There will be time enough tomorrow to deal with the pictures and notes burning a hole in her desk drawer. Today is about the three of them solidifying their bond, capping it off with an epic wedding night.

She sent Freya and her fussy cousin away, claiming she wanted time alone. She practically had to push Freya out the door. The woman's been a tad clingy since she returned from the island, to the point of putting Penny on edge.

A sharp knock sounded, and Penny's heart rate sped up when Xander stepped inside, and right behind him came Lex, who shut and locked the door.

"Holy fuck, Princess. You are breathtaking."

Except for the warmth flooding her cheeks and the smile on her face, Penny stilled under their perusal, letting them take her in from head to toe. Her intricate hairstyle and makeup. When their eyes dropped to what she wore... a white silk robe draped her curves. Lex cleared his throat, his gaze glued to her dusky nipples visible through the material.

"Bellissima. We expected you to be in your gown by now."

"I'll put it on in a few minutes. There's something I need first. I realized I don't have my something borrowed or something new." Penny grabbed a pillow from the bed and tossed it at their feet.

"Princess?" Xander's eyes darkened with desire, and he growled with understanding. He knew what she wanted, undoing his belt buckle.

"Wait." Xander stopped his movements at her command. "Let me...let me look at you both. I want to worship your beauty."

"That's what we wanted to do to you." Lex pouted.

"Oh, you will," Penny promised, circling them while they stood still for her perusal.

Lex wore a tuxedo with a white jacket and black tie. He looked dashing and regal, and Penny trailed her fingers over his shoulders and down his arm. He caught her hand and brought her knuckles to his lips, and she gave him some of her practiced Italian. "*Sei mozzafiato, amore mio*-you're breathtaking, my love."

"Grazie," Lex said, giving her a wink.

Xander also wore a tux, but his jacket was red, and he didn't wear a tie. He'd undone the top two buttons of his black shirt, showing the merest hint of his tattoos. Penny popped another button, showing a little more.

He'd trimmed his beard and twisted his hair into his usual braid. Penny wanted it down. "Take it down for me. Please?" The moment Xander did, Penny sank her fingers into it and pulled him down for a kiss.

No matter what happened the rest of the day in the chapel, or at the reception after, this moment alone with them will always mean more to Penny than anything else.

"Interesting change of plans," Xander grumbled. Penny knew how much he hated being surprised. Guilt over her secret made her want to confess, but the rest of Xander's words captured her attention.

"We wanted to see you in your dress and exchange some words and promises between us, though you appear to be offering us something else."

"You want to exchange vows? I had an elaborate plan to have a commitment ceremony, too. It just included sucking you both off until you came all over me first. I promise you will get me in my gown because you're the ones dressing me."

Both their mouths hung open. Shocked by Penny's bold words, Lex chuckled. "*Oh, Principessa, il tuo piano e molto migliore del nostro*-Oh, Princess, your plan is much better than ours."

"We have little time." Penny removed her robe, and their expressions darkened with desire when she dropped to her knees on the pillow she laid at their feet.

With the boldness they gifted her, Penny cupped them over their slacks and stroked their stiff cocks through the material. Then she looked up and said the words that fueled their rush to free themselves. "Cover me with your cum."

"As you wish," Xander growled, then both he and Lex whipped their dicks out. Penny took one in each hand, wrapping her fingers around their thick shafts. She stroked them from root to tip, spreading their precum down their lengths.

They shuffled closer, holding onto each other's waists. Penny took turns sucking them into her mouth. Desperate for more, she pressed their lengths together and tried to take them both.

"Let us, sweetheart," Xander said, gripping the base of his cock while Lex did the same. "You open your pretty little mouth, and we'll do the rest." Penny dropped her hands to her thighs, and they took over, stroking their dicks, and she opened wide, trying to take as much of them as she could.

"Yes... dolcezza," Lex hissed. Penny licked and sucked them. She moaned and kept her gaze on them while they worked toward their release. Eager to lap it all up.

"You close, brat?"

"Si."

"Get ready to swallow what we give you, sweetheart. Then we're gonna paint your tits with the rest." Xander commanded, always in control. "Fuck yes."

Penny extended her tongue and tried to close her lips around both their cocks.

"Yes. Take what we give you." The first spurt from Xander hit her tongue, and seconds later, Lex added to the cum flooding her mouth. Penny swallowed everything they gave her until they pulled away, leaving the last of their release covering her breasts.

They stroked her breasts, rubbing their cum into her skin, tugging and pulling on her nipples until they became hard, needy points. Penny licked the last of their cum from her lips and moaned.

"Now, it's your turn, sweetheart." Xander scooped her into his arms, then set her on the bed. "You get to cover us with your sweet nectar."

"Oh, god, yes. Please make me come."

"You will, baby." Xander turned to Lex and commanded, "Suck her clit. I want her to come multiple times for us."

"Yes, Sir." Lex gripped Penny's thighs and spread her wider. He latched onto her clit, driving Penny toward her release.

Xander kissed her and slipped his fingers inside her pussy, finger-fucking her and rubbing her G-spot while Lex sucked her clit harder, making her writhe beneath them. “That’s it, Princess. Come for us.”

“Yes.”

To know what it’s like to be worshiped is to be dressed by Xander Ward and Lex Ricci. Penny couldn’t fully describe how she felt, but words like 'pampered' or 'revered' were a start. Soft caresses led to tender kisses placed on every part of her body they covered. All while offering her whispered words of love and praise.

Lex held her hand, helping her balance while Xander dropped to his knees, slipping her panties over her feet and up her legs. He kissed her pussy before sliding her panties into place.

Xander settled the belt of her garter around her waist, and after kissing the tips of her breasts, he covered them with the matching white lace push-up bra, adjusting her tits to sit perfectly in the cups.

Lex urged her to sit on the edge of the bed. Then he dropped to his knees beside Xander. They each took one of her feet and kissed her arches and toes. Then they rolled her silk stockings up her legs and attached them to the clips on her garter belt.

They each picked up one of her ivory and gold stilettos and slipped it onto her foot. She cupped their cheeks, blinking back tears when she said, "I love you both so much. You're both integral parts of my life now, and I never want to go back to a life without either of you in it."

"Princess." Xander looked at Lex and then at her. "We love you too."

"Dolcezza, you own our hearts."

"Come," Xander said, offering her a hand up. "It's our turn to look at you. Stunning."

"*Mozzafiato*-breathtaking."

"Stay there, Princess," came Xander's soft command. "Lex, give me a hand with her dress."

They gathered the material, and Penny lifted her arms while they lowered the gown over her head. Lex fussed and straightened it, and Xander stood behind her, lacing the corset of her bodice into place.

Lex and she shared a secret smile when Xander pulled the laces tight, knowing how much he loved to bind them.

Xander joined Lex to admire Penny in her dress. "I've never seen a more beautiful bride."

"Oh? You've seen your fair share of brides, have you?" Penny teased.

"Funny. You're the first. You and Lex will look perfect together at the altar."

"It's supposed to be you and Penny," Lex said. Ever ready to sacrifice himself.

"No. If I had my way, you'd both stand there with me, exchanging vows for everyone to witness."

Xander cupped her face, holding her gaze with his. "It's okay, Princess. I accept things the way are because it's how they must be. Maybe if things were different, and we didn't need to hide what we are-"

"In a heartbeat," she proclaimed. Xander closed his eyes, breaking their connection and breaking Penny's heart. She wanted to have that and knew Lex did too.

Xander opened his eyes and brought Lex closer by the hold he had on Lex's neck. "It's no longer an issue for me if my part in our relationship is a secret. I'm a private guy, and this is a sacrifice I'm willing to make if it means I get to call you both mine."

Penny bit her lip, trying to stop the words desperate to escape. "What if we're discovered?" The guilt from the persistent danger she's keeping from them, rears its head.

"We'll deal with it if the time comes, but we're fine." Xander sounded almost optimistic, making Penny's guilt worse because they're not okay. *Tomorrow. She'll confess everything tomorrow.* She promised, bargaining to have one more day of uninterrupted bliss.

"For the first time in my life, I feel complete since you both came into my life. Like Xander, I'd lay my life down for you, and promise to love you, respect, and honor you until my last breath," Lex said, trailing his index finger along her cheek. Then he looked up at Xander. "You complete us in such a profound way. There's no one else we'd get on our knees for."

"Those sound like some pretty good vows," Penny whispered.

"Si. They do."

"Agreed. There's nowhere else I'd rather be than here with you." Xander pressed his lips to hers, sealing their impromptu vows with a kiss. First her, then Lex. Then Lex leaned in and kissed her, too. Then they were all kissing each other in a messy collision of lips, tongues, and teeth.

Penny rubbed her cheek against Xander's palm. There was a slight roughness on his skin that wasn't there before. "What-?" She tilted her head and looked at his hand.

Xander gave her a sheepish look. "We wanted to surprise you, and I almost forgot. We got tattoos." Penny pulled his hand closer, examining the intricate design.

"Here," he said, stepping behind her and keeping his palm before her. "You need to look at it from my perspective." Penny could now see their initials hidden in the design.

"Mine's on my left shoulder blade. I'll show you later," Lex said with a wink.

"It's lovely, but-" Penny met their gaze. "You got tattoos with our initials without me?" Lex's smile dropped, and Xander stiffened at her back.

"Shit," Xander cursed. "We fucked up."

Penny spun in his arms. "No, it's okay. I get it. You wanted to surprise me, and there's nothing wrong with the two of you doing something together."

"It's not okay. We fucked up, and when we can take you, we'll make it right."

"Promise, dolcezza."

A knock at her door signaled Freya's return. Penny looked at Xander's watch and scoffed. "Figures she's fifteen minutes early."

"Penelope?" Her muffled voice sounded through the door.

"Give me fifteen minutes," Penny shouted.

"I'll give you ten." The sound of her shoes receding down the hall followed her response.

"Damn, that means she'll be back in eight." Penny let out a frustrated sigh. "Which means you need to go."

Xander opened the door and peeked down the hall. "Coast is clear. Are you sure you don't want me to wait and escort you to meet your father?"

"No, I'm good. I want a... moment with my mother."

"We understand," Lex said, tugging on Xander's sleeve. "Come on."

"Eager are we?" Xander growled.

"Yes." Lex turned, pressing his chest to Xander's. "For the honeymoon."

"Brat."

Penny giggled at their antics. "I love you both. Now, go. I'll meet you in the chapel." With one more kiss from each, she closed the door behind them.

Penny fidgeted in front of the mirror, thankful for the effortless movement of her dress. Tule capped her shoulders, and the laced-up corset kept everything in place. The skirt draped light and flowy, cascading to the points of her shoes. To complete her look, she added a peachy nude gloss to her kiss-swollen lips.

As she admired herself, Penny agreed with Xander and Lex. She'd never looked more beautiful with a satisfied glow lighting up her face. She guessed she had five minutes until Freya knocked on her door again.

Penny took one last look around her room. Someone will be along to move the last of her belongings to the new suite of rooms, and she realized too late that she should've secured the notes and pictures in a better place. Or better yet, Penny should've confessed the whole thing to Xander and Lex.

She decided then and there she'd tell them everything tonight. Consequences be damned. They needed only to get through the ceremony and reception. Then, people will leave.

Penny grabbed everything, planning to shove it all into a garment bag at the back of her closet, when a noise stilled her movements. She swore she'd locked the door when Xander and Lex left.

Unease skittered down her spine because the sound didn't come from the doorway.

Penny turned and sucked in a breath to scream, except her assailant released an aerosol spray into her face. "Why?" she tried to ask when everything went blurry, and the rest of her question faded away as she breathed in the vapor.

Penny tried to take a step forward, and her body didn't obey. She crumpled to the floor, scattering the pages she should've given to Xander, and now it's too late as darkness consumed her.

CHAPTER FORTY-THREE

Xander

Xander teased Lex from across the room, sliding his index finger beneath his nose, and breathing in Penny's heady scent. Fuck. He couldn't wait to get them alone, planning the perfect wedding night for the three of them.

They took turns sucking her clit and finger-fucking her until she'd come for them both. Twice. Lex rubbed his top lip and smirked, giving tit for tat. Any moment, their Princess will walk down the aisle with their cum on her luscious tits, and her rosy glow of satisfaction won't be from makeup.

Between teasing each other, Xander monitored the guests seated in the pews of the tiny chapel in the courtyard. Even more guests arrived to fill the ballroom for the reception.

Unease skittered down his spine. Xander didn't like the fact that Penny didn't have someone escorting her to meet her father. The urge to return to her room made him seek Lex's gaze across the room.

He didn't meet Lex's gaze, though; his eyes were on his watch, for like the third time. When Lex finally raised his gaze to his, concern marred his handsome features. Penny's late.

Xander knew it was not unusual for the bride to keep her groom and guests waiting. However, it's not what Penny did. His stomach knotted; something was off.

They didn't need any words to know what needed to be done. Xander gave Lex a quick nod.

He caught up with Taylor at the door. "If I'm not back in ten, send reinforcements." Xander gripped Taylor's shoulder and brought him close. "Protect him with your life."

"You know I will."

Xander squeezed his shoulder. "Thank you."

He jogged across the courtyard, taking off down the hall to the back staircase. He didn't want to worry her father, nor have him impede Xander's desperate need to ensure Penny's safety.

Xander reached her room in record time and knocked. "Princess?" he called, doing his best to keep his growing panic at bay. He waited, then called her name again, pounding the door louder this time. Xander tried the handle and found it unlocked. "Penelope?"

He stepped inside, knowing right away that he was alone. Despite the emptiness of the room, Xander looked around anyway. Did he miss her going to meet her father because he took the back stairs?

No, Taylor would've texted him if she'd arrived.

He checked the bathroom first because of its proximity to the door. Nothing appeared out of place, and no sign of a struggle.

He moved through the rest of her room when some scattered papers beside her desk caught his eye. Photographs. Xander picked them up, flipping through the images, and his rage coursed through his veins when he picked up a paper.

You will never lead the organization. I'll see you dead first.

"Fucking hell." He gathered everything on the floor and shoved it inside his jacket pocket, hoping they'd get some trace evidence.

Xander clenched his fists. Penny kept a secret. A fucking dangerous one. Why didn't she tell him? And how fucking dare she endanger herself like this? There's a punishment unlike anything else in her future. He needed to find her and ensure she was safe first.

A sudden noise behind him made Xander reach for his Glock. Too late. Xander grunted from the impact, and pain chased the pop of a shot fired through a silencer, and it radiated through his chest. He turned in time to catch the wall inside the closet shift seamlessly back into place.

When Xander first took on this assignment, he memorized the layout of this damn castle, and nowhere did it show a hidden passageway connected to this room.

He staggered, catching himself on Penny's desk chair, the flimsy thing not strong enough to take his sudden weight. It toppled over, taking Xander with it. The pain in his chest worsened, and his shirt grew wet and sticky with his blood. Spots clouded his vision, seconds away from passing out.

It hurt to breathe, though he made one last effort to find his footing without success.

Xander's last thoughts before everything went black were of Penny and Lex, and how he'd failed them.

Chapter Forty-Four

Lex

"P*erché fai gli occhi dolce alla gaurdia del corpo*-Why are you making eyes at the bodyguard?" Roberto asked.

The burning heat of his cheeks gave away how much Lex's brother could get under his skin. "*Non sto facendo gli occhi*-I'm not making eyes," Lex said with a huff. "Penny's late, and I want Xander to check on her."

Lex tracked Xander's every move until he slipped away in search of Penny. When he turned to his brother, Lex found him staring, curiosity twisting his features. "Isn't that what brides do? Build the anticipation?"

"Penny and I are both eager to conclude this ceremony. She wouldn't keep everyone waiting."

Berto snorted. "I can't believe you are marrying the heir to the organization. It's an amazing turn of events for someone who wanted nothing to do with this part of the family business."

Lex glared at his brother. "*Ancora non lo so*-I still don't."

"*Scemo*-Fool."

Lex looked at his watch again. Xander went to check on Penny almost ten minutes ago. *Something's wrong*. Ran on a loop in his mind. Not even his brother's snide remarks distracted him from it. He rubbed his sternum, his heart kicking up as unease pressed in.

The murmurs of the gathered guests grew louder as they shifted in their seats, eyeing the open door to the chapel where Taylor stood with a tense expression on his face.

The clacking of shoes racing along the cobblestone path sounded outside the open chapel door. Seconds later, Freya appeared in the doorway, frazzled and out of breath. "Help," she gasped, collapsing into Taylor's arms.

"Everyone, stay calm and stay in your seats," Taylor said, and Lex had no intention of sitting by. He moved around the perimeter to get to where Taylor still held Freya in his arms. Lex got there in time to hear Freya say, "Penny's missing. Xander sent me to tell you."

What she said made Lex pause. Xander would have called Taylor. Lex has watched him do it plenty of times. Sending Freya to tell them translated into wasted time. Precious time.

It's not just Penny. Xander was in trouble, too.

Taylor looked over at Lex, silently conveying that he also caught the lie. Then he said to Freya, "Thank you for risking your life to tell us. I want you to stay with Steph and Ian." Two members of the security team stepped forward.

"They'll make sure you get checked out when the paramedics arrive."

"I'm alright," Freya said, trying to step out of Taylor's hold.

He held firm. "I insist. You could've injured yourself on your valiant run here." Steph and Ian now stood on either side of Freya. Taylor directed a third guard to come with him.

There was no way Lex was going to stay here while the two most important people in his life were in danger. "I'm coming too," he said, brooking no argument, though Taylor argued anyway.

"Sir, it's not a good idea. At least until we know what's going on."

"Oh, you believe this is up for discussion. It's not. I'm going with you."

Taylor grunted. "Fine. Stay close until we know what we're up against." They'd no sooner returned to the castle when Taylor's phone went off and he stumbled to a stop.

Xander?

"Update now," Taylor demanded the moment he answered. "What? Son of a bitch. Lock this place down. Everyone stay on high alert." Taylor shoved his phone in his pocket and a hand through his hair when he turned to face Lex, and he knew whatever he was about to say was bad.

"What is it?" Lex asked, terrified of the answer.

"They found Xander in Penny's bedroom with no sign of her." Taylor hesitated for a second, then said, "He's taken a GSW to the upper chest."

Blood roared in his ears, and Lex pushed past Taylor, heading for the fastest route to Penny's bedroom. "Goddamnit, Alexandre. Wait," Taylor shouted, close on his heels.

When Lex reached the sweeping stone staircase, it was his turn to stumble to a stop. Penny's father lay motionless, slumped on the floor. "James?" He heard Taylor run up behind him.

"Sir, let me handle this. EMRS is on its way." Taylor gripped his shoulder, leaning close to Lex. He said for his ears alone, "Go. He needs you." Lex met Taylor's earnest gaze, gave him a sharp nod, and ran up the stairs.

Oh God, please be okay.

Chapter Forty-Five

Penny

Her eyes fluttered open only to find more darkness. Panic filled her, almost overtook her. Then she heard Xander's voice in her ear. *'Take a deep breath and focus. Remember everything I taught you.'* Penny breathed deep or tried to. The mustiness of the cloth didn't make it easy.

Kidnapped.

She held still when she heard a muffled voice to her left and used what little strength she'd regained. With the element of surprise, Penny kicked. Her heel struck true when she heard a grunt. "Bitch! God damn it. That spray's supposed to knock her out for hours."

That voice.

Penny didn't have a plan past striking whoever took her, and when the sting of a needle sucked her into unconsciousness once again, she didn't have time to do anything else.

Chapter Forty-Six

Xander

Fuuuuck! Why did getting shot hurt so fucking much? He groaned. The sound of a monitor beeping kept time with the pulse hammering his head. At least he's alive.

"Xander?"

Lex? He tried to say. *Why didn't his mouth work?*

"Shhh, don't talk," he soothed. Lex kissed Xander's temple. "You're okay. You're in the hospital and just got out of surgery."

God, he's thankful to feel Lex's hand in his...then his words hit him like a ton of bricks.

Hospital.

Shot.

"Penny?"

Chapter Forty-Seven

Xander

One week ago.

As they sped down the winding road, Xander's hands tightened on the steering wheel while Lex's hand tightened on his cock. "Fuck, brat, you're going to make me drive into the ditch."

"*Sembra che tu cia teso*-You seem tense. Why don't we find somewhere private to pull over, and you can punish me for putting our safety at risk?" Lex leaned across the console and nipped his earlobe, making Xander groan, already scouting for a place to pull off, so they can get off.

A mile further, and Xander turned into an empty field, parking behind the high stone fence. Forest surrounded the rest of the field, and he knew this would be all the privacy they would get.

The moment he turned the engine off, Lex launched toward him, smashing his mouth to his in an intense kiss mastered by lips, teeth, and tongues.

Xander palmed his cheeks, taking control the way his brat craved for him to do.

Lex tried to climb over the console to get closer, pressing against the car's horn. Xander pulled back. "Let's try not to alert the owners of the field, hm...?"

Lex kissed him again, this time more softly, as an offered apology. "Sorry, when I'm around you or Penny, I can't seem to help myself."

Xander chuckled. "You don't say." When he attempted to shift his seat back, he found he'd already extended all the way. "Back seat?"

"*Buona idea*-Good idea."

They got out, pushed their seats forward to give themselves more room, and climbed in. Xander faced Lex, both on their knees in the backseat. He undid his belt and the button of his jeans when it occurred to him.

"Wait."

Lex froze in the middle of pushing his pants down over his hips. "Get back out and take your pants off, then lie across the back seat with your head here," Xander said, patting the edge by the door where he stood.

"What do you have in mind?" Lex asked. A smirk played about his lips, and Xander believed he already knew.

"We don't have much time. How does fucking your face while I suck you off sound?"

Lex winked. "Perfect, Sir." His cock jerked against his stomach, begging for Xander's mouth.

In seconds, Lex jumped out of the car and shucked off his pants. Xander took off his shoes and removed his pants, tossing them on the driver's seat. By the time he got naked, Lex already lay across the backseat with his head hung over the edge, and his mouth opened wide, ready to take Xander's cock down his throat.

"Fuck, brat. You're going to make me come from your eagerness alone."

"Well, we are on a time limit."

"Always ready with the sass, aren't you, brat?" Xander smacked his cheek, adding a bit of degradation to their play. "Color?"

"Green, Sir."

"Good boy."

Xander ran his thumb over Lex's lips, the tip of his tongue sneaking out to taste him, sending a current arcing across his palm. He stroked his cock with his other hand, bringing it to Lex's lips, painting them with precum. "Open."

Lex parted his cum-covered lips, licking them clean. His seeking tongue dipped into Xander's slit, searching for more. The gentle lap of his tongue brought Xander to the edge, and he wasn't ready to let go yet. "No more teasing, brat."

Lex opened wide. Xander cupped his face with one hand, guiding his cock to the back of his throat with the other. Lex made a garbled sound and then swallowed.

"Fuuuck," he growled, punching his hips back and forth until Lex took his entire length and his balls pressed against his nose, cutting off his air. Xander pulled out of his mouth, wanting to check in before he got carried away. "Is fucking you with a bit of breath play, okay?"

"Si." Lex's voice sounded raspy from Xander using his throat. "I like it. It's giving me a rush."

Xander stroked his cheek. "You have your safeword signal. Double-tap my leg if you need me to stop."

"Yes, Sir. Thank you, Sir." Lex opened his mouth wide and waited.

Xander tipped his head back and slid his cock to the back of his throat, pulling out to let him take a breath. With the steady rock of his hips, Xander leaned forward and took Lex's cock in hand, stroking him with soft pulls, the opposite of how he's fucking his mouth.

Lex whimpered, sending vibrations along the length of his dick, making his balls tighten. Xander held them against Lex's nose, cutting off his air, then he counted to ten, and pulled back to let him breathe.

The next time he held himself deep, Xander counted to fifteen, the entire time Lex whimpered and swallowed around him, bringing Xander to the brink again and again.

Xander kept his touch light on Lex's cock, teasing him until he thrust his hips off the backseat with frustration. He placed his palm on his lower abdomen, holding Lex in place. Xander pulled his hips back, his thrusts shallowing to give Lex a breather and a chance to beg.

He fucking loved the way Lex begged.

Lex thrust into Xander's hand, desperate for his release. "Please...suck my cock. I'm close. Fuck my face, I can take it."

Xander looked down at Lex with his fuck-swollen lips covered in precum and saliva, and his jade-green eyes darkened with arousal. He caressed his cheek, enjoying the prickle of his light stubble. "Take a deep breath, baby. You're not getting another full one until we've both come."

Lex gasped and nodded.

"I need your words."

"Yes," Lex rasped, then he took a deep breath, and Xander slid his cock all the way in.

He rocked his hips and leaned over, taking Lex into his mouth. Xander wrapped his lips around his tip, sucking him hard enough to summon his soul through his slit.

Xander massaged Lex's balls and sucked more of his length into his mouth until he dipped into Xander's throat. He took a deep breath through his nose, getting his gag reflex under control, then worked his mouth up and down Lex's cock, pushing each of them closer to release.

Xander pulled off Lex's cock and growled, "Give me your cum, brat. I'm about to unload mine down your throat."

Lex gripped Xander's thighs tighter, demanding without words that he give him everything. In return, Xander sucked Lex harder, stroking the rest of his length while he fucked Lex's face, and the first spurts of his cum pulsed down his throat.

Xander grunted, and Lex swallowed him, taking every drop. Lex jerked his hips, trying to fuck up into Xander's mouth. He held him down, sucking harder until his balls flexed in his hand, and the first shot of his salty release landed on Xander's tongue. "Fuck yes."

They arrived at West's shop with a few minutes to spare, sporting their 'fresh from a fuck' look when the bell chimed and they stepped through the door. Weston Sharpe leveled Xander with a knowing gaze.

West smirked. The man's too damn good-looking for his own good. Lex and West are the same height, but the similarities end there. With sandy blond hair left loose around his face, icy blue eyes, and a muscular body covered in tattoos, he looked like every person's bad-boy fantasy.

Once upon a time, Xander would've jumped at the chance to have a bit of fun with his friend and former military teammate.

Not anymore.

"Well, well, well." West whistled long and low. "Look what the cat dragged in." Ignoring Xander's green-eyed monster glaring back at him. "Or dare I say look who this fine-ass man brought with him?" West eyed Lex up and down, already picturing him naked and in several positions between them.

A rumble echoed off the walls of the tattoo shop. The growl came from deep within Xander's chest. "Not this one. I'm not sharing him with anyone except our third, Penny."

"There are three of you? Well, look at you accomplishing your poly-loving dream. It's everything you wanted. I'd say congrats, brother, but to be honest, I'm a wee bit jealous." Despite the teasing, West backed off, respecting Xander's boundaries, choosing to focus on the ones he didn't define.

"No worries. You left watching and listening as viable options, and I'm good with those." The smug bastard even gave Xander a wink.

West extended his hand to Lex. "Since we're already talking about some kind of fucking, I ought to introduce myself." West flipped a thumb in Xander's direction. "This big, jealous fool is too busy pissing on your leg to do so. Weston Sharpe, expert sharpshooter and tattoo artist at your service."

"Jesus Christ, West. Enough with the charm, and no watching either."

"Ah, listening, it is then. You know I'll scratch my voyeurism kink any way I can consensually get it."

Lex cleared his throat, disrupting their banter. "If you're finished objectifying me, I'd like to meet your friend."

Xander shoved the green-eyed monster back into the corner of his mind where it sprang from and tugged Lex to his side. He palmed his throat, his thumb and index finger beneath his jaw, where he pressed a kiss to his heated skin. "Sorry, baby. You and Penny bring out my inner caveman whenever someone else comes near."

Lex met his gaze, his eyes already darkening with desire. "I didn't say I didn't like it." Lex took West's hand and shook it. "It's nice to meet you."

"Fuck, the two of you are hot together." Without shame, West adjusted his cock. Then he grabbed his cell and, with a shit-eating grin on his face, sent a message to their group chat.

A second later, Xander's phone buzzed in his pocket, and he shot West a glare. "What did you do?" Xander asked, reaching for his cellphone when more alerts pinged.

West: Hey, you guys, guess who's got himself all settled in a sweet little throuple?

Gray: Is this about you?

West: Nope.

An image followed his response.

West: <picture of Xander with his hand cupping Lex's throat, gazing at him <fire emoji> <egg-plant emoji> <wet emoji>

Fuck. He and Lex looked good together. Xander saved the pic with a plan to send it to Penny and Lex later.

Everly: Who's the third, West? That ship sailed with you and X a long time ago.

Then Jasper chimed in, and all hell broke loose.

Jasper: It's not West. Where's the gorgeous creature you came to Decadent with?

West grabbed his phone again, and Xander watched the text bubbles dancing on his screen with trepidation.

West: Her name's Penny. She's not here. Just the Italian Stallion. <horse emoji> <laughing face emoji>

Xander glared at his friend. "What are you, twelve?"

Jasper: Stop teasing the poor man, West. From the picture, I can tell Xander is in love.

West: Now, who's the one teasing?

Gray: If anyone knows, it's you, Jas. <winking emoji>

Jasper: Tell your 'Italian Stallion' he can thank me the next time you're in New York. I bet you'll thank me, too.

There's something Xander needed to know.

Xander: Did you have something to do with this?

Jonathan: Oh, shit. Jas is working his match-maker magic again.

Everly left the chat.

Gray added Everly to the chat.

Jasper: I'm aware of your stance on relationships, Eve. <smiling devil-face emoji>

Everly left the chat.

Gray added Everly to the chat.

Xander looked at Lex while his friends argued amongst themselves in the text thread. "Did someone point you in our direction at the club that night?"

"Um...yes? This guy caught me staring at you. He said his name is Jasper. He told me I'd thank him someday if I introduced myself to you."

Xander sent another text, cementing his friend's teasing for the foreseeable future.

Xander: If y'all don't mind. How does a bottle of your favorite whisky sound, you smug, match-making bastard?

Jasper: Since we both know how expensive my favorite whisky is...that's quite a thank you.

Xander: Worth it.

"Do you know this guy or something?" Lex asked. Xander turned his phone, allowing Lex to read the exchange. His furrowed brow smoothed, and he laughed. "No way. What a small world. Also, this picture is sexy. Send it to me?"

Everything else disappeared when Xander met Lex's heated gaze. "Of course, brat. I'll wait to send it to Penny. We don't want to spoil our surprise."

"Speaking of," West said, reminding Xander they aren't alone. "What are we tattooing today, boys?"

Xander fished the folded paper out of his pocket. "This," he said, handing it over.

West reached for it and whistled between his teeth. "Nice. I'll trace this onto the transfer paper."

"You don't want to redraw it or tighten any of the lines?"

"Nah, this looks great. Let me trace it up." West laid out a fresh sheet on his drawing table, tracing over the design. "Am I right to assume you're getting the same design, Lex?"

"Si. I am."

Finished tracing, West turned back to face them and clapped his hands. "Alright, since you picked it, where am I sticking it?"

"Right palm for me."

West gave him a knowing look with a quirk of his brow. "You're a better shot with your left, anyway."

"Shut it, fucker. I still outrank you."

West winked, then turned his attention to Lex. "How about you, stud? Where am I inking you?"

"Well...." Lex slipped from his possessive hold, and with a glance in Xander's direction, he grabbed the hem of his shirt and bared a strip of skin that hinted at his V-taper. Then his punishment-accruing brat gave him a coy look. "Maybe here, by my hip." Lex lifted his shirt higher, exposing his stomach and left pec. "Or here, over my heart."

West followed the trail of exposed skin, over his defined abs to his firm pec and pebbled nipple. The tip of his tongue traced his bottom lip, as if he hoped for a taste. A surge of possessiveness hit Xander out of left field, causing an even louder growl.

Such a fucking brat. And West isn't helping matters. Xander's dick is hard enough to hammer nails right now.

It's the Lex effect.

Lex turned, the tension in the room thickening. His jade-green eyes darkened with mischief and desire, and he pulled his shirt all the way off.

Xander didn't miss the way West's gaze traveled over the expanse of blank canvas he exposed. "You know what? I'll get it here on my shoulder. This way, Daddy can run his fingers over it when he--"

Xander stopped him with a hand around his throat. His thumb and index finger added sweet pressure beneath his jaw. "Oh, brat. You've done it now. Though I believe this was your plan all along."

West guffawed. "Fuck, brother. You found yourself a bratty little switch, didn't you? Gotta be honest, I'm now more than a little jealous."

Xander ignored West's teasing and asked Lex, "Didn't you get your fill at our stop on the way here? Now, you've whipped your shirt off in front of my friend, showing off what's mine. Even daring to sass me in front of him? I don't believe you're close to being satisfied."

Lex smirked, trailing his fingers over Xander's arm. "I'll never get enough of you...Daddy," he whispered.

Fuck. Xander needed to lose himself in Lex's bratty mouth again.

West cleared his throat, garnering their attention. Gloved and setting up his station, West ran his gaze over them both. "The back room is yours if you need to release some...tension. I am, after all, a firm believer in tension release."

"I'm game if you are," Lex said. The prominent bulge in his pants made his interest obvious.

Xander glanced at West. He'd removed his gloves and slid his palm over the front of his jeans, and Xander knew he wouldn't be tattooing anyone until he took care of that monster. "You get to listen, nothing else," he said, reiterating their boundaries.

"You're in charge."

"Damn right I am." Xander focused on Lex. "Is this okay with you?"

"Fuck yeah."

"Last door at the end of the hall," West chimed in. "Leave it cracked; my hearing isn't like it used to be."

"Bullshit," Xander muttered, already dragging Lex down the hall to the sound of West's laughter.

When they got to the door, Xander pressed Lex against it. His hand wrapped around his throat, and Xander stepped into his space until nothing separated them except their clothes.

Xander stared into his eyes. "What is it about you and Penny that's got me ready to fuck all the time? I came down your throat not even an hour ago, and I'm already hard as a fucking rock," he said, rocking his hips to emphasize his words.

Lex arched into him. "It's the same for me. Being with you and Penny is like nothing I've experienced in any of my prior relationships." Lex blushed and shifted his eyes to avoid his gaze. "There aren't many...."

Xander moved his thumb beneath Lex's chin and tipped his head back, kissing him with a tenderness he reserved for Penny.

"I don't give a fuck who you have or haven't fucked. I went wild in my twenties. Fucked and played with a lot of people over the years, and every single one of them has ceased to exist the moment I became involved with the two of you. Your past, Penny's past, my past has brought us to this moment in time, and I'd do it all again if it meant I got to be with you."

Lex swallowed against Xander's palm. "Thank you for giving me the tenderness you keep for Penny. Until this moment, I didn't know how much I needed it, too."

His breath ghosted across Xander's lips. "*Baciami, per favore*-Kiss me, please. I need you." Their mouths crashed together in a frenzy of passion and heat. Lex reached for the handle and turned the knob. The door slammed open, and they became more frantic to lose themselves in each other.

"You don't need to break things to have an orgasm," West shouted from the front of the shop.

"I'll cover the damages," Xander called back, breaking his kiss with Lex, trailing hot, wet, open-mouthed kisses down his neck.

"Hey, you keep it loud while you get off, and we'll call it even."

Lex laughed into the crook of his throat when Xander said, "Jesus Christ, West. Enough with the commentary." He pushed away from Lex to look around the room, not finding much to use. A few shelves filled with products, along with a small counter in the corner, didn't leave many options to fuck him over.

Alright, the floor will have to do.

"Undo your pants, take your cock out, and get on your knees," Xander commanded, already undoing his. Lex rushed to shove his pants below his hips. He wrapped a hand around his dick, then dropped to his knees.

Xander stepped between Lex's spread thighs, tapping the inside of his knee with his booted foot to make him spread wider. "Did I give you permission to play, brat?"

"No, Sir," Lex said, not stopping.

"Then get your hand off your dick."

Lex smirked, licking his lips. "Yes, Sir." He slid his hand up the length of his cock one more time, then let go.

Xander grumbled over his insolence and stepped even closer, forcing Lex to spread his knees wider, making the waistband of his pants dig into his upper thighs. He now stood close enough to make Lex arch his back to meet his gaze, and it made his firm ass pop, tempting Xander to take him.

Not yet.

"Don't move. I want you to stay like this." Xander stepped back and walked behind Lex, taking in the perfect way he presented himself. His gaze followed the indent of his spine to his parted cheeks. "Reach back and spread yourself for me."

Lex groaned, parting his muscular cheeks, letting him take his fill. "Fuck, your ass is perfect." Xander dragged his finger along the crease, making Lex shiver. If possible, he arched further, begging without words for Xander to do more. To take him.

Lex looked over his shoulder with such longing. "Are you ever going to fuck me?"

"Not today." The longing on Lex's face shifted to disappointment, and Xander revealed his and Penny's plan, not wanting another minute to pass without Lex knowing how much he wanted to fuck him.

Xander leaned over until his lips pressed against his ear. "I'm saving your sweet cherry for your wedding night. Since you and I took Penny together in one of the hottest fucks of my life. We wanted to give you the same experience."

Lex shivered, and he wiggled his ass on his heels, humping the air, searching for the release he's desperate for. "You're picturing it right now, aren't you, brat?"

"Fuck yes. I can't wait for you to stretch me open and fill me with your gigantic cock."

Xander huffed. "Gigantic seems a bit of a stretch."

"You're fucking joking, right? I know you've seen your cock."

"Alright, you win. I have a big dick, and I have the utmost confidence you can take it." Xander nipped his lobe and growled, "One more week."

Lex sighed. "Yes...one more week."

Xander walked around Lex, standing between his legs again. He kissed him, sliding his tongue past his parted lips, moaning into each other's mouths.

When Xander dragged his mouth away, he said, "You can beg me all you want...in fact, I quite enjoy the way you beg."

Xander gripped his jaw, ensuring he had Lex's undivided attention. "If you believe I'm going to fuck you for the first time in the backroom of a tattoo shop, you are mistaken. You get a bed, and you're getting our girl."

"*Cazzo, ti amo*-Fuck, I love you."

"Love you too, brat."

"Sweet as your love sounds, and it sure sounds sweet. You know I'm happy for you, Xander, but...are the two of you going to do anything besides chat? Are we all getting off or what? The sooner we do, the sooner I can get back to tattooing you." West shouted from the front of the shop.

Damn, Lex made him forget West's presence, something that's very difficult to do. Caught off-guard when Lex palmed his dick and licked the crown, lapping the precum pooling at his slit.

"Time to quit teasing me, sweetheart. Open wide and take this gigantic dick."

"Please...I need it," Lex begged, then he parted his lips and stuck out his tongue, ready to take Xander deep.

"I know you do, brat. Be a good boy and stroke your cock for me while I fuck your face. We don't want to keep West waiting. He gets grumpy when edged for too long."

Xander pushed the head of his cock past Lex's parted lips. "Besides, I can't wait to get back to Penny."

Back to Penny...back to Penny...back to Penny....

Penny's name triggered a searing pain, radiating across his chest.

Shot. Penny's missing. No....

Pulled away from Lex and brought into the harsh light of reality, his eyes opened, and everything came rushing back.

Penny being kidnapped...him getting shot, waking up in the hospital, surrounded by beeping monitors and the sharp scent of disinfectant. "Penny!"

Xander needed to get out of this fucking hospital bed. He needed —

A soft, feminine sniffle followed a choked hiccup. Long slender fingers entwined with his, bringing his hand to be kissed by a set of lips he'd recognize anywhere.

Is he dreaming? It must be the drugs they gave him. Or is he dead?

The lips pressed against his knuckles lifted in a smile. His breath caught. He wanted to see Penny, wanted to look so badly.... *What if it's not real? What if she's not real?*

"Aye, it's real, Xander. You're not dreaming, and you're not dead. Please look at me. I need to know you're okay. Please tell me you're okay."

Penny asked him if he was okay. She's the one who got kidnapped. This can't be real. This. Can't. Be. Real.

"It is, Xander. I swear to god, it is. Please, look at me," she begged.

He sensed Lex on his other side and leaned into his touch when he grazed his temple with his knuckles. "*E vero. Lo giuro, e vero, amore mio*-It's real. I swear it's real, my love."

Xander swallowed hard, his vision becoming blurry with tears. When he turned his head and met her shimmering amber eyes. "Penny? You're...how...?"

"Hi."

Chapter Forty-Eight

Lex

Eighteen hours ago.

Lex ran.

He raced up the stairs and down the hall to Penny's old bedroom. They left the door open, and he heard strained voices coming from within while a couple of other security members stood in the doorway.

Xander.

"Move." The two at the door jumped aside, and Lex skidded to a halt, mortified at the scene in front of him. Xander sprawled on the floor while two other members of the security staff performed first aid, trying to stem the flow of blood.

Blood. Fuck...there's a lot of blood.

"Is he…?" The words jammed in his throat, though he pushed them through because he needed to know. "Is he alive?"

One man cut Xander's shirt open with a pair of scissors from the first aid kit beside him, while the other kept pressure on his wounds. He's the one who glanced his way and answered his question. "Yes. He's been in and out since we found him. The perpetrator shot him twice, and the bullet may've grazed an artery, what with the blood loss. I can't say for sure until he's assessed. Sorry."

"Can I…?"

The man seemed to understand Lex's stilted question. "Aye. The name's Angus. Come sit by his head. You need ta give us room to keep him stable. Alright?"

Lex won't risk Xander's life further. "Yes."

The older man gave him a reassuring smile. "I'm sure Mr. Ward will appreciate a familiar face when he wakes next."

Lex moved around them, careful not to disturb anything, and got on his knees by Xander. He reached out a trembling finger and brushed a lock of hair away from his face.

"What about Penelope? Where is she?"

"We don't know, sir. Others are combing the grounds, searching for her."

Xander stirred, brought around by the other man pulling his shirt apart, or maybe because they'd mentioned Penny.

Angus kept the pressure on Xander's chest with his left hand while he used his right to check for an exit wound. "Give me that towel," he said, and Lex felt grateful to be useful. "It looks like a through and through."

They worked with the efficiency of those with triage and first aid training, and he will forever be thankful for their expertise.

When Angus switched out the blood-soaked cloths for clean ones, Lex took in the full scope of Xander's wounds. Mangled flesh and blood marred the tattoo on his left pec. The image burned into his mind, becoming the stuff of future nightmares. Angus added more pressure, making Xander moan with pain.

Where the hell is the ambulance?

No sooner had the idea entered his mind than Taylor filled the doorway. "Paramedics are here."

"*Meno male*-Thank god."

"Lex?" Despite the roughness of Xander's voice, it was music to his ears.

"I'm here, baby," Lex said, giving Xander all his focus. Everyone else in the room faded away, or perhaps they all fell silent not to miss a word of this conversation. Either way, Lex didn't give a fuck. They can make all the assumptions and judgments they want. He won't hide who Xander is to him.

Not anymore.

"I love you. Penny loves you. You're going to be okay."

"Penny...got to find Penny."

"When I know you're out of harm's way, I will. One crisis at a time, okay?" It's all Lex can handle.

"No...danger...Penny." Despite being shot and the blood loss, Xander tried to get up.

"Oh, no, you don't," Lex scolded, cupping Xander's face to hold him still. He leaned over him and put his face close to his. "I get to protect Penny, too. The tech and software I've created are top-notch. She's wearing a tracker...more than one."

Xander gave him a weak smile. "Figures." His raspy words deteriorated into a coughing fit. Thank goodness the paramedics came through the door with a stretcher and a medic pack. They made everyone get out of the way, stabilizing Xander for transport to the hospital.

Lex knew he'd reached peak panic when Taylor pulled him aside and handed him a small stack of papers. "What's this?" He didn't want to look at them. He didn't want to take his eyes off Xander.

"Tim got these from Xander when he first found him."

Lex tore his eyes away and looked at the items in his hand. "What the hell are these?" He flipped through the photos and threatening notes. "Blackmail? Death threats? Penny kept this from us?"

"You and Xander will need to ask Penny when you find her, and we are going to find her."

"I won't need these ridiculous threats to do it. Let your team gather whatever forensic evidence from them they can," Lex said, handing the papers back to him.

"Get my laptop from my room and meet me at the hospital. I'm riding with Xander, regardless of whether they let me. We're going to find Penny, and Xander is going to be okay."

"Yes, sir. I'll organize the investigation here, and then I'll bring it right over."

Lex clasped Taylor's shoulder, knowing this must be hard for him, too. "Thank you."

"Lex?" Xander's voice drew him, and he rushed to his lover's side.

"I'm here, *amore mio*." The paramedics secured him to the stretcher, ready to get him to the ambulance. Lex followed them down the hall, staying by Xander's side when they made their way downstairs.

"Penny...I didn't keep her...safe."

"Don't. You've done everything to keep Penny safe, including showing her how to protect herself. We'll get her back. I swear."

When they reached the bottom of the stairs, Lex came face to face with another crisis he'd compartmentalized the moment he found out Xander got shot.

They rolled Xander's stretcher past a second one with Penny's father on it, readying him for transport in the other ambulance Lex could see through the open door.

Lex breathed a sigh of relief until he registered the paramedics' lack of action and how still James remained. Then they draped a sheet over him, covering his face. "*Oddio, no*-Oh god, no."

What else will Penny have to endure?

Lex looked from James' covered body to his own father's expressionless face. While the other guests remained in the chapel, his father got past the guards, which didn't surprise Lex in the least.

"Father, you're supposed to be in the chapel with everyone else. I...I'm sorry about James. I don't know what happened."

"Where is your bride?" Marco asked, ignoring his condolences. "It's of the utmost importance to marry her now more than ever."

Lex almost staggered from the coldness of his father's tone. Didn't he care about James' death, or what this would do to Penny?

Lex tried to pull his father aside. They'd made it a short distance when Marco jerked his arm out of Lex's grip. "Enough of this placating. Where is your bride?" he asked again.

More like demanded.

"Father, what is wrong with you? Penelope is missing, and someone shot Xander."

"Missing? What the hell is being done to find her?" This time, Marco grabbed him, and Lex winced from the way his father's grip dug into his arm.

Marco's voice shifted into a hiss. "This union is essential to our future within the organization. The son you will have with Penelope will secure our lineage, running things into the next generation."

Lex allowed his rage to rise to the surface and jerked out of his father's punishing grip. "Is this all you care about?" His father gave him nothing except stony silence, and Lex reached his limit of acquiescing to his father's every whim. "Do you want to know what I care about? What matters to me?"

Lex pointed toward Xander being loaded into the other ambulance. "He's the one I care about. He almost died today. Penny and Xander mean everything to me. I'm going to find her and bring her home. The organization can burn to the ground, for all I care. I don't give a fuck. I never did."

His father's face became mottled with rage. "You have everything you have today because of the organization, and you will honor your legacy."

Lex didn't want to deal with this anymore and got right up in his father's face. "Everything I have today is because of me. I built my billion-dollar company with the software I invented without help from you or the fucking organization. Yet I walked away from it all for you and them. I have a relationship now, with two people who complete me in ways I've never imagined, and I won't walk away from them for anything."

The paramedic turned to Lex and asked, "Sir, are you coming? We need to get him to the hospital."

"Yes," Lex said. His father tried to grab him again, and he shook him off.

"This isn't over," Marco hissed.

"For me, it is." Lex jogged to the waiting ambulance and hopped into the back, sitting where the paramedic directed him to. Not bothering to look back at his father, Lex held Xander's free hand and pressed his knuckles to his lips. The warmth of his skin reassured him that, for now, Xander's okay.

One crisis at a time.

He must have fallen asleep because a noise made him jerk awake. "Xander?" Lex leaned over the bed, and Xander groaned. "Shhh, don't talk," he soothed, kissing his temple. "You're okay. You're in the hospital and got out of surgery."

"Penny?" The whisper of their lover's name from Xander's dry lips sliced Lex open all over again.

"She's...."

Lex checked his watch for the hundredth time. Taylor texted him fifteen minutes ago to say he's ten minutes out. Where the fuck is he? Lex needed his laptop to activate his tracking software. "She's safe. You'll see her soon."

Xander seemed to believe his reassurance and slipped back into the darkness to rest and heal. Lex sent up a quick prayer to every deity he knew of, hoping what he told Xander remained true.

When they wheeled him into the private suite after being in the recovery room, the doctor refused to tell him anything until Lex lied and told him he was Xander's husband.

The literal fear emanating from Lex must've swayed the doctor because he relented and told him both DSWs were through and through. One nicked an artery, though, and Xander lost a lot of blood. They stopped the bleeding during surgery and gave him a blood transfusion.

"If Mr. Ward stays clear of infection and doesn't seem to have any other issues, your husband will make a full recovery."

Glad to know at least one owner of his heart is going to be okay. Hearing someone else refer to Xander as his spouse made Lex more determined than ever to make it a reality.

He just needed to find Penny first.

"If Taylor can get here with my fucking laptop."

"I'm here," Taylor said, bursting through the door, out of breath. "Sorry. Some fucking idiot caused an accident ahead of me and blocked traffic. I left the car with a cop on the scene and ran the rest of the way."

"You're here now, and I'm glad you're okay," Lex said, taking his laptop from Taylor's outstretched hand. When Lex looked at him, he found Taylor staring at Xander with a pained expression, and Lex clasped his shoulder, wanting to reassure him. "The doctor said he's going to make a full recovery."

Taylor pulled his gaze away from his friend. "Yeah?"

"Sí, he lost a lot of blood. They've already given him one transfusion. The doctor believes he'll need more."

Taylor's gaze returned to Xander. "If you don't need me, I'd like to donate. I'm a universal donor."

"Wow, thanks. I'm sure they'll appreciate it, and I know Xander will, too." After his father's behavior, having someone do such a simple thing to help pushed the emotions he suppressed to the surface.

Lex cleared his throat, tapping his foot to release excess energy as he waited for his laptop to boot up. "This is going to take me a few. How about I text you when I get something on Penny's location?"

"Sounds good." Taylor stopped by the door. "I'm sorry about Penny's father."

"I am too."

Taylor left, closing the door behind him, and Lex opened his tracking software. He didn't know how to tell Penny about her father, and his new mantra sounded in his head. *One crisis at a time....*

He'll talk to her when she's safe, and he can comfort her.

He also hoped Penny forgave him for the extra precautions he'd taken to keep those he loved safe. And while Lex didn't possess Xander's size, strength, or skill with a gun, he possessed ways of his own to protect.

The trackers he developed to work with his software are tiny and discreet, and Lex placed one on every article of clothing Penny and Xander owned, including shoes, handbags, and the engagement ring on Penny's finger.

If these motherfuckers didn't strip her bare and transport her somewhere else, Lex will have her exact location in moments. With the software now running, he activated the tracker in Penny's ring. "Bingo," he whisper-yelled, not wanting to disturb Xander when a red dot appeared in the center of his screen.

Lex zoomed in on the location. He didn't have his glasses on and squinted when the satellite image came into focus. "What the fuck?" he shouted this time.

He shot out of his chair and ran across the room to the door, flinging it open. He looked down the hall to his right; however, his name being called from the left made him spin around in utter disbelief.

Penny stood at the other end of the hall. *Is he dreaming? Is she here?* When she called his name, Lex jumped into action.

"*Oh, mio Dio*, Penny!" Lex ran to her, and she limped toward him. Her hair hung half out of her updo, and she had a bruise on her cheek, along with scratches on her arms. Her gorgeous gown, ripped and ruined, showed the scrapes and bruises on her legs, too.

What the hell happened to her?

Later.

Later, Lex will let the rage consume him, and he'll let it out when they apprehend who did this to her. Right now, he wanted to hold her and know she's safe. She crashed into him, and he wrapped his arms around her, holding her tight. "Penny."

Penny sobbed against his chest. "Lex."

"Shhh, Dolcezza. I've got you. You're safe now," Lex said, trailing gentle kisses along her temple. The relief of feeling her against him became palpable. Then Lex heard the running feet coming down the hall toward them. He curled Penny behind him, on the defense until he saw the medical personnel, and their words registered.

"Ma'am...ma'am, please. You need medical attention," the out-of-breath woman said when she reached them.

Lex didn't miss the panic in Penny's eyes and addressed the frantic nurse. "Which room?"

The nurse pointed to the room two doors down. "A doctor can examine her in there."

"Alright. Can you give us a couple of minutes, and then I'll bring my wife in?" Penny's eyes widened at his use of wife, and a quiet gasp slipped past her lips.

The nurse agreed. "I'll page the doctor."

“Thank you.”

The moment the nurse walked away, Lex held Penny’s face, searching her expression for any severe signs of pain. “Principessa, you need to get checked out. I need to know you’re okay, and it’s something Xander will demand to know, too.”

Penny shook in his arms, pushing from his grasp. “Where’s Xander? Is he alright? Dimitri said he’s injured. How bad is it?” She sniffled, and tears streaked her cheeks. “Is he okay? This is all my fault.”

Lex used his thumbs to wipe away her tears. “I promise he’s alright. They did surgery not too long ago to repair the damage from two gunshot wounds. He’s lucky; one bullet nicked an artery.”

“Oh, God. This is all my fault.”

“They repaired it. Xander’s going to be fine, and I know he won’t like the way you’re blaming yourself, and neither do I.”

“And my father, how is he?”

Lex stiffened. “Your father...Penny, I’m sorry. Your father passed away today.”

“I...oh, no.” Penny sniffled. Her amber eyes filled with tears, spilling onto her cheeks. “So much devastation in one day.”

Lex took his pocket square and dabbed her cheeks with the silk material. She took it from his hand, and he pulled her tight against his chest. “I’ve got you, Dolcezza. Our relationship with our parents will always have complications, but we love them because they are our parents."

"Thank you."

When Penny said nothing else, he asked, "Do you want to work your way up to talking about your father?"

"Yes. I can't deal...I mean, there's so much to work out, I don't know where to begin."

"Want to start with how you got a hold of Xander's uncle, and not one of us?"

This made Penny smile, and she wiped away the rest of her tears. "I met Xander's uncle during our time in New York. He gave me his number in case I ever needed anything. Told me to memorize it, and when I got to the pub, his number was the only one I remembered. The bartender let me--"

"Wait, wait. Bartender?"

"Promise, I'm getting to it. Anyway, the bartender let me use his phone, and I called Dimitri. He told me about Xander and which hospital he's at. I got a ride from this nice, older couple having lunch at the pub, and here I am."

Lex eased Penny from the floor where they still sat. Thank goodness the hall remained empty. They made quite a spectacle seated in the middle of it. With her tucked into his side, he gently pulled her to her feet, walking her toward the room where the nurse had directed them.

He kept kissing her and touching her. Beyond thankful she's safe. Between kisses, he said, "Now, we both know there's more to it. You have a lot to tell me, and if Xander's not awake when we settle in to have this conversation, you'll repeat each word for him. Right now, though, you're getting checked out."

Chapter Forty-Nine

Penny

Twelve hours ago.

"Please don't stop," Penny whimpered when Xander's hand slipped beneath the hem of the dress he chose for her to wear. Or what passed for a dress?

The deep V of the leather mini plunged to her navel, and the skirt skimmed the tops of her thighs. Xander's fingers froze when they met her bare pussy.

"I believe I left a pair of black lace panties on the bed for you to wear along with this dress," he said with his lips pressed to her ear. "Why aren't you wearing them, Princess?"

Penny tried to turn in his arms and explain she found no underwear when Xander's grip tightened on her hips, stopping her. "Never mind. I know where they are."

"Huh?" She raised her eyes and found a scrap of lace dangling from Lex's index finger. "Oh." She covered her mouth, her laughter still distinguishable above the beat of the music.

"What? I wanted to ensure we maintained easy access to our slutty little Princess's pussy."

Xander snatched the bit of lace from him and tucked it into his pants pocket. "Don't think your fantastic idea gets you out of a punishment for such insolence, brat."

"Never, Sir." His tone was anything but apologetic.

The opening beats of Nine Inch Nails' "Closer" pulsed through Penny's body. Many of Decadent's members shifted to the dance floor, enticed by the beat of the provocative song.

"Come on, let's dance," Lex shouted, weaving them through the crowd, etching out a space for themselves in the center of the dance floor. Lex pressed to her front, and with Xander at her back, the song's erotic words washed over them while they moved together.

Being back at Decadent without disguises or their faces hidden under masks is incredible. Free to be among others who sought their own pleasure beneath the strobe lights.

Xander and Lex pressed in; nothing except their clothes separated them, and Penny never wanted to leave their arms. She smiled, tilting her head back when soft lips surrounded by a trimmed beard tickled her ear.

"Wake up, Princess. You need to fight to come back to us. We need you...I need you."

Penny's brow furrowed in confusion. *Wake up? Come back to them? She's right there, in their arms...isn't she?* Penny shivered, unable to get warm. *How can she be cold, dancing between her men?*

"Dolcezza, please...wake up. Now!"

"Huh...what?" Penny groaned, the sound of her voice like an icepick to the back of her skull. *Is she hungover? Did she hit her head? What the fuck happened?*

She tried to rub her eyes with her right hand and found herself chained to the bed. "What the fuck?

The memory of her almost-wedding stole her sensuous dream and replaced it with the nightmare she now found herself in. Penny blinked, letting her eyes adjust to the darkness.

Her stomach churned, and she took some slow, measured breaths, in through her nose and out through her mouth. When her nausea eased, her vision hadn't improved. With no window or light, the pitch blackness pressed in on her.

"Stay calm. Remember what I taught you; use your other senses to gather information." Xander's voice echoed in her head.

She can do this.

Penny moved into a seated position and placed her bare feet on the floor, finding hard-packed earth. She took a deep breath. It smelled musty and earthy, like a cellar. A smell she's all too familiar with. All at once, she realized where they'd taken her.

The dungeon is beneath the castle...except this isn't a cell, though at the moment it is her prison. She'd bet all her money; she's in secret passages beyond the ancient cells.

There are three she knew of, leading to the North Sea, the road outside the village, and there's even one going to the village pub. When she came to the end of that tunnel, she got drunk for the first time.

Fun times.

"This isn't the time to travel down memory lane, Dolcezza. Though I believe I'd enjoy such a story." Penny snorted. Her imaginary Lex amused her, like the real Lex always did.

"You're right. Not the time. I'll tell you about it after I get out of here." She talked to the figments of Xander and Lex, not because she's having a mental break. No, her mind conjured them to keep her sane. Penny needed to keep her shit together to get out of here, and she'd use up every trick in her arsenal to do it.

Her cuffed wrist limited her to a few feet from the bed, where she explored what she could reach with her left hand, finding nothing of use. Penny needed a light, and she needed to get out of these restraints. Then she can see the marks she made when exploring these tunnels.

She hoped she wasn't somewhere down the tunnel leading to the North Sea. If they'd taken her there, she would have had to backtrack for hours to get to the passageways leading to the road or the pub.

It's been years since she went to the dungeon and to the hidden tunnels beyond.

When her mother received a cancer diagnosis, Penny needed an outlet, a way to rebel. Somewhere to release the anger consuming her at the unfairness of her mother's deteriorating health. So, she went where her father forbade her to go.

The dungeons below the castle.

The first time Penny went down there, she discovered why her father had wanted her to stay away. She came upon a couple of men who worked for her father, beating another man tied to a chair. Her father stood off to the side, observing with cold, detached interest, before demanding answers from the unfortunate man.

It opened Penny's eyes to a side of her father she never knew existed, and it altered her perception of him forever.

She'd stumbled out of sight. Driven by the fear of being caught, Penny turned left when she should've gone right, finding the tunnels by accident.

Over the next few months, she avoided the rooms her father and his henchmen used to interrogate people, or worse, and explored the ancient passageways, drawing arrows in the dirt floor until she knew where each one went.

Penny devised a basic system, using S for the North Sea passage, R for the village road passage, and P for the passage leading to the pub. She carved them into the support beams with a number to mark the distance. She hoped her captors hadn't explored them to the extent she had. Penny needed all the advantage she could get.

She didn't know how long it would be before their return. Every minute is a gift she can't take for granted. First, Penny tried to work her hand out of the cuff, and when it didn't work, she pulled a hairpin from her ruined updo.

"Remember our lock-picking contest, Princess? Who escaped the fastest?"

"How can I forget?" she muttered. "It took me thirty-seven tries to beat you, and even then I'm pretty sure you let me win."

"You picked the lock in under ten seconds. Don't knock your accomplishment." Dang. Even imaginary Xander offered praise when she needed it. If her subconscious utters a 'Good girl,' she will seek professional help after this.

Penny picked the lock, biting the corner of her bottom lip in concentration. "Ah-ha," she shouted seconds later when the cuff released. She covered her mouth, not wanting to give away the fact that she's awake.

Penny stilled, not even taking a breath. When silence greeted her, she breathed a sigh of relief and rose from the bed. She took careful steps, not wanting her bare feet to land on something sharp while she searched for a lantern or flashlight, or even something she could use for a weapon.

Her missing shoes, maybe?

When she found nothing, Penny slumped to the floor. She'd already made it three-quarters of the way around the room, finding more dirt and dust.

"Don't give up. You're going to need to fight with everything you've got."

Penny needed to remember what Xander had taught her. Hours spent in the gym practicing hand-to-hand combat and how to escape brutal holds. He even taught her how to disarm someone. She's not helpless and still has the element of surprise on her side as she faces the one person she once believed to be a confidante and a friend.

Freya.

Penny didn't want to contemplate Freya's betrayal. She didn't have a choice; she needed to figure out the missing pieces.

"Threats. Blackmail. Kidnapping...."

"You ought to add murder to your little list."

Penny gasped when Freya's voice floated toward her in the darkness. "Freya? What the fuck are you talking about?"

"Language, Princess...."

Penny tucked closer to the wall when a shadow moved in the corner. The one she didn't check yet. So much for stopping to wallow in why all this is happening.

Freya stepped from a hidden entrance, bringing a lantern with her. "Xander calls you, Princess, right? Or at least he used to."

Penny squinted. Her eyes adjusted to the light, glinting off the metal of the gun as Freya held it steady on her. A lead weight settled in Penny's stomach. *No, it can't be true*. "Did you...hurt, Xander?" She refused to use the word kill. Xander is not dead.

"Well, I didn't stop to check his pulse on the way out. People don't walk away from two bullets to the chest."

Penny staggered back, the wall stopping her fall. "No. I don't believe you." There's no way Xander's dead. She'd feel a profound loss. No, Xander's alive.

"You heard me loud and clear, Penelope. I left Anya there to run interference while I came back here to take care of you."

Penny wiped away her tears with the back of her hand. "Anya? Who the fuck is Anya?"

Spite filled Freya's laugh. "Anya's my identical twin sister. I can't believe we fooled you for years. I mean, your bodyguard-lover almost caught us once. Anya forgot to cover the mole near the corner of her mouth. It's our only physical difference. She didn't argue when I made her get it removed."

Freya's brow wrinkled when she looked at the delicate watch on her wrist. "She ought to be here anytime." When doubt clouded her expression, Penny used the other woman's distraction to strike.

With a banshee-like scream, Penny charged Freya, ducking low to avoid any possible shot she might get off, and nailed her in the gut with her shoulder.

"Oof," Freya grunted the moment Penny made contact, knocking the wind out of her and sending the gun skidding in the opposite direction while Penny wrestled her to the ground.

"You bitch." Freya clawed at Penny's arms, drawing blood with her nails. She even landed a half-decent right hook to her jaw, making her brain rattle. Penny shook it off and pinned Freya's arms with her knees. She tried to kick and buck Penny off by lifting her hips, but she was having none of it.

"If I'm a bitch, you're a fucking psycho. If you hurt Xander, I'm going to fucking end you."

Penny fisted the other woman's hair and struck the end of her nose with the heel of her palm, breaking it. Freya screamed and then fainted from the pain such a precise blow caused.

Penny stood, adrenaline coursing through her system, making her limbs tremble when she picked up the lantern and went to detach the chain from the bed. Penny tossed the mattress aside, finding the end of the chain attached to the bed by another steel cuff. Perfect.

"Time for another record breaker, Princess."

Luckily, her ruined hairstyle held more bobby pins, and she pulled another from her locks, freeing the second cuff faster than the first. "Yes." She smiled in triumph, dragging the chain back to Freya, who moaned in pain.

Penny flipped the half-unconscious woman over and pinned her arms behind her back. She tried to struggle, and Penny slammed her head against the packed earth. "Don't you fucking dare."

She locked both of her wrists into one cuff. Not giving a fuck if it cut off her circulation. This bitch deserved every bit of the retribution Penny wanted to rain upon her.

With the lantern in hand, she found the gun across from the bed, checked the chamber, and found it empty. Did she use them all on Xander or lie about shooting him in the first place?

Penny grabbed the chain and jerked it. Hard. “Get the fuck up. Now.”

Freya whimpered in response. Without the use of her arms, it took her a few minutes to shuffle to her knees and stand. “Let’s fucking go,” Penny said, growing more impatient to get out of here.

“I’m trying,” Freya shouted, her voice sounding funny thanks to her busted nose. She’s going to have a lot of other things busted if she doesn’t get moving.

“Wait.” Penny didn’t want this woman leading the way. Who knows what she might try? She brought the chain between Freya’s legs and further restricted her movements.

Penny stepped in front of her and yanked on the chain for good measure. “I’ll lead the way, and if you try anything, I’ll chain-whip your pussy. Now, let’s go.”

She raised the lantern and stepped through the entrance to the room, with Freya trailing behind her. She cast the light to her left, then to her right, trying to decide which way to go. Penny went with her gut and veered left.

They walked for a bit in silence. Every few feet, Penny tugged the chain, reminding Freya who's in control. "Why did you and your sister do it? The threats, the blackmail, kidnapping me...what made you do this?"

Penny caught Freya's glare over her shoulder. Blood dried on her upper lip, chin, and neck. Her eyes swollen and blackening with bruises, Freya looked quite the sight. The silence stretched. Maybe she won't answer, and then she did.

"Revenge. Why else? I've heard it's a dish best served cold." Freya shrugged, rattling the chain. "Or I believed it to be."

"I don't understand. Why do you want revenge on me? What did I do to you?"

"Not you. Your father and the organization. You were a means to an end. Now I'm positive they've captured Anya, and my ditzy sister will sing like a canary."

Freya shook her head. "You know, my family used to be part of the organization, too. Until your father murdered my parents and my brother. Somehow, he didn't know about us. We'd gone to the park with the nanny that day."

They came to a support beam, and Penny raised the lantern a little higher, slowing her steps. P9 caught the lantern light. It meant five more support beam lengths to go, and they'd reach the pub. "Yes," she whispered.

Lowering the lantern, she said to Freya, "Look, I'm sorry for what happened to you and your family. My father didn't want me anywhere near the organization. He's...I'm aware he's done a lot of horrible things."

"Aye, then your father arranged a marriage for you to bring you into the fold, and I put my plan into action," Freya smirked, the expression morbid with all the dried blood on her face.

"Gotta admit, I always believed you to be a goody two-shoes type. Didn't have you fucking the bodyguard *aaannnd* the hand-picked fiancé on my bingo card. Never figured you for a whore, Penelope."

Penny turned and faced her nemesis. She called her a whore, like the term is something to be ashamed of, when Penny knew it wasn't. "Careful, Freya. I've already busted your nose. Don't tempt me to break something else."

Freya opened her mouth to speak when someone else beat her to it. "Freya," a familiar voice whisper-shouted. Familiar because it's an exact copy of the woman standing beside her. Penny tightened her grip on the chain and put a finger to her lips in silent warning when Anya made her way toward them.

"Ugh, it took forever to shake the guard dogs Taylor sicced on me. Wait up," she whined. "Why are you way down here? The castle is back this way. Oh, em gee, you will not believe this." An oblivious Anya carried on like she was about to spill the juiciest piece of gossip. "They called two ambulances. One for the bodyguard you *pew-pewed* and one for Penny's father. Pretty sure the man who offed our family is dead. May he rot in hell."

"My father's dead?" Penny gasped.

"Anya, get your fucking head out of your ass and help me," Freya shouted.

"Huh?" Anya still didn't clue in to the change in their situation. "Frey, why are you chained up, and Penelope's free?"

"How are you this dumb? Help me." The sister clued in, and chaos ensued.

Anya charged toward them, and Penny experienced an actual 'fuck it' moment. "You get no apology from me for what's about to happen." Penny yanked the chain, taking Freya's feet out from underneath her. With her arms pinned at her back, she landed hard. Penny heard a definitive crack, confirmed by Freya's scream of agony.

Not waiting for Anya to reach her, Penny ran toward her. Since the move worked well on her sister, she bent, catching her in the gut with her shoulder. The momentum sends Anya ass over tits to the floor behind her.

Penny used the last of her energy to slide the panel aside and crawl into the basement of the oldest pub in the village. She took the stairs two at a time, eager to reach civilization and desperate to get her hands on a phone to contact Xander and Lex. She refused to believe what Freya or Anya said. Xander is alive, and her father will be okay.

Being held in the tunnels meant Penny didn't know what time of day it was or if the pub was even open when she burst through the door leading from the basement. The man behind the bar dropped a towel, followed by the mug he'd been drying. The sound of shattering glass was loud in the quiet space.

Penny leaned against the bar to catch her breath.

Oblivious to the broken glass at his feet, the bartender said, "Who the fuck are yew, and where the fuck did ya come from?"

"Pen...Penelope," she said between gasps of air.

The man's eyes widened with recognition, taking in every cut, bruise, and scrape when he looked her over. "Yer Fergusson's lass?"

"Aye."

"What the fuck happened to ya?"

Penny didn't have time to explain. "Phone. Please, can I use your phone?"

The man lifted it from beneath the bar and set it on the polished mahogany in front of her. "Be my guest."

Penny dialed the one number spinning on a loop in her head since she left the twins tied up and made her way out of the tunnels.

He picked up on the fourth ring. "Dimitri?"

"Penelope?"

Penny sniffled. "Aye, it's me."

"Thank the fucking heavens. When Taylor told me about Xander and how you'd gone missing, I booked the next flight over."

"Is Xander...?" How did Penny ask if one of the men she cared most about in the world is still alive? But Dimitri knew what she meant.

"I won't sugarcoat this, girlie."

"Okay." Penny braced herself for the worst.

"He got shot, and last I heard, he's alive. They took him to Queen Elizabeth University Hospital," Dimitri confirmed.

The twins lied at least about Xander. Her intuition grew uneasy when she focused on her father. "Did Taylor say anything about my father?"

Dimitri paused for two seconds too long. "You need to get to the hospital. Where are you?"

"I'm at the village pub." Penny looked around. The place was empty except for an older couple nearby, who were eyeing her with growing concern. She tried to give them a reassuring smile, but her face hurt too much. The couple and the bartender seemed to be the sole occupants, leaving her options for a ride limited. She hoped the couple owned a car.

"The...what?" Dimitri asked, drawing her attention back to their conversation.

"Listen, Dimitri. I gotta go. I need to get to Xander and Lex. Find out for myself if they're alright. We can talk more when you get here."

Penny hung up the phone to the sound of Dimitri calling her name. "Thank you," she said, pushing the phone back toward the stunned bartender. "You, uh...might want to call the police. I left the perpetrators of my kidnapping unconscious. Well, I believe they're unconscious. Maybe they're dead...I'm not sure. Anyway, I left the panel open to the tunnel. It's under your cellar stairs."

"Okay," he said in a daze.

She left the bartender to make the call and approached the curious couple with an exhausted smile and an outstretched hand.

"Hi, I'm Penny. Can you give me a ride to Queen Elizabeth University Hospital?"

Chapter Fifty

Xander

Present Day

"How...what?" The monitor's incessant beeping sounded an alarm, and Xander found it challenging to breathe. *Penny's here? No, they kidnapped her.* The door to his room flew open, and in ran two nurses and a doctor, full of concern, to surround his bed.

"Move out of the way, miss," one of them said, pushing Penny aside.

Big mistake.

With Penny no longer beside him, Xander's reaction catapulted into a full-blown panic attack, causing further alarm for the medical staff.

The sound of blood rushed through his ears, drowning everything else out. He tried to talk, but with his jaw clenched tight, Xander worried he might crack his teeth. Every muscle in his body seized, drawing so tight it felt as if they would snap.

Then the sweetest sound reached through the darkness, threatening to pull him under. "Can't you see he's having a panic attack? He needs to know I'm here. He doesn't believe this is real. We've gone through too much already, and Xander needs to know I'm safe. Please, I have to show him I'm safe."

"Miss...?"

"It's Fergusson, Penelope Fergusson."

A brief silence fell. Penny seemed to miss the pause in the conversation. The doctor recognized her name. A throat cleared, and someone spoke. "Ms. Fergusson, please let us do our jobs. Mr. Ward is recently out of surgery, and if he doesn't calm down, he's going to further injure himself. It's best if I give him a sedative."

"No, Xander will hate being sedated. He doesn't like losing control. Please give me a chance to calm him."

Penny's here. She's advocating for him. She's...real.

The tightness in Xander's chest lessened further when Lex added. "Let her, please. If he doesn't calm down, I promise you can sedate him."

Brat.

Xander sucked in what felt like his first deep breath in days.

The doctor sighed and agreed. The medical staff stepped back, and two beautiful faces crowded his vision. Xander took another shuddering breath, and his jaw unclenched. "You're here."

"I'm here," Penny said with a sniffle. One of her tears landed on his cheek. Or is he the one crying?

He lifted a shaky hand to cup her bruised face. A rage so acute flooded every cell in his body, eliciting a calm he hadn't experienced since his combat days. Everything in his body stilled, and his heart rate slowed to a steady beat. "Who did this to you?"

"The same person who did this to you."

"Freya?"

"Aye, and she didn't work alone. Her identical twin sister, Anya, helped. Freya is the one who pulled the trigger and caught me off guard with a mean right hook." Penny dropped her voice to a whisper. "Not to worry, I used the skills you taught me, and neither of them will hurt us again."

"Did you...?"

"Oh, well...no. I mean, I considered it. But in the end, that's not me. I left the two tied up in an unconscious heap in the secret tunnel, and the bartender at the pub called the police."

A throat cleared behind them, and one nurse stepped forward to check Xander's temperature and pulse. "Temperature and heart rate are within normal ranges. It appears you have things under control here. I'll be back in an hour to check on Mr. Ward again. If you need help sooner, please press the call button."

The doctor gave them a pointed look. "Mr. Ward needs his rest to recover. From the looks of it, you all do. Don't overdo it."

“Thank you, we won’t,” Lex said, assuring them when he walked them out. Then his shoulders dropped with exhaustion and relief. The worry and anxiety he’s handled alone...Lex needed comfort and reassurance much like Penny did.

“Lex?” The plea in his voice exposed the rawness of his emotions. Penny crawled into the tiny space on his left, curving her arm above Xander’s shoulder to avoid his wounds, then she did one of his favorite things and dragged her fingers through his hair. “I need both of you close right now. Please come here.”

“There’s no way I’m fitting on this bed, too.” Lex pulled the chair on the right side of his bed closer and sat down. Then he put his hand on Xander’s stomach, Penny entwined her fingers with his, and Xander covered both their hands, linking them together.

“I’m sorry. For everything,” Penny said in a choked whisper, breaking the silence.

Xander turned his head; his nose brushing her temple, and he breathed in her soft, floral scent, kissing her forehead. “No, sweetheart. I’m sorry. Sorry for the hurt and pain I didn’t protect you from.”

“No, I wear these cuts and bruises like badges of honor. You protected me. Everything you taught me saved my life.”

“I’m sorry about your father, Principessa.” Lex kissed her fingertips. “We’ll get through this together.”

“I’m not ready to talk about my father’s death and what it means for us. Not yet.”

"We can talk about your father whenever you're ready, baby. How about you tell us what happened from the time Freya and Anya kidnapped you to the moment you arrived at the hospital, because I need to know how you ended up in the village pub?"

"Yes, Dolcezza. Leave nothing out. I want every detail of how you kicked their asses."

Penny's sniffle morphed into a soft laugh. Lex's words had the desired effect of lightening her mood. "Well, when the drugs they gave me wore off, I found myself somewhere in the tunnels leading to several hidden exits beyond the castle...."

"Damn, Princess. Your bravery and resilience turn me the fuck on, and I can't do a damn thing about it."

Their laughter died off when Lex's father, Marco, burst into the room. His eyes narrowed when he took in how close they sat together. "What is the meaning of this? Why are you lying in bed with him when you're supposed to marry my son?"

Xander opened his mouth to speak when Lex squeezed his hand. Penny took her time, careful not to jostle him when she got up. Lex also stood, neither one letting go of his hand.

"*Padre, non è il momento*-Father, now is not the time."

"*Non lo é, accidenti*-Like hell it's not."

"If you must know," Penny said, interrupting their growing argument. "I was in bed with Xander because he and I are together. Like your son and I are together."

"And Xander and I are also together," Lex said for good measure. "Hey, if we're coming out, we're coming all the way out."

"What you said back at the castle is true, then?"

"Yes, father. The three of us are together, and we are in love. Very much in love, in fact." Xander squeezed Lex's hand, offering silent encouragement. "Also, there won't be a wedding. At least not a traditional one."

"What about the contract your father and I arranged? What about the organization?"

Penny tipped her chin up. "Fuck the organization. I've wanted nothing to do with it."

"Nor have I," Lex added.

Marco's face grew red with rage. "*Non puoi farlo*-You can't do this."

"*L'ho appeno fatto*-I just did," Penny said, surprising Marco with her flawless Italian. "Tell the others I will call a meeting soon. Once I've grieved my father's passing. You know, he used to tell me what good friends you were...."

To Marco's credit, he looked embarrassed by his oversight. "Forgive me. With everything going on...I am sorry about your father, but you must know he'd never stand for this...this situation of yours."

"I guess it's a good thing he's dead then. I am now the head of this organization, and no one is going to bar me from loving who I want to love. We will be in touch. The three of us need to rest and recover. We also have a lot to discuss, and neither you nor the rest of the organization will strong-arm me into upping my timeline."

Xander looked over Marco's shoulder to find Taylor standing in the doorway. "I believe everyone here has gone through enough in the last twenty-four hours. Visiting hours are over. Let me escort you out," Taylor said. The steel in his tone left no room for argument, though Marco tried.

"Do you know who I am?"

"Yes, sir. I do. I also don't believe you know who I am, or what I'm capable of."

"Are you threatening me?" Marco sputtered.

"No, sir. No threat, simply stating a fact."

Xander chuckled, covering it with a cough. He rarely gets to sit back and let Taylor take the lead, but he's too damn weak to get out of this bed. No matter how much he wanted to toss Lex's father out on his ass.

Marco shifted his attention to his son. "Alexandre, are you going to let this...security guard for hire speak to me this way?"

"After the way you've spoken to the three of us? Yes."

Taylor held the door open. "Sir, if you'll come with me, I'll make sure you get back to your guards unharmed. Your son, Penelope, and Xander need time to recover from their ordeals. This conversation is hampering their recovery, and I cannot in good conscience allow this to go on." His insistent words moved Marco toward the door.

"I'll speak with you in a few days, Father."

Marco's gaze sliced over the three of them still holding hands, and he pinned Xander with a haughty glare. "I should never have recommended your services to James."

Xander shifted in the hospital bed, not big enough to accommodate his large frame, and squeezed his partner's hands in silent reassurance. Their united front remained one of unwavering love and commitment.

"Funny how life's like that sometimes. I save one of your sons and fall in love with the other. I'm not going anywhere, and I will protect Lex and Penny with my life."

"This isn't over," Marco said and stormed past Taylor out of the room.

"Thanks, Taylor."

"Anytime, brother." He tipped his chin to the three of them, closing the door behind him and Marco. They expelled a trio of relieved breaths. After everything, Marco's wrath and bigotry were a lot to take.

"So...I guess we're out of the organization, and I'm pretty sure my father just disowned me. What shall we do now?" Lex asked, chipper despite what went down.

Penny's smile grew hopeful when she looked at them both and said, "Let's move to New York."

Chapter Fifty-One

Penny

Six weeks later.

"You ready, Princess?"

A week after they reunited at the hospital, the hospital discharged Xander with strict instructions to rest and allow his body to finish healing. He hated every minute of his confinement, except when Lex bratted, which he did every day. Penny feared he'd racked up enough funishments to last a lifetime. No doubt it's his intention.

James' funeral took place the Sunday after. Laid to rest next to Penny's mother in the small cemetery behind the chapel. She still wrestled a lot between grief and anger, something her therapist told her is normal.

While Xander did his rehabilitation, she and Lex tackled her father's office. It's where Penny received a crash course in how powerful he was at the time of his death.

The holdings, stocks, and bonds she planned to divest would increase her wealth beyond comprehension. She didn't need it and planned to donate sizeable sums to several charitable organizations. It's the least she can do for all the pain her father caused over his lifetime.

Penny's more than ready to begin the rest of her life with these men who have stood by her, showing her every day their unwavering support, love, and strength. "Aye. Let's get this over with. Shall we?"

"Lead the way, Dolcezza."

They strode down the hall toward the boardroom. Penny walked in front. Lex and Xander kept pace two steps behind her. She wore a fitted custom black suit, with a pristine white dress shirt and a black and white pinstriped tie. She styled her auburn hair in a tight bun at the nape of her neck. With a simple coat of mascara and a dark burgundy lip, she looked fierce-as-fuck.

Penny dressed to impress. All to tell them to go fuck themselves. Fuck their misogyny and bigotry bullshit. She planned to walk away from this organization with her head held high and her men by her side.

The hum of conversation subsided when the three of them entered the room. "Good afternoon, gentlemen. Thank you for being here. I won't mince words, nor will I waste your time. As the last remaining member of my family, I'm here to tell you Fergusson's will no longer lead or be a part of this organization. I will divest my father's assets to avoid war breaking out amongst you, and I'm turning over the castle to the village council, who plan to turn it into a tourist destination."

Penny met every disgruntled gaze in the room. "My father kept me isolated from his...business dealings. These past few weeks were quite eye-opening, and I have no desire for any of it. Select someone else or get fucked. That will be all, gentlemen. I'll have security show you out."

She turned and went back the way she came, with her head held high, and her men by her side.

"Since we've dealt with the organization, there's another matter we need to attend to. Right, Princess?" Xander clasped Penny's chin between his thumb and index finger, tipping her head back and giving her no choice except to meet his gaze.

"Are you sure you're well enough? Has the doctor given you the clearance to resume...strenuous activities?"

Xander chuckled. "Oh, it's fun when I have two brats to play with." Using his other hand, Xander pulled a folded piece of paper out of his jacket pocket and bopped the end of Penny's nose with it. "Got my doctor's note right here, sweetheart."

"Of course you do."

"With you, I need to cover all my bases," he said, tucking the paper back into his pocket. Then he removed his jacket and rolled the cuffs of his black dress shirt to his elbows, and Penny swallowed around the desire lodged in her throat.

Damn, his forearms are like literal porn.

His smile darkened. "Did you say something, sweetheart?" Knowing exactly what he's doing to her. Penny glanced at Lex, getting an eyeful of the bulge in his pants. He couldn't stop staring at Xander's arms either.

Xander gripped her chin, capturing her gaze. "What do you think, Princess? How many do you deserve?"

How much punishment did she deserve? Penny kept something vital to her safety from Xander. She kept something from him, which almost cost him his life. Something inside Penny snapped, and she quoted one of the most iconic Mean Girl lines. "The limit does not exist."

"Nonsense."

She dropped to her knees. Her forehead pressed against the tops of Xander's shoes. Her hands gripped his ankles, and she begged for forgiveness. "I'm sorry. You almost died because of me." Her words came with a choked sob, and tears blurred her vision, dampening the leather of his shoes.

Great. Something else she's ruined.

"You've ruined nothing." Xander gripped the back of her neck. "Stand up right now." He didn't give Penny a chance, guiding her up by his hold. Then he marched her to the corner and pressed her nose to the wall like a naughty child.

He let go of her neck and pressed her palms flat against the cool surface. "Don't move," Xander growled against the shell of her ear. Then he turned his head and addressed Lex. "Get on the bed, brat. I'll get you ready when I've dealt with our Princess."

"Yes, Sir." Lex sounded gleeful. He's always excited about an impending punishment. Her? Not so much, though she deserved this one.

Xander grunted, and Penny smiled despite her flowing tears when she heard the telltale sign of Lex jumping on the bed.

"Keep adding to your tally, brat."

"I hope never to run out, Sir." The sass coming from Lex lightened the darkness threatening to close in on her.

She shuddered with anticipation when Xander returned his focus to her and wrapped his hand around her throat. His hard body pressed her against the wall. His hot breath fanned her cheek, making her shudder with arousal.

"Now, Princess, there's something you need to understand. Yes, you kept something vital from Lex and me. And yes, while your deception warrants punishment within the dynamic we share, you are not responsible for my being shot. That's on me."

Penny stiffened and tried to push out of his hold. "No, I...." Xander added pressure to his grip on her throat, silencing the blame she insists is hers.

"Enough," Xander growled. "It's my job to protect you. The day I first met you in your father's office, hell, the day he sent me your photo, I made a vow to protect you with my life."

His forehead pressed against the back of her head when he confessed, "I got distracted and didn't register the creak of the floorboard until she fired the first shot. Not gonna lie, it fucking hurt, but I'll step in front of a bullet for you every time, Princess. You and Lex. I won't let anything happen to either of you. Believe me."

"I believe you," she whispered, overwhelmed by such a declaration, though it didn't surprise her. Xander has shown he'd lay his life down for her, and now he'll do it for her and Lex. Someday, it will include the children they might have.

"Do you know the number of pictures and threatening notes you kept from Lex and me?"

The sudden question made Penny fumble with her answer. *How many...five, six?*

"Six," she answered, though the moment the number left her mouth, she knew it was wrong.

"Mm...I believe you forgot two. Four photos. Four letters. And countless opportunities to tell us the truth. You're going to give me eight, Princess."

"His plan is to kill me," Lex muttered from his spot on the bed, and Penny realized what he meant. He's not taking a paddle to her ass. No, he's going to orgasm her to death. Lex, too.

Penny heard the crack of flesh meeting flesh, followed by a stinging pain in her left ass cheek, pulsing in the shape of Xander's palm. She clenched her thighs, turned on even more.

"Hey," she gasped, trying to turn her head to glare at Xander, except he held her in place, keeping her nose pressed into the corner.

"I never said a sound spanking isn't part of this. Assume nothing is off the table, Princess, unless it's the hard limits we've already laid out between us. Color?"

"Green, Sir."

"Good girl. Now, you're going to stay here with your nose pressed to this wall until I'm ready for you."

"Yes, Sir."

Xander landed a second smack, this time on her right cheek. "You know I'm all about symmetry," he said with a wicked chuckle, then he kissed her shoulders, and Penny shuffled from foot to foot, absorbing the sweet sting.

"Damn, you look fucking good, wearing my marks." He stepped away, leaving Penny to listen while he prepared Lex for his part in their scene.

Like their first night together.

"Look at you making use of the wedge pillow I purchased last week."

"I'm giving it five stars. It gave me an incredible view of you administering those two blooming palm prints on the sweetest ass I've had the pleasure of fucking."

"It's an ass worth worshiping for the rest of our lives. Isn't it?" Xander asked, and Penny felt the heat of a blush warming her from her chest to her face.

"Mm...si, it is," Lex said, and more of her desire slicked her thighs.

"You can admire our Princess more once I get you situated. Move to the center of the bed and place your head on the cushion."

Penny heard Lex groan. "Mm...feels good." Then the sharp sound of a smack elicited another groan from him.

"My handprint looks good on you, too, brat. Don't leave our Princess in the dark. Tell her what I'm doing to you."

Again, like their night at the club.

"He's massaging my arms, getting them ready to be tied to the headboard for an indeterminate amount of time." Another sharp smack preceded Lex's hiss.

"Always with the sass, naughty boy."

"Yes, Sir." And Penny whimpered right along with him.

"He's using the black hemp rope to bind my wrists to the headboard. The rope against my skin grounds me. Oh...fuck." Lex's words trailed off into a long, low moan, and Penny almost turned, wanting to find out for herself when Xander's words froze her in place.

"Tell her, brat. What am I doing to you?"

"He's stroking my cock. Fuck...it's fucking good. Don't stop, please. Goddamn it...he stopped."

"We can't have you coming yet, now can we? In fact, you won't come for a while. For six weeks, you bratted in front of me. Taunting me...teasing me while I recovered, unable to give you the discipline you craved until now. Penny's going to use your cock like her own personal fuck-stick. She's going to milk you through all eight of her orgasms, and you'll come when she gives me her last one."

Penny gasped. Xander's plan is the perfect mix of heaven and hell. Of turmoil and ecstasy. She didn't know if she'd survive it. Lex may not either. Death by sensory overload is a heck of a way to go.

The sound of her men kissing filled the room. Their grunts and groans, the sound of mashing lips, teeth, and tongues, made Penny more and more desperate to turn around.

She swore, by its own volition, the tip of her nose slid away from the corner of the wall when a smack to her left cheek reignited the sting there and stopped her cold.

"You're lucky I'm ready for you; otherwise, I'd put you over my knee right now."

"Sorry, Sir."

"Mm-hm...I believe you will be." Xander glided his hands over her, touching Penny everywhere except where she wanted him to the most. When he ran his fingers over the tips of her breasts, she arched her back, giving his thick erection a place to nestle, and rocked her flesh up and down his length.

It surprised her that Xander allowed her to tease him, keeping it up while he braided her hair. The whole time, he didn't say a word. When he finished, his hands landed on her hips and stilled her movements.

Penny shivered when Xander dragged his nose along her nape. "After I've made you come seven times, I'm going to thank you for teasing me by fucking your face while you give me your eighth orgasm."

"Ready?"

"No."

Xander chuckled. "Color, Princess?"

He loosened his grip, and Penny turned to meet his gaze. "Green, Sir. So, fucking green."

"There's my brave and adventurous girl."

"Fuck, the two of you are beautiful together. Please, can we get on with this exquisite torture?"

Together, they looked over at Lex. The way Xander bound his arms and legs kept his movements to a minimum, and his cock stood straight in the air, begging for attention. He's at their mercy.

"Looks like your ride is ready, Princess." Xander took her by the hand and guided her to the head of the bed, where Penny looked at him with confusion. "We need to make sure you're also ready. Go on now, sit on his face, and get a warm-up orgasm out of the way."

Penny stuttered. "There's no such thing. Pfft...a warm-up orgasm? Are you trying to kill me?"

"Is death by orgasm such a terrible way to go?"

"Please...sit on my face, Dolcezza, I need to taste you."

How could she refuse an invitation like that?

Penny climbed onto the mattress and straddled Lex's head. She hovered there for a second, worried about suffocating him.

"Sit on his face, Princess. Lex enjoys a bit of breath play."

"Please. Dolcezza...."

"Get your fill, brat; every other one happens while she's riding your cock."

"Fuck yes." It's the last thing she heard Lex say because she settled over the lower half of his face.

His tongue slid between her folds, lapping at her opening. "Oh, that feels so good." Lex moaned in response, and she rocked her hips, guiding his skillful tongue to her clit to give her the warm-up orgasm Xander demanded.

"Yes, Princess. Ride his face like the good little slut you are." Xander pinched her nipples, tugging them until they beaded into hard points desperate for more. "Soak his face in your come."

"More," she begged. The tip of Lex's tongue flicked her sensitive bundle of nerves one more time, circling it, giving her just enough pressure to bring her closer to the edge of another release, though not enough to send her over, and she cried out with frustration.

Xander gripped her throat. "I told you, Princess, the rest you give me riding his cock.""Please let me ride him, Daddy. I'll be such a good little slut for you. Please...."

Xander's desire-filled gaze met hers. He didn't take his eyes off her when he kissed her. "Alright, sweetheart. You can ride his big dick, and you'll come when I tell you."

"Yes, Sir."

She went to move off Lex when Xander stopped her. "No, love. You've got to drag your pussy down his chest to ride this ride. It's the price of admission," he said, gripping the base of Lex's straining cock.

"Fuucckk," Lex groaned when Penny slid off his face and down his chest toward her prize, leaving a trail of her arousal behind.

Xander kept hold of Lex's cock and leaned in to reach his mouth, sucking Penny's juices from his lips, and distracting her from her goal of sinking onto his beautiful cock. "So sexy."

Xander broke the kiss with Lex, his lips now shiny with her desire, and Penny wanted a taste. Thank goodness, Xander's one step ahead of her, snaking his tongue past her parted lips. When he swirled his tongue with hers, she swallowed their combined flavor and moaned into his mouth.

"Fuck," he gasped. "Get on his cock, baby." And Penny realized how close Xander is to losing control. She dragged her pussy over Lex's stomach, inching toward his waiting cock. The depravity of it all was turning her on even more.

She whimpered when she took his tip inside her, and Xander guided her down the rest of his length. Oh, yeah. She's in trouble. Her orgasm barrelled through by the time she seated herself on his perfect dick.

Penny didn't have a chance in hell of hiding it from Xander when she spasmed, and Lex shouted, "Oh, fuck, grip me tighter." Giving her away, and by then, she didn't care.

It didn't faze Xander in the least. When he moved to the end of the bed and stared at her, he had the most satisfied grin on his face. "There's one, Princess. And because you came without my explicit permission, I'm going to tie you up, too."

"Nooo...." Penny rode Lex's cock with the ferocity of someone who knew such freedom was about to be taken away. "Fuck, I will not last," Lex warned.

Xander tsked, then smacked Penny's ass several times, making her clench around Lex's cock, closing in on her next orgasm. "Be still," he commanded.

With one more glorious slide down Lex's exceptional pole, Penny seated him deep inside her. Xander wasted no time securing her hands to her ankles, leaving her spread and skewered on Lex's cock.

He kissed Lex and checked in with him, making sure there was no numbness in his hands or feet, ever their attentive Dom. Then Xander rained kisses across her brow and over her cheeks, catching the tears she let slip with his lips. "I hope these are tears of ecstasy, my love."

"They are."

"Good. I want all your tears. In fact, I want you to give me more." Xander stood back from the bed and stripped off his shirt and pants, leaving his gorgeous body on full display. He moved to the corner of the bed, letting them both get a look at how they affected him while he stroked himself from root to tip.

Lex cursed, and Penny moaned.

Xander brought out their desperation like no one else, and when Penny clenched around Lex's cock again, he screamed. "Fuck. Please, Sir. Don't make me wait any longer."

"You've got quite a wait ahead of you, brat. Our Princess, however, is going to give us more." Xander moved between their parted legs and dropped to his knees.

"Oh, fuck yes." Penny moaned the moment Xander circled her clit with his tongue and sucked it past his lips. He latched onto her sensitive bud, taking needy pulls, sending her right to the precipice.

She hovered there, unable to ride Lex's glorious dick the way she wanted, and she whined. Xander let go of her clit and met her frustrated gaze. "Problem, Princess?" he asked, and Lex let out a rueful chuckle.

“I need to come. Please let me come, Sir.”

“You need to, eh? I wonder if you’ll be saying the same thing when you get to orgasm number eight.”

Penny didn’t care what she needed to say or do to get Xander to give her permission to come. “Please.”

“Alright, Princess. As you wish.” A switch flicked, and a steady buzzing filled the room.

Lex whimpered when Xander pressed a vibrator to the base of his cock, which sent vibrations through her core. “Oh, fuck. Oh, shit. I will not make it.”

And just as Xander latched onto her clit, he looked her in the eyes and said the magical, orgasm-unlocking words, “Come for me.”

Chapter Fifty-Two

Lex

Is there such a thing as death by someone else's orgasm, all while being denied one of their own? Because... "Fuucckk," he groaned. Penny's cunt held him in a vise-like grip, coming for the fifth time on his dick. He didn't know if he'd survive three more.

Lex tugged on the ropes binding him to the headboard. Xander's Shibari skills meant the ropes didn't give. Not one inch. The sounds coming from him became more animalistic. Grunts and whimpers replaced his pleading words.

Xander smacked his thigh and said, "Three more, brat, and then I'll let you come."

"I don't know if I can," Penny said, her voice a rough whisper after screaming through multiple orgasms.

"Fuck, Dolcezza, you've got to. I won't survive it either way. Please, I beg of you, I want to go out in a blaze of glory. Let your divine cunt take me to the afterlife."

"No one's dying, and everyone is coming by the time we're done. Three more, Princess, and then you get to swallow my load as Lex fills you with his."

And just like that, Xander righted the ship and got the goal of ultimate pleasure back on track.

He cupped Penny's face between his palms, kissing her, letting her lick her earlier release from his lips. "Yes, Princess. Get your fill. Soon, I'll add my cum to the mix, and Lex and I will get you nice and full at both ends."

He nipped her lips one more time, then Xander turned to him. "You know, brat, I can help you resist until I give you permission to come."

Fuck. Lex wanted to come, but his desire to please Xander far outweighed it. "*Fallo*-Do it. Whatever it takes."

Xander chuckled. "I haven't even told you what 'it' is."

"Doesn't matter. I'll do anything."

Xander picked up another coil of rope. "This will push your limits with pain."

"I doubt it's more than what I'm going through now."

"Hm...don't dare to presume. The pain of resisting your orgasm differs from the pain of my controlling when you'll come."

"I can take it." A moment later, when Penny clenched around his straining dick, Lex felt his balls draw tight to his body. "Oh, fuck. Please do it. Otherwise, I will not make it."

Xander leaned down and kissed him. "If it's too much, use your safe-word and I'll release you."

"I will."

"Good boy."

Xander tweaked Penny's nipples, which made her clench around him again. "Not helping, Xander," Lex said through clenched teeth.

"Is our naughty little slut gripping your dick good and tight?"

"I swear she's trying to choke the cum out of me. Oh...fuck." Lex moaned when she did it again.

Penny giggled, peeking at him over her shoulder. "Does it feel good, baby?" Despite being rung out from the multiple orgasms already, she still possessed the energy to tease him.

Xander lowered to his knees, dragging the end of the rope over Lex's balls. He shivered and tried to rock his hips to get a bit more friction, and he groaned with frustration when Xander's restraints held him in place.

It got worse when the warm, wet heat of Xander's mouth latched onto his testicles. His plush lips surrounded him while his tongue drove him wild, licking his sensitive sac and drawing his balls away from his body, letting them go with a loud sucking pop. "Mm...better. Now you're ready for my rope."

"Please hurry."

Xander looped the rope around the base of his testicles, creating a barrier between Lex and his orgasm. He tightened the slack and fastened the rope to a hook beneath the bed.

Lex groaned, taking in a few deep breaths, breathing through the discomfort until it became a dull ache, walking a fine line between pleasure and pain, which kept him right on the edge.

Xander rubbed his palm over the tight skin of his sac, the sensation almost a sensory overload, making Lex's eyes roll back in ecstasy. His hand didn't linger, sliding his palms up his thighs to Penny's.

"Such patience, Princess, while I took care of our brat. With him under control, I can give you my undivided attention." He cupped her breasts, pinching and teasing her nipples while he kissed a path down her throat to take a stiff peak into his mouth.

Penny moaned. The way Xander teased her sensitive nipples made her vaginal muscles clench around him. His cock pulsed inside her, a sensation like an orgasm, though he knew he didn't release. Xander's bondage kept him from unloading inside her. His hand dipped between them, stroking the base of his cock while teasing Penny's clit.

"Yes, Princess...you're going to give me another orgasm, aren't you?"

Penny's body vibrated on top of Lex. "Oh...yes. Oh...god...yes."

"Then come for me."

Penny's cunt spasmed. Her muscles rippling around him while she gave Xander orgasm number six, and Lex the agony of surviving another one where he didn't.

Xander became relentless, turning the vibrator back on and pressing it to Penny's clit. "Don't stop, Princess. Give me number seven. Now." Penny's sixth orgasm didn't end, rolling into another wave of spasms around Lex's cock with her seventh. This time, she soaked his groin with her release.

Did he experience *la petite mort*-the little death? Because Lex swore he died for a second there and saw heaven. And it's not over yet.

"No more," Penny whimpered, her voice all raspy and rough from all the screaming she's done.

"Are you using your safeword?"

"I-no, Sir."

"Then you can and will." Xander kissed her temple, running his hands in a soothing motion over her limbs, squeezing her biceps and shoulders to relieve some of the tension from being restrained. When he looked at Lex and asked, "Are you ready to have the most intense orgasm of your life, brat?"

Tears of desire and frustration trailed from the corners of his eyes. "Please...Xander. Please let me come."

"The moment I pull the slipknot free, you're going to. Mm...let me get my cock wet in the sweetest mouth first."

Lex groaned, forced to ride the intense edge of release a little longer.

Xander cupped Penny's face. "I know you've got at least one more in you. Daddy's going to give you something to focus on. You give me your eighth, and I'll feed you my cum. What's your colors, pets?"

"Green, Sir," they both said.

Xander guided Penny's mouth to his dick with a hand at the back of her head. Careful to keep her balanced while he slid past her lips. He groaned, rocking his hips, feeding Penny more of his cock with each thrust.

"You're perfect, baby girl. The way you've driven me wild all night, I won't last, which means you can't either."

Xander turned the vibrator on again, reaching beneath them to press it against the base of Lex's cock. "*Oh, fottimi, per favore*-Oh, fuck me, please."

Penny moaned around Xander's cock, and he fucked her mouth faster. Xander dropped his chin to his chest, watching Penny take him, watching Lex lose his hold, knowing they'd all reached their limit.

"Now, Lex."

Xander dropped the vibrator, and the rope around his balls fell away. Lex's vision went white. His muscles seized, and the rush of his release filled Penny's fluttering cunt until it overflowed and dripped down his aching balls.

"Swallow every drop, Princess. Yes...take it all," he said with a guttural groan. Pulling his spent cock free of her mouth. "You did so well." Xander met Lex's gaze. "You both did." Then he pressed a kiss to Penny's cum-covered lips. "I love you both. Every day, I promise to love you even more. Now, let me get you out of these restraints."

Always their caretaker, Xander drew them a bath and brought them snacks. He got in the tub first, and then Lex helped Penny in. She nestled against Xander's left side, her hand going to the healed scars from his bullet wounds while she settled her head beneath his chin.

"Fuck, you sure are pretty together."

"The three of us are pretty together. Get in the tub, brat."

Xander shifted his right leg over Penny's hip to make room. Once settled against Xander's right side, he wrapped his arm around Lex, pulling him close, and he shifted, tangling his legs with theirs, relaxing from the heat of the water and the tender way Xander cared for him and Penny.

Lex traced Penny's delicate cheek with his fingertips and closed the distance between them, pressing a soft kiss to her lips while Xander rubbed their backs, giving them a light massage after such an intense evening.

"Do you want some water or a piece of chocolate?" Xander asked, pressing kisses to the tops of their heads. He's always prepared to meet their needs, placing a tray with water bottles and a dish of chocolate squares within reach along the edge of the tub.

"Chocolate me, please," Penny said, parting her lips for Xander to place a square of dark chocolate on her tongue. The little minx even licked the pad of Xander's thumb.

"Princess, after nine orgasms, don't start something you are in no condition to finish."

"Aye, you're right. I'm in no condition to finish. Check back with me in an hour, though," Penny said with a pout on her kiss-swollen lips. Her fingers entwined with Lex's, and the two of them traced the patterns of Xander's tattoos between them.

"Is this real? Are we really moving to New York?" Penny asked with the hope of a future she once thought impossible. Lex understood her need for reassurance.

"It will take some time. Going through all your father's papers, divesting of his investments in the organization. I believe we can swing the move within the year when all's said and done," Lex said. Extricating themselves from the organization will take time, but their move to New York is going to happen.

"I'm sure there's something we can do in the meantime to make the wait a little easier." Xander met Lex's gaze over Penny's head. "Any ideas, brat?"

Lex knew what he wanted, and with a hint like the one Xander was giving him, along with the wedding-themed sites Penny left open on every single one of their devices, meant he was sure they wanted the same.

"I believe the two of you promised me one hell of a wedding night, and I don't want to wait anymore. Let's get married. Our way."

Epilogue Penny

They shared a beautiful commitment ceremony on the beach at sundown on the last Thursday of September at the island house. Kenneth got ordained online, and Leana served as their witness.

With the last rays of the warm September sun, they linked hands, Penny's held between theirs. Xander curled his fingers, drawing them both around his.

She gazed at their interlocked hands, contemplating what they'd gone through to get here, confident they'd weather any storm to come, and they'd do it together.

Today, they committed their hearts and souls to one another, something which seemed impossible a few months ago. Yet here they stand, speaking words of love, sharing their hopes and dreams for an incredible future.

The moment Kenneth pronounced them husbands and wife, tears threatened to ruin Penny's makeup. Xander kissed her first, then he kissed Lex. Tender presses of his lips expressed his devotion to them both.

Lex went for a bit of flair with his kisses, dipping Penny over his arm. Her laughter shifted into a moan when he trailed open-mouthed kisses down her throat. Releasing her, Lex stepped into Xander, cupped his face between his palms, and brought him in for a powerful kiss, one exquisite enough to soak her panties.

Her turn. Penny looped an arm around each of their waists and tugged them close. Her men were quick to clue in to what she wanted, aligning so that their lips met hers together.

Of course, their ceremony held no legal merit. They entered a civil arrangement, working with a lawyer to complete all the necessary paperwork, tying their lives together in a neat, triangulated bow.

Xander looked forward to returning home, and thanks to Penny's American mother, she held dual citizenship, allowing her to live there whenever she wanted. Lex, however, no longer held any specific ties to the US, having sold the majority stake in his company, and the three of them wanted their move to go without issue.

So, when it came time to sign the official marriage certificate, Kenneth and Leana witnessed, in the eyes of the legal system, Xander and Lex are now husband and husband, and Penny is their sidepiece. Which she planned to exploit at every opportunity.

Kenneth and Leana stayed for dinner, toasting the three of them and their commitment to each other. Penny walked the couple to the front door, assuring them they still planned to return to the island house often. This is, after all, where they fell in love.

When she closed the door behind the couple, Penny dropped her head back against it and sighed. She smiled to herself, admiring the two rose-gold bands framing the engagement ring Lex gave her, when a throat cleared.

Penny looked up to find her husbands leaning against the opposite wall, their lust-filled eyes taking her in. Xander moved first, pushing away and taking measured steps toward her. How a predator might stalk its prey.

"Doesn't our wife look happy, husband?" Xander asked, stopping a few feet away, looking at Lex over his shoulder.

He strolled toward them with his hands in his pockets. His heated gaze raked over Penny in the sweetest caress. "Mm...si, she does. I'd say our wife looks *incredibilmente felice*-incredibly happy. Radiant, even. Much like you, husband," Lex said, meeting Xander's gaze when he stood shoulder to shoulder with him.

Xander returned Lex's lust-filled stare. "And you." Xander's lips quirked. "Husband."

Penny melted. The way they referred to each other as husbands. The way they referred to her as wife...turned her insides to goo.

"I believe it's time to take our celebration upstairs."

Penny squealed when Xander scooped her into his arms bridal style, carrying her up the steps with Lex leading the way. When they reached the door of the bedroom they always used, Xander passed her into Lex's arms, making Penny swoon with how they found a way for them to both carry her over the threshold.

"Isn't this all kinds of romantic?"

Lex grinned. "Get ready for a lifetime, Dolcezza."

Penny cupped his cheek, tracing his lower lip with her thumb, and asked, "Are you ready?" The three of them shared many intimacies, exploring and pushing each other's boundaries, though Xander and Lex never crossed this one.

Until tonight.

Lex leaned in and kissed her, his words for her alone. "I want this. To be connected to you both this way." With one more kiss, Lex lowered her until she stood by the bed, and Xander joined them.

He leaned down and kissed the spot where her throat met her shoulder, breathing her in and making her shiver, and when Xander pressed a kiss beneath Lex's jaw and said, "I will never grow tired of calling you my husband and my wife." Desire pooled low in her belly.

"Mm...my new favorite endearments," Penny said, snuggling between them.

Xander's fingertips teased each vertebra of her spine until he reached the zipper of her dress and tugged. "You are beautiful in this dress, Princess." His lips brushed her ear. "You'll be even more beautiful out of it."

For their private ceremony, they opted for a casual look over a formal one. Penny wore a simple, cream-colored sheath dress, while Xander and Lex dressed in dark slacks and white button-down shirts. They left their collars unbuttoned and their shirtsleeves rolled to their elbows, offering Penny a lethal dose of forearm porn times two.

How her panties haven't melted yet is unknown to her.

Xander tugged the zipper down while Lex pressed open-mouth kisses to each inch he exposed. The straps fell from her arms, and her dress slipped to the floor, leaving her in a white strapless bra and matching thong.

Lex curled his arms around her, his fingers dipping beneath the waistband of her panties. "Wet and needy already."

Penny rocked her hips, grinding her ass against his erection. "I'm not the only one who's needy."

"Touché," Lex gasped, grinding on her some more.

Xander undid the last button of his shirt, pulling it free from his pants, and shrugged it off his shoulders. "Less teasing and more undressing, brat."

Lex dipped his middle finger between her folds, swirling the tip around her clit. When he pulled his hand free, he left her wanting more with a sheepish grin on his face. He sucked his finger clean and moaned. "You taste divine, Dolcezza."

"Never stop being a brat."

"Never."

Xander kissed his lips over the top of her head, cocooning Penny between them. "Now, get your fucking clothes off or I'll take a paddle to your ass, and then fuck it."

Penny snorted when Lex replied, pulling his belt free of his pants. "Don't threaten me with a good time."

Xander turned her to face him. "Use the bathroom here. Lex and I will shower in the rooms down the hall. I'll leave items out for you to use. So, be a good girl and make use of them. Lex and I want to hear your screams of pleasure."

"Yes, Sir." Penny peered up at him from beneath her lashes and asked, "Does this mean I have permission to come?"

Twenty minutes later, Penny emerged from the bathroom, wearing nothing more than the rings on her left hand and a smile, and per her husband's instructions, her hair braided into a single plait down her back.

She didn't get it perfect like Xander did, but it will serve its purpose to keep her hair out of the way. She tiptoed to the open bedroom door and heard the muted sounds of them showering, then went to the nightstand beside the bed.

Xander left a folded little card with *Princess* written in his bold script. It sat beside a small tray covered with a cloth concealing its contents. Penny rounded the bed to find a similar tray and card, this one with *Brat* scrolled across it. She peeked beneath the fabric, curious to find out what Xander had brought for Lex. Her lips parted, and she licked them with anticipation.

Four bundles of rope, lube, a butt plug, and...*is that a cock-ring* placed on the tray? Penny ran back to her side, even more eager to find out what Xander chose for her. When she reached the nightstand, she took a calming breath and lifted the cloth. "Oh...fuck."

Her tray contained a rose clit vibe, Ben Wa balls, another bottle of lube, and a leather harness with a six-inch, flesh-colored dildo attached to it. "I get to fuck Lex, too?"

"You do," Xander said, startling her when he walked into the room with Lex following close behind. "You're also supposed to be in the throes of an orgasm or two."

They wore nothing but black silk lounge pants. The way the material cradled their thickening bulges made her mouth water.

Xander's gaze shifted to the tray on the other nightstand, the one she left uncovered.

"Too busy snooping, I see. I left name cards for a reason, Princess." He shrugged his thick, tattooed shoulders, not seeming to care that she did.

With a snap of his fingers, Xander directed Lex to one of the two chairs next to the bed.

"Doesn't matter because now we get to experience your orgasms in person. Lie in the center of the mattress, Princess. I want you to make use of everything except the strap." His expression grew wicked. "You'll know when it's time for that."

Damn the way this man plans things.

Penny climbed onto the bed and crawled across the mattress, glancing over her shoulder to meet their lust-filled eyes.

"Your glistening cunt is giving your excitement away, Dolcezza."

"Oh? I didn't realize I hid how much the two of you turn me on. I'll do my best to make it even more obvious." Reaching the middle of the mattress, Penny lowered to her elbows, spreading her legs wider, offering Xander and Lex a better view.

Then she flipped onto her back to their accompanying groans. With her legs splayed open, she cupped her breasts and lifted them in offerings, smirking when Xander needed to hold Lex back from joining her on the bed.

She shifted her hand down her belly and between her thighs. Her fingers parted her folds, showing Xander and Lex her desperate need.

Lex bit down on the knuckle of his index finger. "*Cazzo. Guarda quanto e bagnata per noi*-Fuck. Look at how wet she is for us."

"She is," Xander growled. His thick cock tented his pants, not shy about how much she affected him. "Use the toys, Princess. Get off for us."

Penny rolled over and grabbed the vibe, lube, and Ben Wa balls, bringing them with her to the middle of the mattress. She used the vibe first, lining it up with her clit, finding the setting to make her back arch off the bed, an orgasm already tightening her core. "Oh, yes," she said, her eyes rolling to the back of her head.

Her nipples pebbled into stiff peaks, and Penny tugged them with her free hand, letting the jolt of pleasure travel straight to her pussy. "Xander...Lex...I'm going to come."

"Give us your orgasm, Princess."

"Come for us, Dolcezza."

She cried out, and her muscles seized. Her body shook with the power of her release.

Penny shuddered, collapsing onto the pillow beneath her head. She turned the toy off, leaving it suctioned to her clit, knowing they'd want more from her.

"Insert the Ben Wa balls. Give your cunt something to clench with your next orgasm."

Penny followed Xander's instructions, not even needing lube, her own arousal enough to insert them with ease. She pressed the first one inside. Her pussy clenched around it, pulling it further into her body.

"Mm...," she moaned, enjoying the sensation of the weighted ball inside her. The second rested against her opening, and she pushed it in too. Penny rocked her hips, and the Ben Wa balls shifted inside her, making her clench around them.

"Turn the vibrator back on, Princess."

Penny pushed the button, and the low hum of the first setting teased her clit. She didn't even know if she'd make it to her favorite setting before her next orgasm consumed her.

She must've blacked out for a moment because the next thing she knew, Xander and Lex loomed naked over her. "Can you stand, Princess?" She reached between her legs to pull the Ben Wa balls free when Xander stopped her. "No...leave them there."

When they helped her stand, Xander said, "Help our wife into her harness, brat."

Lex shuddered. His part of the evening is about to kick into high gear. "Yes, Sir." He stepped around them and picked up the leather harness.

He held it in front of Penny and then lowered to his knees. She put a hand on his shoulder to balance, lifting first one leg, then the other. Lex pulled it up her legs, and once he got it around her hips, he shuffled behind her to do up the buckle at her waist.

Lex then slipped his hand between her legs, grazing her clit when he reached for a second strap to bring between her cheeks, securing the Ben Wa balls inside her.

Oh...fuck.

Last, he tightened the leather straps around her thighs, ensuring the dildo rose from the top of her mound.

Penny gasped when Lex sucked the tip of the dildo into his mouth. She wrapped her fingers around the base, embracing the surge of power washing over her.

"Fuck, that's hot," Xander said, placing the bottle of lube in her free hand.

"Go sit in the chair. Stroke your rubber dick and show us how much you want to fuck our husband while I get him ready to take us."

"Yes, Sir." Penny sat in the chair and dribbled a bit of lube into her palm. She coated the rubber phallus until her hand moved up and down its length with ease. She didn't touch her clit, yet with each stroke, her clit pulsed.

Lex whimpered, keeping his eyes on her while Xander guided him to the other side of the bed.

"Take the cock-ring, lube, and plug with you to the end of the bed and lie with your ass on the wedge where I placed it." Xander pulled one of the wedge cushions from under the bed, setting it on the end of the mattress, and gestured for Lex to do what he asked.

Xander picked up the coils of rope. "I want your ass in the air, brat," he said, and Lex shifted into place. "Yes...good boy."

The position kept his legs open, displaying the shadowed cleft between his cheeks. Penny shifted in her seat, stroking her rubber cock a little faster, enjoying the tug of the strap between her legs and the sensation of the Ben Wa balls shifting inside her.

Xander cupped Lex's face, staring at him with such love, Penny wanted to weep. "I'm going to put you in the most vulnerable position you've ever been in. Are you ready?"

Lex swallowed, leaning into Xander's touch and nodding.

"Words, brat."

"Si, *sono pronto*-Yes, I'm ready."

Xander kissed him, and it quickly became primal and masculine. Penny loved it when they got like this. The force with which they consumed one another made her gasp and her pussy clench, an orgasm coming out of nowhere, crashed through her.

"Our wife's eagerness to help relieve you of your cherry is turning her on enough to come while watching us kiss. Right, Princess?"

Penny bit the corner of her bottom lip and arched her back, teasing her hard nipples while she rocked her hips against the seat of the chair. "Yes."

Xander gripped Lex's jaw. His lips pressed to his ear when he growled, "Look at the way she's rocking her hips. Your Dolcezza is going to fuck you so good."

"Yes," Lex said with a hiss. "Please, fuck me. Both of you."

"Who's my needy whore now?"

"I am. Please...."

"Patience...we need to get you ready first."

Xander bent his legs until his heels touched the backs of his thighs and made quick work of binding them with a bundle of rope. "I'm leaving your hands untied. You'll be free to touch me and Penny unless you misbehave." His warning was more than clear.

Xander drizzled lube into his palm, slicking Lex's cock and balls, adding the rest to the metal cock ring. He slid it over his length, working his testicles through until the ring circled the base of both.

It made his already hard dick get even harder. "Fuck," Lex groaned. "It's intense."

"That's the point," Xander said, teasing his slick fingers between his cheeks to rub his tight hole. He added more lube, letting it trickle down his crease. Penny played with her nipples while Xander slid his middle finger inside Lex to the first knuckle, taking his time to stretch him open.

Lex dropped his head back, exposing his throat, and Xander trailed hot, wet kisses over his skin, sucking on his Adam's apple, then he nipped his jaw. While he teased him with his mouth, he worked a second finger inside Lex.

"Fuck, you're going to strangle my cock when I get inside you," Xander said with a grunt. Lex curled his bent knees closer to his chest, a low, keening sound leaving his lips. "Hitting your prostate, eh? You're giving me more than one orgasm tonight."

Xander gave Lex another searing kiss, then pulled his fingers free. He lubed the butt plug and seated it inside him with a single thrust.

Lex whimpered. "Full."

"Mm...relax into it, pet, and embrace the way the plug presses against your prostate. Besides, it's nothing compared to taking my cock." Xander studied Lex, then his stormy blue eyes raised to meet Penny's. "Come suck your husband, Princess. I need to wash my hands."

Penny stood on shaky legs, yet her stride when she approached was one of sultry confidence. Lex stared at her, captivated. Xander didn't take his eyes off her either. The way they wanted her gave Penny the confidence to embrace this part of herself. The one who wanted to be in control sometimes.

Penny dropped to her knees and took Lex into her mouth. He pushed onto his elbows, watching her take his length to the back of her throat. He reached out a hand and cupped the back of her head, holding her in place while he rocked into her mouth.

"Fuck yes, Dolcezza. Suck me. If it becomes too much, tap my leg."

Tears blurred her vision, yet she hummed her agreement and placed her hands on his thighs. Breathing through her nose, Penny tongued his cock while he did his best to fuck her mouth in the position Xander tied him in.

"Fuck, I'm going to come."

"Oh, no, you're not," Xander said from the doorway of the bathroom. Penny didn't know how long he stood there while Lex fucked her face. The stranglehold Xander held on his cock implied he'd been there for a bit.

Lex loosened his grip, and Penny lifted off him, gasping for breath with a huge smile on her face. She turned to face Xander, wiping her saliva and Lex's precum from her chin, sucking her fingers clean.

"Dirty girl."

"Yes...I'm your dirty girl, and you like it."

"No, sweetheart," Xander said, grabbing her by the waist and pulling her close to kiss her. "I love it." His tongue swept past her lips in search of Lex's flavor, moaning when his tongue curled around hers. When he broke their kiss, he asked, "Are you ready to fuck our husband?"

Xander turned her until her back pressed to his front, and the length of his cock nestled between her cheeks. He walked them both over to stand between his splayed thighs.

His hands held her hips, and he trailed kisses along her throat until he rested his chin on her shoulder, and they stared down at their prey. "He's beautiful like this, open and waiting to be fucked like he never has before."

"So beautiful," Penny said, trailing her fingers along the inside of Lex's thighs toward his straining cock still slick with her saliva. She traced her finger up his length, circling his crown. She gathered the precum pooling at his tip, lifting her finger to Xander's lips for a taste direct from the source.

"Thank you, baby." Xander reached around her and gripped the base of the slender plug, pulling it halfway out. He fucked Lex with it for a few pumps, then pulled it free.

Xander shifted Penny until the tip of her dildo pressed against his opening. "Shift your hips forward. Not too fast," Xander said, guiding her movements with a firm hand at her waist. "Yes…nice and easy. Let him get used to you."

"Feels good, Dolcezza. Don't stop. Stretch me, get me ready to take our husband's thick, veiny cock. The idea alone is going to make me come."

"You'll come for our wife, and then you'll come for me when you're deep in her cunt, and I'm deep in your ass."

"Yes," Lex hissed when Penny pushed all the way inside him. Her mound pressed against his spread thighs. She gripped his hips, much like Xander gripped hers, finding a rhythm, pulling out almost to the tip, then thrusting inside his stretched hole. The sight was so erotic, she nearly orgasmed again.

"Fuck him hard, Princess. He can take it. Can't you, brat?"

"I promise, Dolcezza. You're going to make me come."

"Take his cock in your hand when you're ready. Nail his prostate on each downward thrust, and he will go off like a rocket. Then…it's my turn."

Xander stepped back, taking a seat in the chair. His muscles flexed when he took himself in hand. His cock looked even bigger in the low light of the room. Penny's movements faltered, staring at the man she'd wanted for years, and now, he's theirs. Their protective Dom.

Xander smirked. "Fuck, I love the way you worship me with your eyes, sweetheart. Give our husband what they need. Make him come and rock his world."

"Yes, Sir."

Penny found her rhythm again, stroking Lex while she thrust hard and fast. She stared into her husband's jewel-colored eyes and said, "Come for me."

Lex grunted, arching into her, and Penny thrust into him one more time, holding the dildo deep inside him. She rocked her hips, grinding the tip against his prostate.

"Shit. Fuck. Yes. Penny," Lex chanted, lost in the throes of his orgasm, coming all over his stomach and chest.

"Mm...you're such a good boy," Penny said, pulling out, leaving him gaping and ready.

Xander approached her on silent feet, wrapping his arms around her waist. He pulled her close.

"Love the way you opened him up for me. He's fucking beautiful like this." Xander undid the buckles holding her strap-on in place, letting the harness fall to the floor, forgotten. Then he reached between her legs and tugged on the cord, pulling the Ben Wa balls from her greedy pussy.

They joined the harness on the floor, then Xander lifted her into his arms and laid her beside Lex on the bed. "I need to taste you," he said, dropping to his knees between her thighs.

Penny gasped and arched into Xander's mouth. He ate her like a starving man, and her fingers sank into his loose waves, holding him to her while he tongue-fucked her pussy.

She turned her head, finding Lex enthralled with Xander pleasuring her. "Hi."

"Hi." A sensual smile spread across his face.

"I love you." She'll never tire of telling them she did.

"I love you, too."

"Kiss me. I'm going to come." Lex swallowed her cries as Xander sent her careening over the edge into bliss.

When he lifted his head from between her legs, his lips and beard were wet with her release. "Sweetest pussy I've ever tasted." He wiped his mouth with the back of his hand and loomed over them, joining in their kiss and letting them lick her cum from his lips.

"Ready for me, brat?" Xander asked, reaching over, he tugged on the ropes binding his legs. "Can you last a little longer in your restraints?"

"Yes, fuck me, Xander. I need you inside me," Lex pleaded, holding onto both her and him.

Xander got to his knees and kissed her one more time. "Stay here and love him for a bit, sweetheart. This may be a little uncomfortable at first. Once we're good, you're going to ride his cock."

"I will. I love riding our husband's cock, and I love you."

Xander chuckled. "Love you too, Princess. And you too, brat."

Penny held both their hands, pressing kisses to their knuckles. "Fuck our husband, Daddy, and fill him with your cum."

"Goddamn your dirty mouth," Xander growled, and she giggled. He stood and grabbed the lube, adding more between Lex's spread cheeks, then he poured a liberal amount in his hand, coating himself, then he worked two fingers into Lex's softened hole, getting him nice and slick.

Penny kissed Lex, raining kisses along his throat and across his chest until she reached his pebbled nipples, sucking one into her mouth while Xander lined up his cock with Lex's hole. "You ready?"

"Yes, Sir."

"I'll go slow. Promise."

"Xander, I won't break, and I know you won't hurt me. Please fuck me. Fuck me hard, I can take it. I want to take it."

Penny lifted her head, watching as Xander pushed the tip of his cock into Lex for the first time.

"Oh, fuck," Lex moaned, making Xander freeze. "No, no, no. Don't stop," he panted.

"The way you're gripping the head of my cock is fucking amazing. I don't want to hurt you. Are you sure?"

"God, yes. Please move."

When Xander still hesitated, Penny chimed in. "He's sure, baby. Lex can take it, you know he can."

"Kiss me, Pen."

Penny kissed Lex, and Xander moved, fucking him deeper and a little harder with every thrust. Lex broke from her lips, tipping his head back in ecstasy. "Fuck yes...more. Please give me more."

"Greedy brat. I love it when you beg." Xander undid the binding on Lex's right leg, never faltering in the steady pace of his thrusts. He eased his leg down until he placed his foot on the bed. Then he did the same to his left leg. "Time to go for a ride, Princess."

Xander hooked Lex's freed legs around his waist, making room for her to hop on his dick. She kissed Lex, who looked blissed out and ready to come. This won't be a long ride, but it will be a good one.

Penny got up on her knees and kissed Xander, then she straddled Lex, hovering over him while Xander wrapped his fingers around the base of Lex's cock, lining him up with her entrance. The muscles in her legs gave out, and she dropped, seating him deep inside her, even trapping Xander's fingers to rub against her clit.

"Such a clever little whore." Xander bit her neck, making Penny moan. She tilted her head, giving him better access. She wanted him to bite her harder. To mark her.

"Please...."

Penny loved the way Xander always seemed to know what she needed. She cried out, her pussy clenching around Lex when he sank his teeth in a little deeper. Not enough to break the skin, but enough to leave a mark for a few days.

Speaking of permanent marks, Penny wanted to know. "When are you taking me to West's? I want my tattoo."

"You want to discuss this now?" Lex asked, rocking inside her while Xander kept a steady beat of slapping skin, pounding his ass.

Xander wrapped his arm around her chest, cupping her breast, and whispered in her ear, "I already booked an afternoon at West's shop. Don't worry, Princess. You'll have one to match ours in two weeks."

"Sweet." Penny glanced at Xander over her shoulder. "Can we come now, Daddy?"

"Fuck, yes. Come for me. Both of you."

They moved together in synchronicity born of love and familiarity. Lex gripped her throat with one hand, his other sliding between them to circle her clit with his thumb. It took very little to make Penny explode. The muscles of her core, fluttering around his length, milked the release from him when Xander also let go, coming deep inside Lex.

Their cries filled the room along with their panting breaths. Penny fell to Lex's side, collapsing on the bed while Xander pulled free of him, removing the cock-ring from around his spent cock. When Xander tossed the wedge cushion aside, Lex curled against her, wrapping his arms around her to hold her close.

"Relax, loves. Let me get something to clean you up." Xander stepped into the ensuite, and a moment later, Penny heard the water running.

She snuggled deeper into Lex's embrace. "Will it always be like this?"

Lex kissed her temple. "We might slow down in our twilight years...."

"Speak for yourself, brat," Xander said, sliding into the bed and taking care of them. "I'm fucking both of you every day for the rest of our lives."

Funny, Xander always keeps his word.

Thank You

Thank you for reading. If you enjoyed this book, please consider leaving a review on Amazon and/or Goodreads. Reviews help Indie Authors so much, and I appreciate every one of you. Happy Reading!

Also by K.C. Ford

Club Decadent Series

One Night at Club Decadent (prequel) (MF/FF/FFM/MFM/MMF Married Couple Polysexual Romance)

Their Protective Dom Bk 1(MMF Bodyguard Sword-Crossing Age-Gap Romance)

Addie & Gray Bk 2 (MF Older Woman/Younger Man Romance)

Jess & Jasper Bk 3 (MF Second-Chance Married Couple Romance)

Their Valentine Dom (novella) (MMF Holiday Smut-filled Romance)

Kari & West Bk 4 Coming Soon (MF Bi4Bi Age-Gap Romance)

Their Primal Dom (novella) (MMF Primal Play Lactation Kink Smut-Filled Romance) Coming Soon

One Weekend in Connecticut (novella) (MF/MMMF/MFM/MMF Married Couple Polysexual Romance) Coming Soon

Standalones – Wide Releases Available Everywhere

The Contract (novella) (MMF Married Couple Cuckhold Bi-Awakening Romance)

It Started with a Gym Crush (MF Older Woman/Younger Man Age-Gap Romance) Coming Soon

Follow Me

Follow my Amazon Author Page to get notified of my latest release.

K.C. Ford Author Page

Visit my website for First Chapter Previews, Content Warnings, and Bonus Chapters.

Author K.C. Ford Website

www.ingramcontent.com/pod-product-compliance
Lightning Source LLC
Chambersburg PA
CBHW030239030726
47493CB00023B/192
* 9 7 8 1 0 6 9 1 3 2 8 1 9 *